Hellyon's Stand

JULES FRUSHER

Other Books by Jules Frusher

The Devil To Pay

Copyright © Jules Frusher 2015

All rights reserved. No part of this book may be reproduced or transmitted in any form or by any means, electronic or mechanical, including photocopying, recording, or by any information storage and retrieval system, without permission in writing from the author.

This is a work of fiction. Any resemblance it bears to reality is entirely coincidental.

Produced by Jules Frusher at Whitethorn Books

Acknowledgements and Author's Note

This is my first novel, the one I started writing in the mid nineties and didn't finish until 2002. I part published it in PDF form for a few people only but now, after editing and rewriting some bits I have decided to publish it on a wider scale. The idea for this story originally came from a dream I had, the content of which forms part of the first paragraph. At the time I started writing this, I was part of a Medieval Re-enactment society and I co-opted three of the other members to help me develop the characters and some of the story arcs of Jak, Torassin and Fenim. So I must say a special thank you first of all to Paul Smart, Andrew O'Leary and Dai Rees for helping bring to life such memorable characters. This book is dedicated to you. I also must thank my mum and dad for encouraging me. I gave this book, printed out in A4 to my dad, who was in hospital, dying of cancer. After reading it, some of his last words to me were: "Promise me that you will keep on writing." And so I have. Finally, a huge thankyou to Tony Wait, my lovely partner for believing in me and pushing me to get this done as well as supporting me with my other writing and projects.

Hellyon's Stand

1

The sound of her feet pounding into the hard ground and the fight to get air into tortured lungs filled her world as Aris plunged down yet another woodland path. She had now been running hard for over an hour, the quarry of a Balaatan hunting party. Two of the trackers were dead — she had shot both of them — which would hold the pursuit team for a while, but it wouldn't be long before they closed in again. Ahead the trees began to thin into a clearing. Two hundred yards away, surrounded by a rusty mesh fence, was a group of derelict buildings. It looked like an Old World college campus, long abandoned by its students. Not perfect, but at least she could hole up there while she got some energy back.

Breaking from the treeline she realised that she was now in the open. This was no training exercise like she'd been through hundreds of times in the City Special Operations division. This was for real, life or death. Rules went out of the window. The perimeter fence, constructed from chain link wire and posts was already down in a few places. She made for one of the gaps and sprinted the rest of the way across the cracked concrete yard towards the building, her senses stretched and ready to snap at any movement. Panting, she had just reached the doorway when a grenade round hit to the side of her. The rotten brickwork exploded with the heat, a piece of shrapnel cutting her face as she threw herself to the ground. Now what? She had not bargained on them catching up with her so fast. She knew that it would only be the remaining trackers together with a few runners at the moment, but she didn't know how many there were and she had not prepared a defensive position in the building yet. Getting to her feet again, she ran along the corridor and into the main building's hall. Other corridors led off to the right and left and she could see staircases rising to higher floors. No, she thought, go up and I'll be trapped for sure; my only chance is to reach the other end of the buildings first and make a run for the woods on the other side. With luck they'll tire first.

Her feet echoed on the tiled floors and kicked up little clouds of dust and debris as she ran, her breath now ragged and catching in her throat. Soon the main entrance doors were ahead. She slowed a little to check for traps, but it seemed clear enough. Even so, it would be madness to rush straight out into the open. She checked her ammunition and with a shock realised that she was running very low. Now she was going to have to make every shot count.

Out of the doorway she could see tall square columns holding up the front facade. A good mixture of shadows and light. Cautiously she moved out of the building to one of the columns. A bullet hit the ground in front of her. It had come from the direction of the roof of what she assumed had once been the gymnasium, which meant that she was exposed where she stood. Taking a chance, she edged out and dived behind another of the pillars. A hiss of heated air next to her cheek told her that the guy up there was a good shot — too good for her just to make a run for it. And soon someone else would be coming up behind her; she didn't really have time to play a waiting game.

Something caught her eye to the right. Another man now stood on the roof of the main building's annex, the sun glinting off the metal armour-plates on his shoulders, his eyes searching the shadows below. Shit, with two of them, she couldn't hide; she'd have to take at least one of them out now. It was possible, even with only four bullets left but she knew her chances of escape still remained pretty low.

The second man must have been alerted to her position by the first, for his eyes suddenly found her and he brought his gun up to aim through his sights.

Aris didn't have time for sights. She just pointed her own weapon and hoped. Her shot hit first, knocking him backwards before he had time to fire. Deciding to risk it, she dodged around the corner and aimed at the man on the gymnasium roof. Again, her aim was more intuition than skill, but he, too, fell backwards, the left-hand side of his head exploding away from the rest. Easy enough. Maybe she did still have a chance.

There were now running footsteps coming up the corridor behind her. Slinging her almost useless weapon over her back, Aris began to run for the perimeter gate, aware that more of Pock's soldiers would now be in the grounds. But it was do or die and she'd rather die than be taken prisoner. Her legs pumping but her mind focused on the gate in front of her, she made a break out into the open.

A shout from behind told her that her escape had been seen and she pushed herself even harder as a hiss of air sounded off to the right. Another hiss and then a singeing pain flared across her right thigh. Looking down she saw that a round had sliced through the outer part of her thigh. At least it had missed the bone. Running now on adrenaline and closing her mind to the pain, she forced herself on, beginning to get out of range of her pursuers. She reached the open gate and sprinted up the grassy track into the woodland beyond. She was sure she had at least killed the front-men — the fastest trackers and runners in the patrol, which meant that their hunt would now have to become a little harder. But she would still have to put more ground between them before she stopped. She tried to run faster, the stinging in her leg becoming a throb as the damaged muscle began to stop working. It wouldn't carry her much further. Gasping for breath, she stopped and saw a break in the undergrowth to the side of the track. A wood-rat trail ... it would do. Trying to block out the pain, she dropped to her hands and knees and crawled through the tunnel, exposed skin being stung by needle-wort and lacerated by the thorn-brush. Her progress was slow, but careful; Pock's soldiers may not have been wonderful shots, but his trackers were some of the best in the Outlands. Her only hope was that they wouldn't be expecting her to hide so close to the path.

The tunnel opened up into a small clearing with a wood-rat burrow on the one side and a thorn-covered thicket on the other. Gritting her teeth against the spines, she pushed her way into the clear centre of the bush. Waiting for the party to pass by, she checked her wound through the torn material of her trousers. It was more than a flesh wound but not as bad as she had feared. Even so, if she didn't find a way of treating it soon, infection would set in and she would surely die a slow and agonising death.

Running feet alerted her to the first of Pock's soldiers coming down the track in pursuit. They ran past, obviously thinking that she was still ahead of them. A few minutes later and the sound of more feet, this time slower, walking, stopping now and again.

Trackers.

Aris held perfectly still, hardly daring to breathe as they approached the wood-rat track, but they walked on past, apparently not noticing anything amiss. Behind the trackers came the bodyguards, and in their midst, Pock, Balaat's mutant-human leader. Maybe she should have felt honoured that such an important personage was present for her intended death but she had heard that his participation in such entertainment was common: he had a predilection for watching fear and death. In himself, he was repulsive enough, with his over-muscled torso, his grey hide-like skin and his strange, musky smell. But what he had with him shocked Aris even more, for attached to a chain wrapped around his one fist was what was obviously his latest pet: a naked woman, her body disfigured by bites and bruises, her face tear-stained and her eyes that of a madwoman. So the stories were true.

The mismatched couple passed within a few feet of where Aris was hiding and she had to exert strong self-control not to draw back out of repulsion. She still had one shot left in her weapon and at this range she could certainly seriously injure him, if not kill him, but she suppressed that urge too. Her common sense told her that to escape without further incident was the most sensible of options.

The whole entourage passed by and finally disappeared up the track. Aris took a deep breath and exhaled with relief. Her leg screaming pain, she began to crawl out of the thicket to the clearing with the wood-rat sett. Once out in the open, she shakily tried to stand up.

Her arms were immediately grabbed and pinioned to her side and a knife blade was pressed against her throat.

'About time,' said a low, cracked voice at her ear. 'Lord Pock is anxiously awaiting to meet the one who nearly escaped his best hunters.'

The holding cell in Balaat Fort was cramped and dirty. Just twenty-four hours ago, she had been in another cell, only this time in her native City. Accused of murdering a fellow Special Ops officer in a drug deal gone wrong, she knew she'd been set up. At her trial it had been obvious that her lover and the man she thought she trusted, Commander Lennard Tiern, had been behind it all. The detailed evidence supposedly found on her at the time of arrest and the fake prosecution witnesses, all so convincing to the military court, had signs of Tiern's handiwork all over.

Shit, a few weeks ago she would never have thought him capable of such ruthless manoeuvring, let alone of leaving her die in Balaat. She thought that they were close enough not to have secrets. That all changed when she came across some papers in Tiern's study by accident. Papers that betrayed him as being a man in the pay of Balaat. She had long suspected him of having sympathies for the Balaatan cause, especially as he was always defending the country's morals by insisting all the stories were just myths. And he wasn't the only one. Aris's unit had recently received information that a hard core of men in the ruling senate were in favour of a close alliance with Balaat. An alliance like they had once had with their closest neighbour, the now beleaguered Hellyon. But for what reason, Aris could only guess.

The information contained in the papers was blatantly incriminating, even though she had only managed to read the first couple of paragraphs. At that point Tiern had suddenly entered and caught her reading them. The look in his eyes told her that there could be no going back. She tried to reason with him, even suggested that maybe she could forget what she had seen. She left for her duty shift with his warning ringing in her ears; if she mentioned the smallest thing about what she'd seen to anyone, she'd be dead. Eight hours later, walking back to the house she shared with her sister and little daughter, a man stepped out in front of her brandishing a weapon. She reacted quicker and it wasn't until he lay dead on the concrete roadway that she identified him as a corporal from another ops unit. Almost immediately she was pounced on by men dressed in unit colours she had not seen before. Arrested and searched, the evidence planted, and from that moment on she knew she was as good as guilty.

After the trial, she had sat in her cell waiting to hear her fate. The door opened and Tiern had entered.

'What the fuck are you doing here?' she spat

Tiern looked at her. 'Official business, Desun. I've come to tell you what the military judges have decided. You're to be exiled to Balaat, as slave labour in one of Pock's camps.'

Aris had sat down in shock. It may as well have been a death sentence. The policy in Balaat was to treat women lower than animals.

Feelings began to boil up inside her until they exploded in an upward movement, her fist flying towards Tiern. Years of experience and training had already taught him to expect such a reaction and he side-stepped it easily, taking hold of Aris's arm and tripping her so that she tumbled into a heap on the floor.

Aris's emotions were in turmoil. 'But I don't understand. Why couldn't you trust me? After all we've had together?'

Tiern raised his eyebrows. 'You really believed that we had something together?'

'It was two years, Lennard. Two full goddamn years. I thought you felt something for me.'

He shrugged. 'No, Aris, to be brutally honest you were little more than an entertaining distraction to fill my off-duty hours. The fact that it lasted two years is perhaps a testament to your... qualities, but no more than that.'

'But what about my daughter? What about Ani, Lennard? What is she going to do without me?'

He shrugged. 'Stay with your sister no doubt. It's not my problem Aris. You are. Or rather, you were.'

He turned to go. She grabbed hold of his arm. 'No. You just can't walk out on me like this. Not everyone will believe I'm guilty. I have friends that will come looking for the truth.'

'Have you? Last I heard, everyone you worked with had turned their back on you. You're finished, Desun. Except in Balaat. Maybe your charms will find a new and ready audience there.'

This time, he didn't see the blow coming; her fist had hit hard, splitting his lip and knocking his head backwards.

'Bitch!' he managed to spit out before another blow to the side of his head sent him reeling across the narrow confines of the cell. The door burst open and three guards crowded in. Aris suddenly found herself on the receiving end of punches and kicks as Tiern was dragged clear. Eventually through blurred vision and the taste of blood, Aris heard the cell door closing again and she was alone, lying on the floor in a small pool of her own blood. A strangled noise escaped from her throat as the dammed tears finally overflowed, making rivers across the skin of her face. All she could think of, all she could see was the face of her six year old daughter. The thought of never seeing her again had caused her far more pain than any number of beatings.

A key rasped in the lock of her Balaatan cell, startling Aris out of her memories. She sat up, uncertain of what to expect. One of the guards entered and gestured for her to follow him. Shakily she rose to her feet, only to be grabbed roughly by the arm and pushed out into the corridor. She was taken to a different building. After more corridors, the guards knocked at a solid-looking door before pushing her through into the room beyond. At the far side, close to a large oak desk, stood a tall, well-muscled man. The bare skin of his arms sported large blue tribal tattoos, unknown to Aris and therefore probably having an origin beyond the far mountains. His head was shaved, except for a sleek black ponytail at the back.

He smiled, displaying yellow teeth, the two canines filed into points. 'Welcome to Balaat.' His green eyes bored into hers for a second as he tried to sound her out. She quickly dropped her gaze, not wishing to provoke any reaction at this stage. 'I am Tall't, the Commander of Balaat Fort and Lord Pock's vizier. I hear you gave his Lordship's hunting party quite an entertaining morning.'

Aris kept silent, her eyes on the floor.

'Aris Desun,' he continued, as she looked up, startled at the mention of her name. How the hell could he know...?

It was as if he read her mind. 'Tiern sent us a message saying that you were about to be exiled in Balaat for your... misdemeanours. He made it very clear that he did not want any chance of you returning to City in the future. In fact it was Tiern who suggested that his Lordship might enjoy a little sport.'

'So, I was supposed to die?'

'Yes. It was decided that the captain of the City patrol vehicle should give you a weapon, just to make the chase a little more exciting. However, no-one realised what a good shot you were. Do you realise that his Lordship lost some of his best trackers and runners today?'

Aris swallowed hard, her throat feeling very, very dry. Her next words were a struggle to get out. 'And I suppose I am to be executed now?'

Tall't laughed. 'That's what Tiern would want, if he knew you were still alive. But what Tiern wants, Tiern doesn't always get. He may be an important ally, but his Lordship will not bow down to anyone else's plans but his own. His Lordship has not seen a woman with such... fighting spirit. He has asked me to keep you alive, for the time being at least.'

A sudden vision of the mauled woman on the leash came into her head. Shit, if that was to be her fate, she would have to find some way to kill herself first. After a few seconds she found her voice. 'I will not be his pet.'

Tall't raised his eyebrows, taking a few moments to understand her meaning. Then he laughed again. 'Oh, you won't be his Lordship's chosen one. Oh no, you're not his type. His Lordship specifically asked that you be kept aside for Circus.'

'Circus?'

'Let's just say you'll need every one of your fighting skills to stay alive in there. And at least this time, his Lordship will witness every moment, instead of just the results.'

There was another knock on the door.

'Come in,' said Tall't in a tone that indicated he had been expecting the interruption.

The man who entered was short and stout, his grizzled hair close-cropped, his face smeared with dirt. He looked Aris up and down, his mouth twisting into a sneer.

Tall't effortlessly placed himself between her and the man. 'Aris, I would like to introduce you to Dirik, our chief interrogator and the Master of Ceremonies in Circus. His eldest son was one of the trackers you so easily terminated this afternoon. Under Balaatan law, he has the right to extract a blood price from you. However, Lord Pock's instructions limit him as to how far he can go — until Circus anyway. I am a fair man and Dirik has served me well for many years. I would hate to see his grief go completely unheeded. Therefore I have granted him the duty of slave-branding you.' Tall't switched his attention to Dirik. 'Apart from branding, you are not to touch or injure her in any way. Is that understood?'

Dirik grunted, clearly unhappy with the arrangements.

'You must wait until the next Circus,' Tall't continued, seeing the man's mood, 'then you will be allowed revenge. His Lordship was most specific about this.' Dirik looked as if he was about to spit at his commander then thought better of it. Tall't gave a little smile and nodded. Dirik moved forward.

Tall't seemed to have one last thing to say: 'After branding make sure she is allocated a bunk in the women's' barracks and some menial duty. Don't try to escape, Aris: as the women will tell you, there is no way out. Apart from in a burial bag that is.'

Aris felt Dirik's strong hand around her arm in a bruising grip. She turned and happened to look into the darkness of his eyes and she knew her nightmare was about to begin.

2

(Six months later)

'Still no sign of life over the edge,' Torassin said as he manoeuvred his body to lie flat on top of the rise. From here he had a good view of Hellyon's border with Balaat.

'It doesn't mean nobody's there though,' mumbled Jak as he pulled himself alongside and searched the horizon through his viewers. 'If anything, it's been too quiet to be healthy. Pock's up to something.'

'Well, I wish he'd hurry up and do it,' said the younger man. 'I wouldn't mind a bit of action ... might liven up patrolling a bit.'

'Speak for yourself. I was fighting Balaat while you were still having your backside wiped, and I, for one, am glad of a short break.'

A sudden movement to Jak's left caught his eye. He grabbed Tor's arm and pointed to a figure running on the track below. It looked like a woman. She was wearing a baggy shirt and trousers like one of Pock's slaves. He frowned. But no woman had ever escaped from Pock's strongholds, not that he knew of anyway, and certainly one had never got this far. Warning bells rang in his head: could this be a trap? There was some more movement from the direction she had come from and a pursuit party of about ten men came into view.

They were coming over the border.

Tor started to move, but Jak grabbed his arm and pulled him back down.

'Aren't we going to help her?' asked Tor.

'Don't be in such a hurry to die. Have you ever heard of any woman escaping Pock and getting this far? It's a trap, it has to be; they're trying to draw us out. Let's watch and see what happens.'

Around a bend and out of sight of her pursuers, the woman suddenly disappeared into the undergrowth. Jak strained his eyes to see where she had gone but it was useless. A few seconds later, he saw a movement in the bushes to the left of her previous position. She had doubled back, but why? The trackers would find her eventually, wherever she had hidden herself.

The first of the pursuit party neared her position. Two men, a tracker and a runner about a hundred yards ahead of the rest were following her footprints in the muddy ground. As they drew level with her new position, she suddenly rose out of the undergrowth at the side with a hefty fallen branch in her hands. Before they had time to react, she had swung the piece of wood at their heads, connecting with both and knocking them off their feet. The encounter hadn't been without noise and the two watching men saw the rest of the pursuers suddenly halt and take up defensive positions in fear of what lay around the corner. Presumably it could have been a Hellyon ambush.

This gave the woman enough time to finish the job. One of the men was unmoving, the other trying groggily to get to his feet. Running over to the still one, she picked up his weapons ... a knife and a rifle and continued past him to where the other man was now on his feet, trying to gather his wits. Swinging the butt of the rifle, she smashed him over the head, bringing him down, lifeless, in the mud. In one graceful movement she had slit his throat, before turning back to his partner and repeating the action. Then, taking advantage her pursuers' caution, she hared on up the track, now armed.

'That's no trap Jak,' Tor exclaimed, 'she's just killed a couple of them.'

Jak shrugged 'So? Makes it look more realistic. They're probably only acting.'

The pursuit team had made up their minds that they weren't about to be ambushed and set off after her again. The sight of their two prone comrades only seemed to make them more determined. They began to gain on her as she slowed up, tiring. Suddenly, she turned, aimed the rifle and fired off two shots, each finding its mark. Two more down.

The shots had caused enough confusion in Pock's men to enable the woman to put a bit more distance between her and them. Rounding another bend, she disappeared once more into the undergrowth. Through the binoculars Jak could just about make out her position as she crawled through the thick fronds to hide behind a fallen tree trunk. The pursuers had obviously lost their best trackers, for they seemed to have difficulty in locating where she had come off the path, let alone where she was hiding. They spread out either side of the path, separating. A tall, rather slouched soldier approached the fallen tree. He turned to look behind him and she seized the opportunity to jump up and put her hand over his mouth. Stabbing the knife into the side of his neck, she then supported his lifeless body as it fell back into the greenery. It had been done so fast and with such skill that he had not had time to cry out.

But his absence had not gone unnoticed; one of his companions came cautiously over to investigate, his knife ready in his hand. She must have known her position was about to be compromised, for she waited until he was nearly on top of her and then jumped up, once more swinging the butt of the rifle so that it connected onto his jawbone with a loud crack. He screamed and she brought the weapon to bear again on the side of his skull. The scream stopped. He went down.

By now the others had been alerted to her position and she made a break for it. As before she suddenly swung around and aimed her rifle at the nearest of the men. She pulled the trigger. Nothing happened. Either the magazine had jammed or there had only been two rounds in there to begin with. She flung the useless weapon away and began to run again, but this time she was noticeably slower. It didn't seem that she could go much further.

Tor looked at Jak. 'Acting, you say?'

Jak grunted and, motioning for Tor to cover him, began to move towards the track. Silently they both made their way down the hill, keeping the woman in sight.

One of the Balaatans had now caught up with her and launched himself at her body, bringing her to the ground. She managed to turn and slash upward with the knife, but missed her target. The weapon was wrenched from her grasp, and, before she could struggle, the other Balaatan soldiers had arrived and pinned her down.

An older man, who appeared to be in charge, gave a terse order. Immediately hand and leg restraints were put onto their captive and she was hauled to her feet.

Jak trained his weapon on the commander. Tor took the prompt and sighted up his first target too.

A soldier in dirt-soiled kit rummaged in his belt bag and took out a sacking hood, stained with blood. He rammed it over the woman's head, causing her to start struggling again.

And then he took his baton out of his belt ...

As the first blow landed, Jak fired, taking out the commander of the patrol, just as Tor fired another lethal shot at the thug giving the beating. The two men holding the woman let go and prepared to make for cover, leaving the battered, hooded figure to fall to the ground, presumably unconscious. But they never made it: one took a direct body hit, the other a disabling wound in the groin. The remaining three in the party made it to the trees and let off five or six shots, all hopelessly wild of their targets. Then there was silence as if they, too, had only had a couple of rounds each in their magazines.

Jak fired off a couple more rounds and then signalled for Tor to move forward under his covering fire. Not that cover was really that necessary for when Jak next looked for his partner, he appeared to have vanished.

'Bloody Sharm tricks,' he mumbled, but secretly he admired the man's ability to seemingly disappear—it was a useful skill to have. Cautiously he moved forward until he came to the clearing: apart from the wounded man, screaming his pain, nothing else moved. Jak took careful aim and finished off the job. The hooded figure also lay unmoving, possibly dead. He gave her a kick. No response. Well, she wasn't going anywhere for a while; he could leave her there for now.

Walking down the track, he met Tor coming back up. The younger man signalled the all clear. 'Got another one as they were getting away,' he said. 'I also checked her earlier kills—she made a pretty neat job of them.'

'Hmm. How about the ones that got away?'

'Last seen running for their lives over the border; probably heading for one of the watchtowers.'

'Best not hang around then. They might come back with reinforcements.'

'What about the woman?'

'We may be too late.'

'She's dead?'

'Well, she's not moving much. Could be just unconscious, I suppose.'

Tor jogged over to where she lay. He jerked the hood off and felt for a pulse. A large bruise was already discolouring her forehead. 'She's alive. What do we do?'

'Three options: one, we leave her here — let fate take its course; two, we shoot her now — it'll save us a lot of bother later; or three, we take her prisoner and see what she has to tell us.'

Tor raised his eyebrows. 'I think Hellyon Command would prefer option three, Jak. And so would I.'

'Yeah, well, I suppose you're right. It'll still be hassle though. I prefer the shooting option myself.'

He caught the look on Tor's face. 'Okay, okay, we'll take her prisoner. Shit, I must be going soft in my old age. Take the leg restraints off, but leave the hand ones on—you saw what she was capable of. Any trouble though and she's dead. Agreed?'

'Agreed.'

Tor reached down to unfasten the leg restrainers and did a quick body search for any hidden weapons.

'Her clothes are wet,' he said, his voice concerned, 'and she seems very thin.'

'So?' Jak snapped.

Before Tor could reply, the woman started to move, regain consciousness. Jak immediately levelled the muzzle of his RD10 rifle at her head.

Her eyes opened. She blinked, took in the situation and closed them again. 'Hellyon?' she asked, her voice barely audible.

'Correct,' answered Jak.

'Asylum ... request asylum ... '

'First things first. You're coming back with us to answer a few questions. Can you walk?'

She nodded.

'Good, because there's no way I'm carrying you.'

She began to struggle to her feet. Tor took hold of one of her arms and pulled her up.

'Right,' said Jak, 'walk in front ... follow that trail. Any wrong moves and you're dead. Understand?'

The woman nodded again. 'I'll be no trouble, I promise.'

Jak grunted and prodded her forward with his gun. He noticed that she was now limping badly and a bloodstain was slowly spreading down the outside of her trouser leg. She was hurt, but so what? It wasn't his problem at the moment.

Progress back to the PV, the Patrol Vehicle, was slower than Jak would have liked, despite the lack of any signs of pursuit. Reaching the vehicle, he went on ahead and did a quick recce to check for any ambush or traps that might have been laid since. Finding none, he signalled Tor and his prisoner forward. Handing his partner the sacking hood that he'd stuffed into his belt, he said: 'better put this on again. We don't want her knowing where we're taking her.'

There was the briefest flicker of fear in her eyes as the hood was replaced, but she stood calmly. Jak opened the back of the PV, picked her up and rolled her in. She must have landed on her injured leg, for she cried out. Then she was silent, unresponsive. He wondered if she'd blacked out again.

'I'll ride in the back with her, Jak,' Tor said, leaping in beside her. Out of the corner of his eye Jak noticed that he turned her over so that the pressure was off her injury. That boy's too soft he thought. At this rate he won't last long.

Jak didn't drive straight back to their base at Hellyon Camp as Tor supposed he would. Instead he went on to the next border watchtower, where he jumped out. 'Just watch her Torassin. I won't be long.' He disappeared into the tower.

'Are you going to get me out of this hood yet?' said a muffled voice at his feet, the woman was obviously conscious again.

'Not just yet. Won't be long though.'

'Oh, come on, you seem the reasonable one. Just take the hood off and untie me. I'll be no trouble, honest.'

Tor smirked, and let the muzzle of his rifle rest against her forehead. She stopped struggling to sit up.

'I may be more reasonable than my friend,' he said, 'but that doesn't mean I'm stupid. I'll shoot you just the same if you give me any trouble, and I won't have any guilt trips about it either.'

The figure slumped back on the floor and muttered an oath. 'No harm in asking.'

Tor smiled. Even in the state she was in she had a bit of spirit; which had the potential to piss Jak off no end. He was going to have his work cut out today.

Jak returned with a couple of men from the watchtower. 'These two will take over for the rest of our route while we do a little interrogation of our own,' he said.

'That's a bit irregular isn't it?' asked Tor. 'Felson won't like it and Sean will tear your head off.'

'And how are they going to hear about it? Look, I'm not going to let what happened before happen again.'

'You mean ... ?'

'Yes.' Jak's voice was terse enough to dissuade any further discussion on the subject.

Between them, they hauled the woman out of the vehicle. She was either unconscious again or else being uncooperative and so they had to half-drag, half-lift her up the steps to the darkened tower room. Below, the PV revved up and moved off. Apart from the guards on sentry in the upper room, they were alone.

The woman was placed on a chair and the leg restraints refastened. Jak took off the hood. She took a few gasps of clean air, looked up at her captors with angry eyes and then looked away again.

'Alright, what do you want to know?' she asked.

'Name first.' Jak began.

'Aris Desun.'

'Where are you from?'

'Balaat Fort. I escaped'

Jak snorted. 'What a load of bullshit! No woman has ever escaped from there.'

'I'm here aren't I?'

'How did you escape?' asked Tor.

'I was on latrine duty when I noticed a breach in the wooden swill-gate — the shit must have rotted it or something. Anyway, it's under the water level, so generally it can't be seen. I got out through there.'

'You don't look — or smell like you've waded through shit, Desun,' Tor commented, walking around her.

'I took a little swim in the river, not far from here. I was trying to shake off the trackers.'

There was a pause before Jak said. 'That was quite a display you put on back there. You've had military training but you wouldn't have got that from Balaat so where are you really from?'

Aris took a deep breath. 'City.'

'City,' Jak repeated softly. He turned his back on her and walked over to the observation slit, suddenly dangerously silent. Tor read the signs and hastily took over the questioning.

'So how come you ended up in Balaat?'

'I asked for asylum, not an interrogation,' she spat.

Jak suddenly swung round from the window. You're Special Ops trained aren't you?'

The surprised look on her face told him the answer.

'So how did you end up in Balaat?'

'It wasn't my choice.'

'Then whose choice was it?'

She stayed silent.

'Who was your commander in City?'

'Why should I tell you? I have asked for asylum, therefore I should be taken straight to your command's headquarters, not questioned in the field.'

'Give me his name!' Jak shouted.

'Tiern, Lennard Tiern.'

'Ha! There it is Tor — the reason her story is bullshit.' His hand was suddenly in her hair, pulling her head back. A knife blade flashed in his other hand. 'Let's get this over with right now.'

'Jak, stop.' The voice was Tor's, but it sounded different, more commanding. Jak suddenly found himself unable to move. His face registered shock that the Sharm had used some sort of mind trick on him — frozen him. 'Bastard!' he mouthed with effort in Tor's direction.

Tor refrained from smiling; he was surprised himself that some of his Sharm training had actually worked on the first attempt. He bent down on a level with the woman. 'Desun, do you remember a joint operation between City and Hellyon about five years ago?'

'Which one?' Aris asked, puzzled.

'Detachments 6 and 9 of Special Operations, were mobilised

from City by Tiern to aid Hellyon's forces in wiping out a small Balaatan camp close to the border at a place called Berryn's crossing.'

Aris suddenly went white. 'That was an accident ...'

'That was no fucking accident, Desun!' Jak suddenly found his voice again. 'Those units from City deliberately turned their fire on Hellyon at Tiern's command. I know because I was there and I lost many, many good friends. Hellyon lost a lot of good soldiers!'

'Were you there Desun?' Tor asked.

She paused before answering. 'No, I was elsewhere that day.'

'Oh really! How bloody convenient!' Jak said sarcastically. He looked at Tor. 'Is she lying?'

Tor knew his answer would either be her death warrant or set her free. He chose carefully and decided to lie: she was still too intriguing to have it end here. 'No, from what I can sense, she's told the truth so far.'

'That doesn't make her — or her kind — any less guilty,' Jak mumbled, but the edge had gone out of his anger now. Finding he could move again, he let go of her hair and replaced the knife in its sheath. For now.

Tor continued the questioning: 'So, tell us — how did you end up in Balaat Fort?'

'I was exiled from City for a crime I didn't commit.'

'What sort of crime?'

'Murder, but I am innocent, I swear.'

'Isn't that what they all say?' Jak said sarcastically. 'So supposing I believe in this... set up — what did you do to deserve it in the first place?'

'I got in Tiern's way. So he made sure I got sent somewhere where I couldn't speak against him'

'So why not just make sure you got killed?'

'That was what he wanted. Pock wanted me for entertainment.' She looked away. 'There are worse punishments than execution.'

'Like what?' asked Tor.

She didn't answer. Tor sensed something dark, something beyond fear in her mind. He decided not to press any further with that line of questioning for now.

'So how is Tiern these days? Does he manage to sleep well at night?' asked Jak.

'Well enough,' she answered.

Jak snorted. 'I bet he does. How well did you know him Desun? Obviously enough to know some of his secrets.'

Tor tensed in an automatic response to the signals he was picking up from her body language. The woman's next answer might not bode well for her future. She also seemed to sense it, for she picked her words carefully.

'He was my commander.'

'And a friend?' Jak asked.

She stared back at him. 'I would say he's not the sort of man you'd want for a friend, wouldn't you?'

'But Tiern's clever. What if all that we saw back there was a set up so that he could send in a spy. It would make an excellent cover story, wouldn't it?'

'Do you really think that everything you saw was set up? That they let me kill some of their men just so I could get rescued by a patrol that no-one even knew was there? If I was going to infiltrate into Hellyon as a spy, there are damn far easier ways of doing it.'

Jak shook his head. 'I still don't think you're telling us everything Desun. I know your type.'

'My type? What the hell do you mean. Look, if asylum here means being treated like this then you'd better shoot me now.

Go on, just get it over with!' She hung her head in defeat and exhaustion.

There were a few moments of silence and then Jak took a few steps back, brought his rifle to his shoulder and lined her up in the sights. Tor waited, holding his breath. He felt he couldn't interfere anymore, Jak would never forgive him.

In the stillness of the room they heard an engine far off but coming closer. The PV was returning.

Slowly, Jak lowered the gun, his face set. Tor could tell he had made his decision, uncomfortable though it was to him. It would now be up to Felson, their commanding officer, as to whether she lived or died. And knowing Felson, he'd probably be wining and dining her within hours.

'Okay, untie her from the chair,' Jak said, his voice rough, 'but keep the restraints and hood on like before. Let's get back to Hellyon Camp.'

Unseen by Jak, Tor gave a little smile.

3

There was only the faintest light in the sky when two figures strode through Hellyon Camp, making for a small circle of tents nearest the south side of the perimeter fence.

'Wake up, you lazy bastards!' the tallest one called as he neared the first tent. 'Thought you could have at least welcomed us home.'

'Piss off.' Jak's head appeared from out of the tent.

'Charming. Some way to speak to your captain.' Sean feigned hurt feelings but a smile still played around his lips.

'Well, bugger off instead then.'

'Oh come on Jak, you know you missed us really.'

Jak grunted and looked up at the lightening sky. He yawned. 'I suppose it's just about time to get up anyway. I might as well get a brew going.'

Sean's companion smiled. 'That sounds like a mighty good idea my friend.'

'I thought you'd say that somehow,' Jak replied.

'Fenim has been craving one of your brews since we left camp; I don't know why he prefers yours to mine,' said Sean.

'Perhaps it's the bitter after-taste,' Fenim grinned.

Jak hauled himself out of the tent he shared with Tor and lit the cooking block. Once the flames started to curl upwards and heat the billy, he turned back and flung the front of the canvas open.

'Time to get up Tor — the village idiots have returned.'

The heap of blankets within gave a grunt and moved slightly. Jak kicked it but still got no response. He gave up and sat down, reaching out to stroke the taggy-eared tabby cat that had silently appeared by his side. 'So, how did you get on?' he asked of the other two.

For the first time since his arrival, Sean was serious. The smile dropped from his face and he began to look his age. 'One big cock-up from start to finish. The other patrol didn't have a clue ... they were careless and managed to get caught in an ambush. Nearly compromised us too. We got away but ended up in the middle of the Darrit marshes, way off our recce point. It was only through Fen's navigating that we got back to the border at all. As if that wasn't bad enough, the Balaatans had doubled the border patrols and we had a hell of a time avoiding them. Shit, Jak, I tell you, having just two men on patrol isn't enough; we need to go back to having at least four.'

'Felson's orders.'

'Maybe I'll have to tell Felson where to stick them.'

The water in the billy started to boil. Jak took it off the fire, added a few handfuls of dried leaves from a sack and stirred it.

'I must admit,' he said, 'we could have done with you two on our patrol a few days ago.'

Sean grinned again. 'Yeah, one of the guys on sentry duty said you'd picked up a female prisoner. I would have thought that the two of you could have handled a woman without our help. Not that I would have minded; I heard she's quite ... '

'She was from City — Special Ops,' Jak said tersely.

'Oh.' Seeing the look on Jak's face, Sean fell silent.

'So what was she doing alone on our border?' asked Fenim.

'She said she'd escaped from Balaat Fort.'

'Balaat Fort? No woman I know has ever got out of there,' said Sean.

'Exactly, but she seems to have managed it, despite the pursuit party on her tail.'

'Good thing you were there,' said Sean.

Jak scowled. 'Is it? Personally, I'd have her shot.'

'Why?'

'Remember our friend Tiern? She was under his command.'

'Berryn's Crossing?' Sean raised an eyebrow.

'She said she wasn't there, and Tor believes her, so I suppose it might be true.'

Sean's eyes narrowed with suspicion. 'Hang on a minute. How do you know all this? I can't believe she told you in the context of a cosy chat along route.'

Jak said nothing.

'You didn't do some interrogation of your own on the way back did you?' Sean asked, his voice rising. 'Shit, Jak, you know the rules!'

'Fuck the rules!' Jak spat back. At the fury in his voice, the cat jumped off his lap and disappeared. 'For all we knew, she could have been an infiltrator, a saboteur ... anything. I wasn't going to make another mistake—not after last time.'

Jak turned away so that his face was hidden by shadows. The silence was eventually broken by Fenim.

'Ardaya wasn't your fault, Jak. She was very clever ... had everyone fooled.'

But the older man didn't answer and the others knew better than to press the issue.

As if on cue, Tor stuck his pale, sleep-bleared face out of the blanket. 'Brew ready yet?' he asked.

'It's amazing how he wakes up when all the work is done, isn't it?' Jak said sarcastically.

Throwing off the blankets, Tor crawled from the tent and sat beside the fire, gratefully accepting the brew as it was passed to him.

'Got enough for another one?' a female voice asked. They looked up to see a tall woman with close-cropped, carrot-red hair.

'Macker!' smiled Sean. 'Come and join us.'

'So when are you going to come and join our unit then?' asked Jak.

'When you guys stop being such assholes,' she grinned. 'Anyway, you've got one medic, you don't need another.'

'We'd swap Fenim for you any day,' said Sean with mock seriousness. 'With all the time Jak and I have known you, you're almost family.'

'Thanks a bunch Sean,' Fen countered. 'You just wait until your next toothache.'

Macker laughed. 'As much as I love you all, I am quite happy with my own unit, thank you.'

'So why do you keep coming over here and drinking our brew?' Jak grunted.

'It's the way you make it, Jak.' Macker grinned at Sean. 'Nice holiday over the border was it? Heard you did some sightseeing.'

'Piss off,' he growled, but his eyes were still smiling.

'Tor said you're treating that woman we brought in,' Jak said, handing her a refilled mug.

'That's right.'

'So what's the story?'

'She certainly has had her fair share of injuries.'

'Like what?' asked Tor.

'Well, most of them have healed ... just scars. It looks like she was tortured while she was in Balaat.'

'What about the bleeding on her leg?'

'She was stabbed in the thigh a few weeks back, in what looks like an older wound, and it hadn't healed properly. During that tangle with the pursuit party she must have taken a hit to it, opened it up again. The state she was in, I'm surprised that she got this far at all.'

'So she was in Balaat Fort?' Tor asked.

Macker nodded. 'No doubt of that.'

Tor smiled at Jak. 'Still think that she was lying?'

Jak threw him a dirty look but declined to answer.

Macker leaned forward and put her hand on Jak's shoulder. 'She wasn't lying Jak. Look. I know the whole thing might have brought back a few bad memories but trust me, Aris is not Ardaya, and she's been through a pretty rough time.'

Jak's whole body tensed. He knocked her hand off his shoulder.

'I think it's time to change the subject,' said Fenim.

Jak stood up. 'Don't bother, Fenim. I'm going for a walk. You can all talk about anything you like then.'

He strode off through the tents.

'Sorry guys,' said Macker. 'I didn't think he was still so touchy about the whole thing.'

Sean rubbed his chin reflectively. 'I'm surprised at how raw he still is. After all, it was four years ago.'

'Yeah, but perhaps the circumstances are too similar,' said Tor.

Fenim shook his head. 'Not all, Tor. Jak's not as soft as he was back then.'

'Did she tell you exactly what happened to her in Balaat?' asked Tor.

Macker looked at the ground. 'No. She won't talk about it ... even when I asked her how she got some of her wounds. Whatever it was, she seems determined to forget about it.'

'Can we help?' asked Sean.

'I don't think she wants any attention. At the moment she's too busy trying to prove that she's okay.'

'Hmmm. That could make things difficult.'

Macker smiled. 'Well, considering that most of the soldiers in Hellyon are on the brink, she should fit right in.'

Aris lay on her bed listening to the first hesitant notes of the dawn chorus and thinking she really should be getting up. Of course, there was no reason for her to get out of bed at all; she was supposed to be recovering, but she just wasn't used to lying in. On the other hand she still felt so tired, so weak and it was good to be able to enjoy the feeling of having a full stomach and to not have the fear of being beaten or killed.

But now her mind started to turn to other things, things she had not wanted to think about whilst in Balaat. Ani. By now she would have been told that her mother was never coming back. Aris wished that somehow she could reach her daughter—tell her that she was safe and well, and that one day, however long it took, she would return for her. But was that true? Could she, in all reality, ever get back to City again? In the back of her mind, doubt ruled on that one. Even if she did find a way of getting past the defences, she would be a fugitive among her own people. Maybe they had even turned Ani against her ... it was possible. And if Tiern ever discovered that she had returned, well, she didn't hold her life expectancy to be very long. No, her chances of getting back to her old life were as non-existent here as they had been in Balaat. But at least here she could relax a little.

Felson had accepted her account without too many questions — well, he couldn't really argue with Macker's medical evidence. Aris closed her eyes again. It would be breakfast soon. It seemed that all she had done in the past few days was eat and sleep. And answer questions. So many questions. In some ways she had preferred Jak and Tor's style of interrogation to Macker's: at least she had become used to fear.

She wasn't used to sympathy.

And sympathy had been in Macker's eyes as she examined Aris's wounds. She had been gentle, holding off every time Aris tensed thinking that she was causing more pain. But it hadn't been the physical wounds that had caused her distress: every touch brought back a memory — a dirty blade, the taste of dust and blood, the deafening screams of an hysterical mob, the creaking of the A frame as well as…. She shook her head ... best not thought about.

Best forgotten.

She forced herself to relax, take a deep breath and unclench her fists. She tasted blood on her lip; she must have bitten it to stop it from trembling so much. No, whatever nightmare she may have been through, it was over now. At least for a while. Hellyon would be a place of sanctuary.

A slight sound gave away a movement by the tent flap. Her eyes flew open and caught the briefest glimpse of a face before it disappeared. Even in the half-light she recognised who it was.

Jak.

But what the hell was he doing here? Had he intended her some harm? She certainly didn't think he'd come to play nurse. How long had he been there?

She took a deep breath, tried to slow her heart rate a little. He had certainly given her a shock, but perhaps that was what he had intended. What was that guy's problem anyway? What had she ever done to him? Maybe, she thought, it's best if I just keep out of his way as much as possible. Things will settle in time.

Felson's tent, although larger, was no more comfortable than those of the men he commanded; it was stifling in the close, thundery heat that had enveloped Hellyon Camp by mid afternoon. Sean, Tor, Jak and Fenim sat in front of the silver-haired colonel, a hint of anxiety on their faces. For all of them to have been summoned was unusual, and Felson was giving nothing away. In fact he seemed almost to have forgotten they were there as he sat shuffling papers behind his desk. Sean watched a fly lazily navigating circles above his head. Why is the old man making us wait, he wondered? It's almost as if he doesn't know how to tell us. Perhaps it is a suicide mission or something.

At last Felson cleared his throat and looked up.

'Right lads,' he said in his usual soft-spoken manner, 'I thought you might like to know about the woman that Jak and Torassin brought in the other day. She's been given full security clearance and will be joining us in our fight. So, first, well done to you both ... ' he looked at Jak and Tor, ' ... on saving her life and bringing her promptly back here.'

Sean shot Jak a look, but the other man's face was impassive. Tor looked down at his feet and started to fidget.

Felson continued. 'From what I've heard, she'll be a valuable asset to our forces. In fact I've already had half a dozen fighting units ask me to place her with them. However, as your unit was the one, which found her, I feel that she really ought to placed with you, at least for the time being.'

Sean had been expecting anything but this and was almost at a loss at what to say. He knew Felson valued his unit highly and that the addition of another good soldier would make it even better. But, close as they all were, could they accommodate an outsider, especially this one? And what about Jak ... ?

'I ... I don't know sir,' he said. 'It's certainly an honour for you to consider us like this ... .'

'But ... ?' asked Felson.

'We are a very tight knit unit and I don't feel I can make a decision until I have asked my men.'

Felson nodded. 'I didn't expect any different. Well, go on, ask them then.'

Sean turned to Fenim first, avoiding Jak's eyes as long as he could. 'Fen?'

Fenim shrugged. 'If she's passed security checks, then I don't have a problem.'

'Tor?'

Tor smiled. 'Yeah, okay by me.'

'Jak?' Sean waited for the response he knew would come, but he was to be surprised.

Jak nodded, a strange smile hovering around his lips. 'Okay,' he said.

Sean raised a quizzical eyebrow but said nothing. He looked back to Felson. 'Well, my men seem to think it's alright.'

'And you?' Felson asked.

'Well, I haven't met her yet, but I'll trust she'll be okay. Can I ask that she be removed if it doesn't work out?'

'No problem,' said Felson, 'but I don't think it will be necessary. Well, I suppose I'd better go and tell her who her new unit is and that she is to report to you in two days.'

Sean nodded and they filed out of tent. Once outside, Sean turned to Jak.

'Why the sudden change of heart?' he asked.

Jak gave the strange smile again. 'I have my reasons,' he said

HELLYON'S STAND

and wandered off, whistling.

4

Sean sauntered back from the operations briefing, his mind already on the task given to him. Back at CU11's encampment, he could see them all around the central fire, preparing their evening meals. All except Aris: as usual she was sat in the opening of her tent, checking and cleaning her rifle.

He frowned. She had been with them for a week now and she still didn't seem to be fitting in. It wasn't that there was any hostility between her and the others; in fact if anything, everyone was being too damn polite, even Jak. It didn't feel right without the usual banter, the atmosphere was becoming uncomfortable. He couldn't fault her contribution so far within the unit, but it seemed that she did what she had to do and then withdrew into the safety of her tent or went for a long walk, instead of trying to integrate with the rest of the men.

He cast his mind back to their first meeting, when she'd reported to him for duty. She hadn't been what he'd imagined, although he wasn't sure what he had expected either. Her face was strong and determined but not unfeminine. He been puzzled at first by her olive skin, which marked her out as a Jerregishan, like Fen. But then he remembered that many Jerregishans had fled to City at the beginning of Jessyn's regime

—her parents must have come from that exodus. She was fit, strong and certainly looked well enough after her ordeal, but her eyes told a different story: they had a darkness about them that told of unimaginable savagery, of fear and anger. He'd seen it before—Jak had been the same after Berryn's Crossing, but Jak at least had had the support of people he knew, of people who had also felt the same kind of pain. People he could trust. Aris had no one here. He'd talked to her and she came across as self-confident, even cocky. He knew, though, it was merely a mask.

In fact her attitude worried him: CU11 were about to embark on another operation, deep in enemy territory and the last thing he needed was a potential loose canon on his hands. Still, at least it would sort the situation one way or another: either she'd start to fit in, or he'd have to send her out with Jak—and only Jak would come back. Whatever, he was not going to put the rest of his unit at risk if she started behaving strangely.

Reaching the tents, he called them round.

'Felson is sending us out to Balaat,' he said. 'We leave tomorrow evening at dusk so that we reach the border in the dark. Then we head for that new fort that's being built twenty taks southwest of the B2 watchtower. One of the scouting units reported an escalation in vehicle movements to and from there. There are trucks—large trucks—going in from City.' Here he paused to look at Aris to see her reaction but she was looking into the fire. 'We are to do a short recce and see if we can discover what's in one of those vehicles.'

'It's weapons,' said Aris tonelessly. There was an uncomfortable silence broken only by the crackle of the fire.

'How do you know?' Sean finally asked.

'Tiern was trying to set up some kind of deal with Balaat, according to what I read in those files he was hiding. Then there was this woman in Balaat — she was often given to this officer as his ... companion. He got quite fond of her, told her things he shouldn't have.'

'Like what?'

'That Balaat was about to be supplied with weapons and ammunition from certain people within City. By all accounts this was quite a big thing because Balaat was starting to run low on materials to make their own bullets.'

Sean frowned. 'But why? What does City get out of it'

Aris shook her head. 'I didn't read that far, but I do know that City — well, Tiern in particular — is supplying Pock with some of the most advanced weaponry it has developed.'

'Maybe there's something in it for Tiern,' said Tor.

Aris shrugged. 'He's always had political ambitions, but I'm sure he's teamed up with someone in higher office on this one. I don't think that even he could pull off this sort of deal all by himself. But who's behind it all, or why, I really don't know.'

'Pity you didn't stay closer to him for a bit longer then, wasn't it?' Jak said caustically.

Aris chose to ignore him.

'Anyway,' Sean said quickly, 'we'll see what we can do when we get there. Seeing as there are only five of us, we'll have to organise ourselves as best as possible. Fen, I want you to take us in, with Jak behind you. I'll follow on next, then Aris. Tor, I want you to watch the rear. We'll go over the border on foot tomorrow after dark and make our way to a good observation point near our target. Then we'll take one day, maybe two, to see what we can before coming back again. Any trouble at any point and we call the whole thing off and head back to Hellyon. Any questions?'

'Are we to have a radio?' asked Jak.

'No. All available sets are in use elsewhere. Anyway, we

don't really need one for this mission. If we get into trouble, there isn't enough manpower in Hellyon to expect someone to come and get us out.'

'Thanks to Berryn's Crossing,' muttered Jak.

Sean knew Jak was trying to provoke a reaction from Aris but thankfully she showed no emotions at all. In fact, her overall silence worried him. It was a routine mission for his unit, but he'd expected at least some questions about operational procedures from Aris. However highly trained, she must have some uncertainty about what was going to happen. Maybe she was trying not to look stupid in front of the others by asking a dud question. Whatever the reason, he hoped he wasn't going to regret including her in his team.

Later, as they were all preparing for bed, Sean took Aris to one side.

'Do you feel up to this?' he asked.

The look she gave him was defensive. 'I'm fine,' she replied. 'I'm as physically fit as I've ever been, if that's what you're worried about.'

'And mentally?'

'What do you mean by that?'

'Look, we all know you've been through some nasty shit. Things like that can affect you for quite a while afterwards — ask most of the men and women around here. All I'm saying is if you're not up to a mission yet, that's fine. You don't have to prove anything right now.'

Her answer was firm, defiant. 'As I said, Sean, I'm fine. And I'm not trying to prove anything — just doing my job.'

He nodded. 'Good. I just don't want any unnecessary dramas in Balaat.'

She gave him a tight smile. 'Don't worry, I'm not going to let you down, if that's what you mean.'

The first quarter of the closest moon, Geia, was hidden behind a ragged collection of clouds as the five of them crossed the Hellyon/Balaat border the next night, walking silently in line along one of the smaller trackways. Every now and again Fenim would stop and the others behind him would halt also, looking and listening, alert for anything that signified danger. Once, a rustling had them all diving for the nearest cover, ready for action, but it was only a blue-fox that trotted across their path on his nightly territorial round. Their relief had been tangible; no one wanted a scene so soon after infiltration into Balaat.

At least Sean could be confident in his unit's ability to pass through enemy territory silently and without getting lost. Fenim guided them well, his knowledge of the geography of Balaat better than any map and compass. Jak, too, knew the area well: the ruins of the village of his childhood lay only a short distance away. He'd often played in these woods as a small boy — played soldier games. Now he was doing it for real.

Fenim stopped again. They all waited, alert. As usual, they heard nothing, but this time Fen stayed still for longer, as if he felt that something was not quite right. There were still no strange noises and Sean began to wonder what he was doing: Fen usually had a good reason for everything he did.

Suddenly all hell let loose from the rear.

'Get down!' yelled Tor as bullets began to fly past them. Tor, Aris and Sean hit the ground, turning to face the enemy. Jak and Fen managed to dive behind a couple of trees and began to blast their weapons into the darkness.

'Move back, move back!' Sean shouted to Tor and Aris in front of him as he desperately wriggled backwards on his stomach. Glancing up, he noticed that Tor had already disappeared ... God, how he wished he could do that, he thought as a bullet hit the ground not far from his shoulder.

Then, for one short moment the firing ceased and Sean could hear a thudding that was his heart. He felt fear in the pit of his stomach and his mind raced: how many of the bastards were there? Were they just at the rear, or had his unit somehow allowed themselves to be outflanked in the darkness? If so, then they would be lucky to get out of it.

The firing restarted. Behind him, Jak put down another round of fire and under it, Aris darted backwards and landed in the bracken next to Sean.

'You okay?' he asked.

She nodded, pulled out a new magazine from her belt pouch and slammed it onto her rifle.

'Good. Put down some cover for me, will you?' he said and ran into the darkness as she let off a volley of bullets. The unseen enemy answered, but Sean had already disappeared into the undergrowth. Keeping as low as he could, he ran for all he was worth, hoping that he wouldn't trip. The moon appeared from behind the clouds just as he reached the safety of a tree. He stopped, panting for breath and looked back. Aris was trying to inch her way back, but had attracted enemy fire, the bullets exploding into the ground around her; he was amazed she hadn't been hit. He saw Tor, directly behind her and in better cover, put down a hail of fire, giving her time to move out of her precarious position. Then when he looked again, Tor had vanished once more, or so it seemed. He heard RD10 fire from even further away; his unit was retreating fast, trying to find a more secure place they could hold. He just hoped they weren't being pushed into a trap.

In the muted light, he could see other shadows moving forward in front of him: four of them, as far as he could tell. A slight movement beside him made him spin around, his heart in his mouth, but it was only Tor.

'I'll get behind them,' the young man whispered, and Sean nodded. Then he had a thought:

'Was Fen back there with you?'

'I didn't see him,' Tor answered.

Sean looked back at the enemy soldiers who were now coming into line with him. 'Well, if ... ' he started, but when he turned back, Tor had already moved off. Shit, he thought, knowing Fen, he's moved up into a similar position on the other side. Let's just pray we don't shoot each other.

He lined up the enemy's leading man in his sights.

A gun cracked from the other side. Sean's target went down. So Fen was over there, but at least he wasn't in direct line of Sean's fire. The rest of the enemy soldiers hit the ground, but from where Sean was, it still left them open. He sighted up another and fired, making a direct hit. To his right and in front, the rest of the unit also opened up. When they stopped firing, there was total silence.

Sean slowly moved forward, as Fen emerged from the other side and crept towards the bodies, his weapon ready for any movement.

But there was none. They were all dead.

Sean whistled softly to bring the rest of the unit together.

'Right,' he said, 'we need to get out of here quick in case someone heard the shots.'

'We're some distance from the nearest watchtower,' said Jak. 'Even if anybody did hear anything, we should have some time. So what do you reckon, was it a normal patrol?' he asked Sean.

'Yeah, why?'

'It's just that they're a bit far west of the watchtower line.'

'Well, perhaps they felt like a change of route and it was just our bad luck to run into them.'

Jak glanced at Aris and muttered under his breath, 'Bad luck? Yeah, I'd say so.'

They reached their destination an hour before first light and set up an observation post under an overhang on the rocky high ground that overlooked their target. Adding a few small boulders for extra cover, the unit settled down and waited for dawn to break.

As the sky lightened, the features of the land in front of them became more defined. A road ran up to the well-defended gates of the camp, which was itself enclosed by a high, metal-stranded fence. Five large wooden huts stood in a row to the right facing an old stone building. In the northeastern section, a disorderly array of tents was gathered into a small area bordered by piles of planks and building materials. Other than the gate sentries and a few other guards patrolling the perimeter, it seemed quiet.

Sean decided that he, Jak and Aris would take first watch while Tor and Fen rested in the back of the overhang. They gratefully laid out their sleeping packs on the rocky floor and were soon asleep, their weapons still within reach.

Not long after, a truck rumbled along the road below. The camp's gates were opened and the vehicle rolled through, soon becoming surrounded by people spilling out of the tents. Jak noticed that Aris had tensed, her eyes never leaving the vehicle.

'From City?' Sean whispered to her.

She nodded. 'That's a GPV — General Purpose Vehicle — of the type used by Special Ops.'

The lackeys surrounding the truck were now being organised into a long line that reached from the vehicle to one of the wooden huts. They were obviously about to unload the cargo.

'Those look like PN30 rifles and boxes of ammo,' said Aris, peering intently through the viewers.

'There are a lot of them,' observed Sean.

Aris frowned. 'And they're the newest City have — laser-sighted and with high velocity ammunition—but why would Tiern supply Pock with so many new weapons when Balaat is still a potential threat to City?'

'You tell us,' said Jak softly. Sean gave him a dig in the ribs.

Soon the last of the rifles had been taken off and eight men entered the vehicle. They emerged, carrying two larger, heavier field guns.

'Shit, PN3s,' breathed Aris. 'Serious firepower.'

'Just what we haven't got,' Sean muttered, suddenly thoughtful.

Down below, the GPV, now empty, turned around and headed out through the gates, back towards City. But the activity in the camp didn't stop: two Balaatan vehicles, smaller than the GPV were brought out and were each loaded with a quantity of rifles and ammunition and a PN3. The lackeys now seemed more organised for they had the job completed in less than an hour. The two vehicles then headed north out of the camp, in the direction of Balaat Fort.

Three hours later, Fen and Tor took over the watch and Sean, Jak and Aris retreated to the back of the overhang to get their heads down. The mid-day heat was beginning to build, and after the exertions of the night, Sean and Aris quickly fell asleep. But although Jak felt drowsy, he couldn't sleep; there were too many thoughts bothering him. He turned on his side to face Aris and watched her, studying her face. There was a familiarity about her, all the more disturbing because she was lying by his side. Like Ardaya, she had Jerregishan blood, but that wasn't all that reminded him: it was also her eyes, and the way she smiled. It brought back too much of the past, a past he'd rather not remember at all.

Even when he'd first seen her, with her face swollen by the beating she'd received, something had tugged at his memory. A few days later he had found himself outside where she was being treated in the medical encampment wondering why he was there. He'd watched her sleeping then too, at least until she'd woken with that nightmare, and again wondered at the similarity. It was a bittersweet reminder of the love he had thought he had found again and also of the greatest humiliation of his life. He thought he had put it all behind him, got on with his life; now this woman had appeared from nowhere, like an avenging angel and he felt disturbed, torn up all over again. It was all too much to be just a coincidence, surely.

But Ardaya had had a totally different personality from Aris and was no soldier, or so he'd thought. What if City, Jerregish, Balaat, or even all three were playing the same trick again and sending in a wolf in sheep's clothing? In which case they had miscalculated because she had been placed in a unit with a man who had a very long memory. She wouldn't be able to breathe without him seeing. He would be onto her every move, watching, waiting. All it needed was one mistake and he would pounce. As he saw it, fate was giving him a chance to replay his hand, only this time he would make sure that he wouldn't be the loser.

His mind wandered back to the interrogation in the watchtower: he should have killed her then, when he'd had the chance. That way it would have been over quickly and cleanly; not this long drawn out war of attrition that seemed to exist between them. But he hadn't and now he was going to have to make the best of it. Sean and the others already seemed to have taken her side against him. Any move he made against her would have to be on his own and done in such a way as to bring no suspicion down upon himself. He studied her face again: it looked so beautiful, so feminine when she was asleep. All the hard lines and tension disappeared. It was then he knew with a certainty that if he wanted any peace of mind, he would have to deal with her, and soon. To kill his past, he had to kill her first.

Fen and Tor's time had seen two more City vehicles coming into the camp. One had contained what looked like supplies and medical equipment, the other, like the first of the day was loaded with more weaponry.

Just before last light, Sean gathered them all together.

'Right,' he said, 'I think we've seen enough here. We have three choices: we can either stay here another day; we can go back to Hellyon, or we can move further south along the road and try and pick up one of those vehicles coming out of City — get it back to Hellyon.'

'Are you crazy?' Jak asked. 'We'd have to drive in daylight, through enemy territory, in a vehicle we aren't familiar with and on roads that we're not used to.'

'Driving the GPV's no problem,' said Aris. 'I can do that. But the biggest problem will be getting it to stop in the first place. If it's got a full crew of six, they won't be easy pickings.'

'What will they be armed with?' asked Sean.

'PN30s,' she answered. 'Just like the ones you saw on that truck earlier. And you'll have to be careful that you don't hit the truck with any of your fire just in case it's got ammunition in it.'

'That's it, then. We can't do it,' said Jak. 'Let's go home.'

'Hang on a minute,' Torassin interrupted. 'When Fen and I were watching, only three men got out of the vehicle, and with all it was carrying, I don't think they could comfortably have fitted any more crew in.'

Aris nodded. 'That's possible. They would probably only need a half crew for this type of assignment, but they'll still be armed with better weapons than us.'

They were all silent, thinking.

Aris took a deep breath: 'I ... might have an idea,' she said. 'If they are Special Ops then there is a chance that they will know me. I could try to stop the vehicle — lure them out.'

Sean shook his head. 'And what if they don't recognise you, or shoot you anyway. No, Jak's right: it's too dangerous, we ought to go home.'

'Look, it's a chance I'm prepared to take,' she insisted. 'I know these people ... '

'Yeah, we know,' Jak interrupted. 'What if you suddenly decide to change sides again?'

The anger in her eyes was unmistakable as she turned on him. 'For fuck's sake Jak, will you never let up? Hellyon badly needs weapons, or supplies, or whatever else those bloody trucks are carrying and I'm prepared to go out there and risk my life to get them.'

Fenim spoke up. 'For what it's worth, I say let's go ahead with her plan. She's certainly right about Hellyon needing more weapons. Whatever the risk, it's worth it.'

Tor nodded. 'I agree. There are enough of us and we're all good at what we do.'

'And if anything goes wrong, we get out immediately, right?' asked Jak.

Sean nodded. 'Right, we'd better get ourselves sorted.'

They reached their ambush point on the road without incident and lay in the cool undergrowth listening to the sounds of the night and for anything that might indicate present danger. But all seemed peaceful and it was decided that they would take it in turns to watch while the others got some rest.

There were no more vehicles that night, but as the first fingers of light crept across the sky, they readied themselves: the first GPV they'd seen yesterday had arrived not long after dawn.

Aris suddenly stripped off her combat jacket and with her knife put some rips into her shirt and trousers. The others stared at her in disbelief.

'It'll look more convincing,' she whispered. Then, gathering up handfuls of dirt, she rubbed them into her clothing, hair and skin. By the time she'd finished, she looked as if she'd been living rough for months.

'You don't want a couple of bruises as well, do you?' asked Sean, grinning. 'I'm sure I could persuade Jak to do the business.'

She grinned back. 'Thanks, but I think I'll pass on that one.' His light-heartedness may have seemed flippant, but she hadn't mistaken the new respect in his eyes.

Jak looked at her with a different expression: the way she had disguised herself so quickly, and what she had said about being convincing only served to arouse his suspicions even more. As he thought, she was more than capable of pulling the wool over other people's eyes. Automatically he checked that the safety catch on his rifle was off. Maybe it was time for her to make that mistake. Ten minutes later they heard a low rumbling noise in the distance.

Aris crawled out to the edge of the road, where she could see the vehicle's approach. It was another GPV, and was moving fairly slowly over the rutted ground. Faking an injury, she limped out into the middle of the road and gave the hand signal to halt. The truck stopped a short distance away. Behind the reflective glass, Aris could see nothing and she suddenly became aware of how exposed she was. A man wearing the black Special Ops uniform got out of the truck, his rifle raised. Aris held her arms out to show that she was unarmed and slowly limped forward. As she got closer, the man's face became familiar: it was Taj, Captain of Unit SO2. She had been through military academy with him, trained alongside him although thankfully they had never been close. She suddenly wondered how she would have reacted if it had been someone from her own unit. She didn't want to think about it.

She moved slowly forward, her arms still raised. 'Captain?'

The man squinted at her, trying to recognise the dirty, dishevelled but familiar creature in front of him. Suddenly the look on his face changed from one of careful curiosity to one of loathing.

'Desun. So you managed to stay alive did you? How can you fucking well live with yourself after betraying your own people? Bitch. I ought to shoot you right now – finish off the job.'

Aris's breath caught in her throat; she hadn't been prepared for such hostility. Tiern must have done a good job on destroying her reputation within Special Ops.

'Wait, Taj, it didn't happen like you think. I was set up. I would never shoot one of my own, you know that.'

Taj laughed. 'So you're claiming that Tiern made something up on a whim just to get rid of you? I hardly think he'd go to such lengths to get rid of a little slut who had outstayed her welcome, do you?'

'You have to believe me; I know I can't prove anything...'

'Damn right you can't.' He turned and beckoned towards the truck. Another man got out and walked towards them. 'Nelmes, I want you to meet former sergeant Desun of SO4.'

'Wasn't she...?'

'Yes, exiled to Balaat for crimes against City. As you can see, she's still alive.' The other man looked her up and down, his lip curling into a sneer. 'Do you want me to take care of her?'

Taj shook his head. 'No. We'd better go by regulations and hand her over to the commander of the camp when we get there. I'm sure Pock's men will know what to do with her.'

Aris felt herself go cold. Shit, she thought, this whole plan is falling apart. Start thinking, Desun, how the hell are you going to get them off this track and into the ambush area?

'In that case you won't be interested in what I have to tell you.'

'Like what?' Taj looked at her with suspicion.

'Do you really think I flagged your truck down just to get threatened and spat at? No, I still have some loyalty to City, no matter what's been done to me. I wanted to prove that loyalty by saving whatever little scheme you've got going on here from attack. However, if you're going to kill me or hand me over to Balaat, I suddenly don't feel so inclined to save your asses any more.'

Taj looked at Nelmes for some reassurance; she had thrown him off stride, she could tell. 'How do we know your information is sound? This could just be a trick to make us let you go.'

'True. But until you trust me a little bit, you'll never know will you?'

Taj nodded. 'Okay, we'll do a deal; you tell us what you know, and prove that it's for real, and we'll let you go again. I can't say any fairer than that.'

Aris nodded. 'It's a deal. Now I've been around these parts for a couple of weeks now and I've seen things that could bring this little arms deal of City's to a halt, at least for a while.'

'Like what?' asked Nelmes.

'Hellyon have inserted a covert advance assault force and

are bringing in weapons ahead of a larger offensive to take out that fort just down the road. And it wouldn't take much, would it gentlemen? It's not particularly heavily defended, considering its purpose, and it doesn't look very organised either. I'll bet a small, disciplined force of Hellyon soldiers could easily take the place, wipe it off the map and take out any City convoys in the area at the time as well.'

Taj grinned. 'Nice story, Desun, but stories alone aren't going to get you off the hook.'

'You don't think I'd just give you a story do you?' Aris replied, trying to keep the sudden fear she felt under control. 'I know where at least two of the weapons caches are. I can take you to them right now.'

Nelmes glanced at Taj. 'Can we trust her?'

Taj raised his rifle again, as if to make a point. 'I have a weapon pointed straight at her head. If she so much as moves one step out of line, she's dead. You stay here with the vehicle while I go and investigate. Damn, we could have done with a full patrol for this one.'

With Taj behind her, Aris turned and headed for the treeline. There was still a risk she might get shot when the unit attacked; she would just have to hope they were quick enough in disarming him.

A hundred yards into the vegetation and nothing had happened. Where are they? thought Aris. Surely they wouldn't have abandoned me?

There was a blur of movement to her right as something heavy ploughed into her and took her to the ground. Almost simultaneously, Taj's weapon discharged, the bullet flying through the empty space where she had been a fraction of a second before. She was aware of a weight on her back, pinning her to the ground.

'You okay?' the weight said.

'Sean, what the hell?' she said, struggling to get her breath back.

'Is that all the thanks I get for saving you? We could see that as soon as Jak attacked, that man was going to shoot you. That's why I decided to get you out of the way as well.'

He rolled off her and she sat up. 'I suppose I should be grateful then,' she smiled.

Turning around, Taj's body lay on its back, open eyes staring into an empty space. He had died without making a sound — Jak's speciality. However, Nelmes had surely heard the shot; he could be radioing back to base any second.

'We'd better get the other one,' Fen growled, as if reading her thoughts. 'Do you want me to take him out like this one, or can we use our guns now?' He looked at Sean for a decision.

'We could always take him prisoner,' Aris said softly, 'he might have had some useful information about what's going on.'

'Don't be so fucking crazy!' said Jak. 'We haven't got the time to take prisoners.'

'Not your favourite past-time, is it Jak?' she snapped back, but the usual edge was not in her voice. He was right. They had been compromised and time was running short.

Sean nodded. 'Take Tor with you. Take Nelmes out the quickest way you can, but just keep your weapons away from the ammo.

Fen nodded and sprinted away in the direction of the truck, Tor following closely behind. Sean turned to Aris, extending his arm to help her get up. 'I should have asked you if you wanted to finish the bastard off.'

Aris shook her head. 'I wouldn't want to waste the energy.'

She turned away from him in case her true thoughts were

mirrored in her eyes. Even if she had been innocent before, she had now indeed become a traitor to City: her actions had caused the deaths of two men from her operational detachment. She shook her head. *Maybe I'm no better than Tiern after all*, she thought.

By the time they returned to the GPV, Nelmes and the third man in the vehicle were dead and Fen and Tor were busy checking over the load. They were grinning like idiots.

'Alright, what have we got?' asked Sean.

'Two PN3s,' said Fenim.

'Lots of PN30s.'

'And don't forget the ammo — masses of ammo.'

Sean held up his hands. 'Okay, Okay, I get the message. Seeing as it seems to do something for you two, you can ride in the back, on top of it.'

'That's probably the best offer Tor's had all year,' Jak laughed.

'At least I get offers!' Tor retorted.

'Have you two finished?' asked Sean. 'We are still in Balaat, in case you hadn't noticed. It might be a good idea to think of getting out.' He turned to Fenim: 'Fen, what's the best road out of here?'

Fenim's answer was immediate. 'The old Sorris road.'

'But that leads past a watchtower!' protested Jak.

Fen shrugged. 'It's the only road wide enough to get this thing back into Hellyon.'

'He's right,' said Sean. 'We'll just have to hope they're all asleep and get it past.'

'Some hope,' answered Jak. 'Do you want to get us all killed?'

'I've another idea,' Aris spoke up. 'Taj's uniform wasn't too bloodstained. Sean's about the right size to wear it and could easily pass for a City Officer.'

'But why would we be going to a watchtower in the first place? And how do we explain the bloodstains?' asked Jak derisively.

'We encountered a small Hellyon recce patrol en route, killed all but one who we're delivering to the watchtower as a prisoner, she answered. 'Sean and one other should be able to get inside the tower, get them off their guard and then a PN30 should take care of everyone up there quite easily. We can handle any outlying patrols as well as take out the watchman on the roof.'

Sean nodded thoughtfully. 'It's still going to be a hell of a risk but I can't think of a better way. Who did you have in mind to be the prisoner?'

She smiled sweetly at Jak. 'I think there's only one man for that job, don't you?' Aris drove the GPV as carefully as possible along the road to avoid causing too much discomfort to the men in the back; she was sure that they'd get their share of that later. An hour later, the watchtower came into view, its wooden bulk rising above a well-defended metal base. The two men on the top were already aiming their rifles at the oncoming vehicle.

Sean did the buttons up on his City combat jacket and swivelled around to the back of the truck.

'Right, here we go. Tor, get ready to ghost your way over to the far side and take out the two men on the roof. Aris and Fen, I want you to stay here and guard the truck. If anything happens to us up there, just get the goods back to Hellyon.'

'Are you okay with the gun?' Aris gestured towards the PN30 in his hands.

'Yeah,' he replied, sounding more confident than he felt, 'piece of cake.'

Two more men with weapons emerged from the base of the

watchtower. Grinning and holding his hands up, Sean got out of the truck.

'It's okay guys,' he shouted. 'Don't shoot. We're from City. Got a prisoner for you.'

The Balaatans stopped, lowered their guns and beckoned him forwards.

'What happened?' asked one, his face surly.

'We were heading for the new fort when we were jumped by a Hellyon patrol. Killed 'em all, except this one—thought he might have some information. However, there isn't much room in that vehicle with all the weapons so I decided to bring him here.'

The surly one glanced at the truck then back at Sean. Shit, if he thinks to look in the truck ... thought Sean. But no, the man seemed to relax. He turned around and waved Sean towards the watchtower.

'Okay, bring him in,' he grinned.

Sean dragged Jak off the truck and pushed him forward, a rifle at his back. Jak's hands were fastened with restrainers, but Sean knew that they were still loose enough for Jak to go for his knife concealed in a trouser pocket if necessary.

They passed through the tower door and began to climb the stairs.

'Did you take any injuries?' asked the other man who was much younger than his comrade.

Sean laughed. 'No. They didn't give us any trouble at all really.'

The older man also laughed. 'Not surprising. They're all a bunch of pussies over the border. Anything of substance got wiped out at Berryn's Crossing—thanks to you guys of course,' he added hastily.

'Yeah, right,' Sean grinned, trying to cover the fact that he had a sudden urge to knock the guy's block off.

The watchroom, like all other watchrooms, was dark, lit only by a couple of methlamps. Wooden boxes and crates of stores were stacked untidily against the walls, leaving little comfortable living space. In the middle of the room, two young men sat around a battered table drinking from a shared cup and playing Pukka. They looked up as the group walked in.

The older man, who seemed to be the leader, spoke to them. 'It's only our good friends from City. They've brought us a Hellyon boy to play with.'

A young, dark man at the table spat in Jak's direction. Jak glared back at him.

'He don't look too playful, do he?' the man said and laughed. 'Never mind, when the patrol gets back, Baggel will make him dance and sing.'

Sean pretended to take an interest in his surroundings. 'Never been in a Balaatan watchtower before. Do you still have a ten man crew?'

The older man handed him another cup filled with a brown liquid. 'Yeah, but four are out on patrol at the moment. Don't know why we're all needed these days; Hellyon hasn't even got the balls for a raid, let alone a full attack.'

You stupid bastard, you don't know how wrong you are, Sean thought, but he just raised an eyebrow and said: 'Best not underestimate the enemy though.'

He drained the cup, identifying its contents as Balaatan chag and trying not to grimace at its bitter taste. 'Well, must be off before they wonder where I've got to.'

On cue, Jak pretended to struggle. Sean brought the rifle up, but suddenly turned and kept it on repeat fire as he scoured the room with bullets, hitting every Balaatan soldier more than once. Unfamiliar with its power, Sean briefly found his aim thrown upwards, the rounds hitting both of the meth-lamps in the ceiling. Glass shattered and flaming meths liquid spread across the room, setting the rotten wood of the walls and floor alight. The crates, too, caught fire and within seconds the two men were surrounded by a wall of flame.

'Shit!' yelled Sean, as Jak hastily released himself from his bonds. 'Let's get out of here!'

They were halfway down the stairs when there was suddenly a fearsome explosion and scorching heat as something, probably a box of ammunition, exploded in the watch-room. The shockwave threw them to the bottom of the steps, landing against the tower door.

After a few seconds Sean sat up, dazed but otherwise unhurt. Jak lay face down next to him, unconscious and with blood pouring from a gash on his arm. Taking a deep breath, Sean stood up, unbarred the door and stuck his head out of the doorway to call for help.

A barrage of shots passed close to his ear. He stuck his head back inside again and tried to clear his mind. The other patrol must have come back, he thought. And then he looked up. Above them, the whole floor of the watch-room was alight and threatening to come down on their heads.

Sean looked up and felt a surge of panic: they had to get out or else they'd be burnt alive. He didn't want to die like that. His heart hammered in his chest and he forced himself to slow his breathing, to take control of his fear.

Outside, he heard the sounds of a fierce firefight: the FD4s favoured by the Balaatans and the more comforting noises of the RD10s of Fen and Tor. He also heard the dull retort of a PN30: Aris must have reverted to a weapon she was familiar with.

The battle seemed to go on forever. Sean started to cough as the smoke became thicker, the acrid stench burning his throat and lungs. Above him, he could hear the ominous crackle of timbers burning through and with a jolt he realised that death wasn't far away. At least in the open, they might stand a chance. He pushed the door open, and, keeping low, dragged Jak from the doorway, any moment expecting to feel the punching thud of a bullet.

But nothing seemed to be happening.

He looked up. All was silent. The battle was over and Tor was running up to help him. As they pulled Jak out of reach of the inferno, there was a loud cracking noise behind them and a large portion of the watch-room floor crashed, burning, where they had been only second before.

Tor looked at Jak. 'What happened to him?' he asked.

'The explosion ... ' muttered Sean. 'I think he hit his head on the way down'

Between them they carried Jak's inert frame back to the GPV, where they laid him on the wide front seat, his legs bent up. Tor squeezed his tall frame into the foot-well and began to apply pressure to the wound on his arm. Fenim, still in the back of the truck, stuck his head through into the cab.

Torassin waved him away. 'It's okay, Fen, I can handle this. You take a look at Sean.'

Sean, pale and visibly shaken, wandered around to the back of the truck, where Fen helped him in.

'Okay guys,' said Aris, quieter than usual, 'the road's going to get a little rough from now on, and I don't want to be hanging around until we're over the border.' She glanced down at Jak, concern in her eyes. 'Will he handle it?'

Tor nodded. 'Jak'll be okay, Aris. Just get us home.'

They'd only been back in camp a few hours, when Felson summoned them to his tent. Only Jak stayed behind in the encampment: he had mild concussion and a deep flesh wound, but the damage hadn't been as bad as it looked and Fen soon fixed him up. As soon as they arrived, the truck and its contents were taken away by SU3, one of the supply units, and suddenly they felt empty-handed, with no trophy to parade. They were all exhausted, but the last thing they felt like doing was resting — the adrenaline buzz hadn't worn itself out enough for that. Therefore, it was almost a relief when they were called in by Felson — at least it gave them something to do.

Sean gave the debriefing, the others throwing in comments and observations from time to time when he omitted something. Felson listened carefully, nodding and 'hmphing' at intervals. At the end, he smiled. 'You've all done very well,' he said. 'I certainly didn't expect you to bring a truck back, let alone a consignment of weapons. As we've been so low on heavy artillery since Berryn's those PN3s are particularly valuable. Do you have any experience with them Aris?'

'Yes, sir. I was trained on all City weapons.'

'Good. Well, perhaps I could ask you to train some of the unit commanders to use them too.'

'It would be a pleasure,' she smiled.

'Your brew sir.' Felson's valet appeared with a mug in his hand. Felson took it off him and the man set about tidying at the back of the tent.

The valet casually looked up and caught Aris's eye. For a second he froze, his eyes growing wide, and then he looked away. Hastily gathering up an armful of blankets, he disappeared behind the partition into Felson's living quarters. Aris frowned, puzzled at the man's behaviour. She looked around at the others, but they didn't seem to have noticed anything amiss.

Why had he reacted so strongly when he saw her? She didn't

know him, but yet the face was somehow familiar. She tried to recall where she had seen him before, but nothing came to mind. Maybe she was mistaken or maybe he had thought she was someone else too. At the moment she didn't have the energy to think about it.

As they left Felson's tent, Sean took hold of Aris's arm and waited until Tor and Fen had gone on ahead. He smiled down at her.

'I apologise,' he said.

'For what?'

'For having doubts about you. You've more than proved me wrong.'

'As I said before, I am just doing my job.'

'Even so, you did excellently. Remember, you're part of the team now, and if you ever need someone to talk to about what you've been through ... '

She fixed him with a hard stare. 'Listen Sean, I appreciate your concern, but I don't need mothering. I'm okay—really I am.'

She turned on her heel and walked off in the opposite direction. Sean watched her go, a worried expression on his face. Sure you are, he thought. The trouble is, I don't believe you. Never mind, you'll open up sooner or later; I can wait.'

5

Tor sat beneath the rock face on the western edge of the camp and tried to relax. Unable to sleep, he had crept from the tent, leaving Jak snoring softly. His feet had brought him here, the one place in the whole of Hellyon Camp that seemed relatively deserted. He tried to recall the dream that had awoken him only to find vague images of hunting dogs running through a thick forest, their coats matted with blood, fear in their eyes. He remembered hearing their desperate howls as they tried to call to each other, to keep the pack together. But that was all. And yet it had left him with a great unease, a feeling that he had to find the meaning behind it, that it was somehow important.

He lay down, feeling his back mould into the solid security of the earth beneath him and closed his eyes. An ancient mantra from his childhood floated into his mind and he began to quietly chant it, feeling his mind relax. The mantra had been one to help children calm down and drift off to sleep; he hadn't thought about it in years. But now, as peace began to steal over him, he felt a floating feeling as if he wasn't quite flesh and bone any longer. It was peculiar and yet somehow still pleasing so he continued.

Beautiful colours filled his head, danced and merged,

making patterns that could not possibly exist in the real world. He smiled, allowing himself to be lulled by his self-made entertainment. The shapes ebbed and flowed, then started to take on a vague form, at first an upright blob and then a defined human shape. The shape became clearer and clearer until at last Tor could make out the features of his father. The old man raised an arm and pointed straight at him.

'Only you can bring them all together,' he said.

'Who?' Tor asked silently, puzzled and almost annoyed that his father had managed to invade his space even here.

'Your people. When the time is right you will know what to do.'

The man's figure began to fade as quickly as it had appeared.

'What do you mean?' Tor called after him. But it was too late; his father's form had dissolved back into the colours and even these were beginning to fade and swirl off into the distance, chased away by Tor's agitation. He found himself sat bolt upright again, back in the real world. The dawn was just about to break over the horizon..

In the distance, an ul-bird hooted in defiance of the rising sun, and Tor could not resist a smile: Ul was the totem of his father, the bird who ruled the shadow-lands of night, who knew everything, saw everywhere. Wise old bird, thought Tor, but not even your tricks will bring me back again, father. My life is in Hellyon now. It may be harder, with less privileges, but at least it is of my choosing.

The memory of the day he left the tribe still sat uncomfortably with him. His father had turned away in disappointment; not only was his son refusing to follow him as Tribe leader but the young man was also going away to fight in someone else's war. But Tor had always held different beliefs to the rest of his people, had always been wilful. He knew that he had the Sharm-singing power within him but it had scared him and he had rejected all attempts to train it. Added to that, his father was respected as a powerful, wise man and that, Tor felt, was too much to live up to. At least here in Hellyon he could be who he wanted to be. Feeling the damp working its way through his trousers, he got up and stretched his stiff legs, brushing off the dust clinging to the wet material. Seeing the smoke rising from the various cooking fires, he decided to walk back, before he was missed.

As he approached the unit's tents, he could see Jak sitting in the opening of theirs, mending a tear in his shirt. Aris was shaking out her bedding. As usual, they weren't talking to each other, but at least they weren't fighting either. Seeing his approach, she waved at him, then wandered back into her tent. As he reached Jak, Sean and Fenim appeared from the other direction bringing the day's water rations in two large holder-cans.

But there was something wrong: there was none of the usual bantering between them. Instead their faces were grim, and Tor could sense their anger. Jak stopped what he was doing and looked up, registering the expressions on their faces.

'What's up?' he asked, his tone wary.

Sean answered, his voice tight with rage. 'It looks like we have a saboteur in camp. The water filtration plant was damaged last night. All water now has to be boiled until further notice.'

'Wasn't it guarded?' asked Tor.

'The sentry was found with his throat cut. It seems like a professional job. The repairs will take at least a week, probably longer.'

'A bit of a coincidence, isn't it?' asked Jak coldly.

'What do you mean?'

He jerked his head towards Aris. 'She's only been here a couple of months and then this happens. It's just like last time.'

'Last time?' Aris had overheard him. 'What do you mean, last time?'

Jak was just about to reply, when Sean held up his hand, warning him off. 'Jak, leave it out. Aris had nothing to do with this.'

'Too right I didn't!' She rounded on Jak, outraged. 'Now, if you don't like me, that's fair enough; I'm not that fucking keen on you either, mister. But don't start throwing around accusations that you have no proof to back up.'

'I don't need proof. I know what I know.'

'Know what, Jak? What do you know? You don't know the first fucking thing about me!'

His eyes, cold, hostile, bore into hers. 'I know enough to regret not slitting your throat that first day.'

'Jak!' shouted Sean. 'That's enough!'

Jak backed off. A cold smile spread across his features, promising that this was by no means finished. Aris drew back her fist, intending to smash it off his face, but found her wrist gripped hard by Fenim.

'Stop it, both of you!' hissed Sean. 'Jak, I'll see you in my tent in five minutes. Aris, I suggest you go and cool off somewhere.'

Throwing one last furious glance at Jak, she marched out of the unit's encampment.

She found herself walking towards the damaged filtration plant. Felson was there, talking with another commander, his face grim. Members of the maintenance units swarmed over the machinery, assessing the damage and fixing whatever they could: some of the pipework had been dismantled or twisted, other parts seemed to have had some type of corrosive substance poured over them. It was clear to Aris, although she was no engineer, that much was busted up beyond an easy repair.

'Not looking good, is it?' said a voice at her ear.

Aris turned and saw Macker with two empty holder-cans in her hands.

'But it can be fixed?'

'Yeah, although it'll tie up most of the maintenance units for a while which will mean general vehicle and weapons repairs won't get done.'

Macker began to walk to the stream to fill her cans; Aris walked with her.

'How are you getting on with the lads?' Macker asked.

Aris tried to give a convincing smile. 'Oh, alright. They're friendly enough.'

'Even Jak?' Macker questioned.

Aris stayed silent and Macker grinned, showing her straight white teeth. 'I thought so. Oh just ignore him; he can be a grumpy little bastard at times.'

Aris shrugged. 'It's more than that: he hates me.'

Macker shook her head. 'If that were the case you'd be dead by now — Jak doesn't mess around.'

'Maybe he just hasn't found the right opportunity.'

Macker looked at her intently for a minute, then handed her one of the holder-cans. 'Come on,' she said, 'help me back with these and I'll do us a brew.'

Macker was lucky enough to have been detailed to one of the solid wooden buildings within the camp; part of the Old World town that had been left behind here. Her room was filled with bits and pieces that looked as though they'd come from the various semi-nomadic peoples in the Tribe-lands: rugs, jars, weave-pictures …. She ushered Aris in and pointed her towards one of the seats.

Aris looked around her; there was something about the room that reminded her of her own apartment back in City. It was a comforting feeling.

'Nice room,' she commented.

Macker smiled, appreciating the compliment. 'Thanks. This is my little oasis. When I get leave I like to travel a little bit and do some bartering at the tribal markets; it's one of my few pleasures in life. I just hope I never get transferred back to tentland.'

'It's a pity there aren't more of these buildings,' Aris said ruefully. 'I'm sure getting fed up of living under canvas.'

Macker handed her a mug of char and sat down on her bed. Immediately a small grey cat, one of the camp moggies, ran out from underneath and sat on her lap. 'There again, the way things are going, no-one will be living here for much longer.'

Aris's head snapped up. 'Really? You think Hellyon's lost?'

Macker sighed. 'That's something I don't even want to think about but, yes, it's a possibility. When Balaat was our only enemy, we stood a good chance of fighting them off as they were totally disorganised and badly supplied. We had the upper hand as we were supported and supplied by City.'

'But then City started withdrawing.'

'Yeah, and Pock took immediate advantage, with constant raiding. He also seems to suddenly have better weaponry than before. Over the last seven years, Balaat has taken half of what Hellyon used to be, burning most of the towns and massacring or enslaving the inhabitants, and then of course there was Berryn's Crossing. Sean says you weren't there.'

Aris shook her head, her expression suddenly guarded. She still couldn't bring herself to admit her presence, even if it had only been as rearguard support.

HELLYON'S STAND

Macker drew a deep breath. 'Then I'll tell you what happened. Hellyon was starting to lose ground badly and our scouts had discovered a new Balaatan camp on our borders which contained a large contingent of troops, and a massive amount of weaponry and supplies; it was all intended for another assault into Hellyon. Commander Morranis appealed to City for help in destroying the camp, never expecting that City would agree. After all, it had been some time since we'd done any joint operations. But City did agree and sent some of their most elite troops and advanced weaponry under the command of Lennard Tiern.

'The night before the attack, Tiern and the Hellyon Commanders formulated a battle plan. The Hellyon forces would be split into two, flanking the artillery of the City Ops forces. The plan was that the huge field guns would destroy most of the Balaat defences and then we would go in and take out the rest. Anyway, the next morning at dawn, we were all in position where Tiern had wanted us. The signal for the attack to begin was given and the cannons moved forwards and fired a few shots at the fences of the camp.

'Balaatan troops suddenly appeared to be retreating and we were given the signal to move forward. Then just as we reached the centre ground, the field guns opened up again, but this time on us.'

She closed her eyes, recalling the memory. 'We were trapped between Tiern and Balaat, fired on by both sides. Our battalions tried to retreat, but it was chaos — panic had taken over and it was every person for themselves. Because I was a medic, I was seconded from my unit of that time, CU3, to join the other medics at the back of the battle-lines. Fenim also was at the back of the lines with me, although he rarely stayed for long. He showed a great deal of courage that day: time and time again he went into the battle to drag wounded men and women out and pass them on to the evacuation vehicles and medics. It was only when Jak and Sean came out — Jak had been wounded in the shoulder with small arms fire — that he heard the rest of CU11, as well as CU3, had been wiped out.

That dawn, our battalions had gone into battle 15000 strong; only 3000 got out. We returned to Hellyon covered from head to toe in the blood of our friends.'

Aris lowered her eyes, shaken by the emotion in the other woman's voice. 'I'm sorry,' she murmured, not knowing what else she could say without giving away her lie. She felt sick.

Macker shrugged. 'Anyway, because of City's behaviour some people may be a bit antagonistic towards you.'

'Well, I haven't had too much trouble so far, except from Jak.'

'Jak's got a lot of stuff to sort out.'

'You're not kidding.'

'Seriously, Jak's had it rough. His wife and children were murdered in a Balaatan raid 16 years ago, when he was miles away on the Jerregishan border. He's always blamed himself for not having moved them to a safer place when he had the chance months before. I think he didn't believe it could happen to them. And then there was Ardaya. She was a woman from Jerregish who came over the border four years ago seeking asylum. Jak found her and brought her back to camp, vouching for her character. She seemed lost and rather vulnerable, so Jak, who was different in those days, took it upon himself to look after her. He ended up falling in love. It was all looking great for him: he was planning to marry her and settle down again and he had also been offered the captaincy of CU11. Then things started going wrong around camp — little things like equipment not working or disappearing. Soon, some of our patrols began to get ambushed even when their routes had been known only by the highest in the command. Still no one guessed.

'And then one night, there was the sound of a terrible struggle from the tent of Commander Leese, Felson's predecessor. Ardaya was caught, literally red-handed, and charged with his murder. At her trial all the facts came out: she had been sent as a spy by the Jerregishans, and had quietly been going around doing small acts of sabotage to lower morale. She also had managed to find her way into Leese's bed, where she had found out details of patrol routes and so on. Leese had begun to suspect something, so that's why she had to kill him.'

'And Jak?'

'He was found not guilty of conspiracy, but couldn't accept what had happened. He couldn't handle that he'd made such a bad error of judgement let alone the sympathy and snide remarks that followed. He refused the captaincy and swore never to take any position of responsibility because he felt that his integrity had been so badly compromised. Losing his family had hit him hard enough, but after Ardaya he changed even more—became harder, more cynical about life.'

Aris nodded. 'I see. So I suppose he thinks that I'm another Ardaya.' She paused, 'This woman ... what was she like?'

Macker stroked the cat who was now rubbing its cheek affectionately against her face. 'I was kept too busy on other duties at the time to be around CU11 all that much, but I saw her now and again.' Macker paused for a minute, and gave Aris a strange look. 'Actually, she looked a lot like you: the hair was longer and she was fuller in figure and face, maybe a little shorter. However, she was no soldier, always looked like a little girl lost. Everyone said how sweet she was and how gentle; I guess that's why Jak fell for her. Unfortunately it was all an act—underneath she was a hard-edged murdering bitch.'

Aris got up, moved to the window and looked down on the

drill square outside. 'That certainly explains a lot although I don't think it will help me like him any more.'

Macker smiled. 'Give it time. You will, I promise.'

A man crossed the square below, catching Aris's attention. It was Felson's valet. She motioned to Macker to come to the window.

'Who's that?' she asked.

Macker peered out over her shoulder. 'Vallen. He started looking after Felson about nine years ago, when I first met Sean, and he's been doing his washing, cleaning and cooking ever since.'

Aris narrowed her eyes. 'I'm sure I know him from somewhere.'

'Maybe he's just got the sort of face that seems to be everywhere.'

'That's what I first thought, but it doesn't explain why he looked so frightened when he saw me in Felson's tent the other day.'

Macker shrugged. 'Perhaps it's your fearsome reputation. No, honestly Aris, Vallen's been here a long time.'

Aris turned around. 'Well, I'll just have to take your word for it. Thanks for the talk, Macker, it's good to know I've got someone on side.'

Macker took hold of her hands and smiled. 'I'm always here Aris, when things get a little rough. Don't forget that.'

By the time Sean got back to his tent, his anger had cooled. Jak, waiting inside, was quiet too, as if he realised he'd gone too far. Or that was what Sean hoped. He didn't really want to give the man a formal reprimand — after all they'd been friends for too long and rank never usually entered the equation. Sean had always been uncomfortable about the question of rank between them anyway: he was too conscious of the fact that Jak had been offered the captaincy of CU11 before he had. If the Ardaya thing had never happened, Jak would be his commander now, not the other way around.

'Sit down Jak,' Sean said wearily.

Jak sat in one of Sean's folding chairs.

'You don't really think Aris destroyed those water plants, do you?' he asked.

'Yeah, I do.'

'Look, I understand your reasons, and to be honest the same thought even passed through my mind to begin with. But my instinct tells me that she had nothing to do with it.'

'Instinct!' spat Jak. 'Are you sure it's your instinct?'

'What are you implying?' Sean's voice was distant, cool.

'Oh come on Sean, I've known you long enough: she's an attractive woman — you want to get your leg over.'

'Don't be so bloody ridiculous Jak. Even if that were true, I wouldn't put the unit at risk for it.'

Jak shut up and looked away; he couldn't contradict Sean on that without dragging his own past into it. He took a deep breath and his next words to Sean although quieter, still contained a sharp edge of sarcasm. 'So you have an instinct. Do you know you're beginning to sound like the Sharm?'

'Maybe, but Torassin's often right about a lot of things. In fact ... ' Sean broke off for a minute, a thought entering his head. 'Maybe there is a way that we could settle this question about Aris's past with Tor's help.'

'How?'

'A mind to mind.'

Jak looked at him as if he had gone mad. 'Mind to mind? You are joking aren't you? Even if there is such a thing Tor probably hasn't got the ability.'

'It might be worth a try though, if Tor's prepared to do it.'

'I tell you now he won't be; he's not that stupid.'

'Well, I can ask him ... '

'Yes, you can, but as far as I'm concerned it's Sharm mumbo-jumbo, and I want no part of it.'

Sean frowned, his anger beginning to show again. 'You won't have to. Earlier this morning Felson asked me to field two unit members for an extra night patrol. You and Fen have just been volunteered.'

Jak glared at him. 'Oh thank you very much!' He got up. 'Is that all? Can I go now?'

Sean nodded. 'But I want no more fighting with Aris inside the encampment, is that clear?'

'Yes, I think you've made your point.' Jak turned to leave.

'One more thing ... ' Sean called him back. 'Send Tor in when you see him.'

A few minutes later, Tor entered, looking puzzled.

'Jak said you wanted to see me about something?'

'Yeah. Look, it's okay, you haven't done anything wrong. I'll come straight to the point: can you do a mind to mind?'

Tor was silent. Finally he asked, 'Why?'

'I want to find out once and for all if Aris is for real.'

'Well, for the record, I think she's genuine.'

'So do I, but unless we can convince Jak, there's going to be trouble.'

'But isn't there some other way? I mean, a mind to mind ... '

'Is difficult, I know that, but I can't think of any other way.'

Tor sighed. 'And I wish I could help you, I really do. But a mind to mind is not something I've ever done or even been trained to do. I've only ever watched others do it. It's not just difficult, it can be dangerous too—for both parties. And Aris would have to be relaxed enough to let me into her head ... I can't do it by force.'

'Hmm,' Sean frowned. 'Leave that detail to me.'

'And there's no guarantee that it'll work either.'

Sean sighed, threw his hands up in the air. 'Okay, it was just a thought. I can see that you don't really want to do it.'

The young man was suddenly silent, as if he was remembering something. 'The vision,' he said and gave a half smile.

'I beg your pardon?' It was Sean's turn to look puzzled.

'Never mind. I'll try it, but no promises, okay?'

Jak and Fenim had already left on their patrol when Aris returned in the evening. With Jak absent she seemed more at ease, laughing and joking with Tor. Sean, sensing the time was right, dipped into his tent and emerged carrying a bottle of kotch he'd managed to liberate from Felson's personal stores. Opening it, he took the first swig, relishing the burn of it on his tongue. Steady, he told himself, must keep a clear head tonight.

He strolled up to the central fire and pulled up a crate to sit on.

'Aris?' He offered her the bottle.

She took it from his outstretched hand and looked at the writing on the label. 'Kotch, Sean? And from the Chapter-lands too. What's the special occasion?'

'Oh nothing much. I just fancied a drink, and seeing as Jak's not around, I might even get a fair chance of having one before it's all gone.'

She smiled and took a swig, also savouring its warmth before handing the bottle to Tor. He waved it away.

'Not for me, Aris. I don't feel like drinking tonight.'

Halfway down the bottle, Sean found he was beginning to feel light-headed, mellow. Aris seemed to have loosened up considerably too; she had lost that defensiveness and had even started to talk about her life in City, her daughter, her sister, her work. But never once did she mention anything of what happened after—in Balaat.

Sean heard her words but found that he was listening less and less. Instead he watched her face, fascinated by her eyes, her smile. Get a grip, he told himself. Maybe Jak was right, maybe he was attracted to her more than he should be. However she was part of the unit, not one of his usual women. It would go against every rule. But no matter how he tried, he still couldn't leave the idea alone. Perhaps he could get her transferred to another unit, another section, and then ... .

'Just going off for a while,' Tor said, his words breaking into Sean's fantasy.

'What ... ?' Then Sean remembered that the Sharm had said something earlier about having to prepare himself first for the mind to mind. 'Oh, yeah ... right.'

At last, he was alone with her.

As if aware of the change in atmosphere, she stopped talking and gazed into the fire, her mind elsewhere, her brow furrowed with a frown.

'The memories will fade in time,' he said gently, guessing at her thoughts.

She looked up at him sharply. 'Will they, Sean? Can you promise me that?'

He was silent for a moment. 'No. No, I can't promise, I can only go on experience.'

'Experience!' She gave a harsh laugh. 'Your experience bears no relation to mine, I promise you. Tell me Sean, do you have any scars that still remind you of what happened?'

'Of course, but scars are the marks of healed wounds, Aris. They fade in time.'

Sitting straight, she undid the top buttons on her shirt and pulled the material aside to expose the raised red flesh that formed itself into the numbers 15618 above her right breast.

'But brands don't fade, Sean,' she said bitterly. 'I will always have this number to remind me that for a short time I ceased to be a human being and instead became a commodity, an object to be used.'

Sean found himself staring at the mark, feeling a sense of revulsion. He had known that Pock branded his women slaves, had even guessed that Aris had been subjected to it, but facing the reality sent a shiver down his spine. He raised his eyes to hers; even with the firelight and shadows altering her features, they seemed black, desolate. Shit, he thought, what did they do to you in there? Suddenly he wanted to reach out and hold her, stop her trembling, but there was a barrier between them, thick with ghosts from the past and fears of the future. Now he had no doubts about the truth of her past.

He didn't know what else to do or what else to say and was glad to see Tor returning, a strength and surety about him that now seemed out of place. Aris saw him too, and suddenly straightened up, smiling. The mask was back in place. Thinking quickly he intercepted the younger man on the pretext of having forgotten to give him a message earlier.

Once they were out of earshot, Tor turned to his captain, looking puzzled.

'What's wrong?'

'We can't force a mind to mind on her — she's telling the truth.'

'But what about convincing Jak?'

Sean threw his hands up in the air. 'I don't know. We'll just have to bend the truth a little, say we did it and she's okay.'

'You mean lie?'

'Well, er… yes, if you put it like that. But it's all in a good cause.'

'Well, if you say so, but I'm all prepared for the mind to mind now.'

Sean frowned. 'Can't you un-prepare yourself?'

'It's not as easy as that. All the energy I've built up has to be discharged somehow.'

'I'm sure you'll think of something.'

They walked back to Aris, apologising for leaving her alone with the bottle.

'God, the hangover's started already,' she said. 'My head's beginning to pound.'

Tor saw an opportunity to dissipate some of the magical energy which was now pulsing its way through his body: 'I could give you some Sharm healing, if you wish.'

'Okay,' said Aris, smiling up at him, 'what do I have to do?'

'Just sit and relax,' Tor answered. 'I'll talk you through it.'

Sean watched as Tor slowly lowered the palms of his hands until they were only a little bit above Aris's head.

'Just relax,' the Sharm said, and by his tone, Sean realised that he was using a voice method to control her. He continued speaking in the same voice: 'Aris, I want you to relax, feel yourself sinking deeper and deeper into relaxation. That's right. Your whole body is tired, heavy, so relaxed and you are sinking — drifting deeper and deeper and deeper. You are warm, safe, relaxed, and all tensions are lifting away. Your headache is clearing and you have no more worries, no fears. You are totally relaxed.'

She began to lean back, so that it was only the support of Tor's body stopping her from slipping to the ground. He brought his hands to rest on the top of her head.

For a minute Aris seemed to relax, a smile on her face, but

then her expression turned to horror. She began to hyperventilate, a look of terror on her face. Her whole body went rigid. All of a sudden she let out a scream that turned Sean's blood to ice.

Tor twisted away from her in the same instant, clutching at his own head and letting her drop backwards on to the earth. The impact seemed to partly shock her out of the trance state, for within seconds she was back on her feet, her hands around Tor's throat.

'You bastard!' she yelled. 'What the fuck did you do to me?'

For Sean it all seemed to happen in slow motion, and as he tried to get up, he realised that he'd had more to drink than he thought. By the time he reached them, Aris already had Tor on the floor trying to choke the life out of him. The Sharm, locked in some crisis of his own, seemed unable to defend himself.

Sean dragged Aris off, holding her in a close grip to stop her struggling. Soon she began to calm down and the fury faded from her eyes to be replaced by a look of bewilderment.

'What did you do to me?' she asked Tor again, her voice sounding small and lost. Tor didn't answer, just stared at her as if he'd never seen her before.

'What happened?' Sean asked, a puzzled look on his face.

She pointed to Tor. 'He was in my mind. Why?... How?... Did you plan this?' she asked in disbelief, shaking her head.

'No, well, not as such. I don't know what happened. Something went wrong.'

She looked at the ground and began to shake. When next she looked up at him, her lashes were wet, her voice strained. 'How could you? I trusted you Sean. You don't know what your stupid scheme has released.'

'I'm sorry Aris, please believe me.'

'Let me go Sean. I need to be alone.'

'I ... I don't know if that's such a good idea.'

She pushed him away and he let her go, not really sure of what to do next.

She walked off into the dark, towards the south gate.

'Shit!' He swore under his breath as he watched her retreating figure. Maybe he ought to go after her — she was clearly in no state to leave camp on her own, but then he looked back at Tor. The young man sat silent on the ground, his face deathly pale. He was clearly in shock. No, Sean couldn't leave him, either. He was going to have to get some help.

6

Aris knew she was in the woods outside the perimeter fence, but how she'd got there, she wasn't sure. She couldn't remember passing the guards on the gate; in fact she couldn't remember anything between leaving Sean and arriving in this place. Her memory had not been the only casualty of the evening—her whole body felt weak and uncoordinated. The steps she took down the dark, narrow path were far from straight.

She stopped and took a deep breath. The pain in her head had gone, but it still felt bruised, and she was confused about what had happened. She didn't know how he'd done it, but somehow Tor had forced himself into her mind and sprung the locks that had held her memories of Balaat locked away. Unfettered now, they all tumbled out, filling her head with horror, fear and the smell of blood. A hideous monster had become unleashed, one which she knew was capable of devouring her, body and soul.

Had Tor meant to do it or was it just a terrible accident on his part? The more she thought about it, the more everything slotted together like a jigsaw puzzle. The bottle of kotch, Sean's soft words and the fact that Tor remained sober. It had all been planned from the beginning.

The bastards! Why couldn't they have just left her alone instead of prying into her privacy? She knew she rarely talked about her past, but hadn't she done enough yet to prove her loyalty? Surely Sean wouldn't have tried this with Jak or Fenim: he wouldn't have dared. There again, he had no need — they were not the outsider. Maybe she should leave Hellyon and go. But where? No, wherever she went, the memories would follow, she'd still be alone and even further away from Ani. She couldn't bear the thought of that.

From what she could remember, Tor seemed to have come off badly from the encounter too. Whatever he'd found in her head had affected him as well. She recalled the fear in his eyes, a mirror image of the fear she'd seen in the eyes of the girls in Circus. Her head began to spin again and a feeling of nausea overwhelmed her. Being out here was not going to help matters: she needed to get back to the camp and sort things out.

From behind her there was the quietest sound of a safety catch being released.

She froze, and then hurled herself forwards in what was more of a reflex than a planned move. She heard the crack of the pistol and the track of the bullet passing overhead, just where she'd been standing. Rolling off the edge of the track, she fell into a deep ditch, a swathe of needle-wort stinging her into a state of semi-alertness. Above her there were footsteps on the track and she could just make out the silhouette of a figure against the clear night sky. At least in the ditch it was all darkness; if she stayed put there was a chance she could remain hidden until one of the perimeter patrols came to investigate the shot.

Slowly she moved her hand to her belt, expecting to find her knife. It wasn't there. Shit, she thought, I must have taken it off earlier. How could I have been so bloody stupid as to come out unarmed?

The footsteps stopped above her. If the man, and she was sure it was a man by the way he moved, saw her then all he had to do was chance one more shot. But who the hell wanted her dead badly enough to follow her? Macker's words suddenly came back to her: 'It can't be too bad, you're still alive.'

Jak? No, she decided firmly; Jak would have been quieter and she would have been dead by now.

Her assailant was bending down now, peering into the darkness of where she lay. Aris didn't even dare to breathe. She saw his hand move, heard the steely sound of a knife being drawn ...

So this was it. She was trapped like a rabbit in a snare. At any other time the man's clumsiness would have proved fatal to him. She would have jumped up, using the advantage of surprise, and taken him out, but her head still spun from the drink and she knew that if she tried to stand she would probably lose her balance, and then her life.

Suddenly there was a shout, other footsteps running down the track. The man straightened up and darted away.

She heard another man's voice, not far away: 'They've gone sir.'

'Keep on searching down the track,' a familiar voice ordered. It was Sean.

'Sean,' she called out, struggling to get to her feet.

'Aris?' he answered. 'Where the hell are you?'

'Down in a ditch, just over to your right.'

She heard the faint rustle of clothing as he came over.

'Are you all right?' he asked, peering down into the blackness as the gunman had done.

'Yeah, I could do with a hand out, though. I'm still a bit

unsteady on my feet.'

He reached an arm towards her. 'Can you grip my arm? Ah, Shit! You never mentioned there was needle-wort down there!'

'Sorry.' She gripped his wrist and pulled herself up the bank.

'What happened?' he asked. 'Did you fire that shot?'

'No, someone tried to put a bullet in me.'

'Did you see who it was?'

She shook her head. 'It was too dark. But it was a man and by the way he moved, not one used to doing this sort of thing. Maybe an older man — certainly older than you.'

'Thanks, I'll take that as a compliment. Look, is there anyone who might want you dead?'

'Other than Jak you mean?'

'You're not suggesting ... '

'No, it definitely wasn't Jak. But it may well be someone with the same idea — that I'm the one who busted those filtration plants.'

Sean was silent for a minute. 'That's a possibility. Whatever the reason though, if someone is out to get you, they won't leave it at this.'

'I can take care of myself.'

'All the same, you're going to need some extra protection. I want you to move into my tent for a while. Fen will have to move into yours.'

She looked at him in disbelief. 'You are joking, aren't you? Can you imagine what people are going to say?'

'I don't bloody care about other people. What I care about is your safety.'

'It'll never work. Sorry Sean, but I'm staying put.'

'Then I'll have to make it an order. Look, Aris, we can rig up some kind of partition if it makes you feel better. I can promise you that there's no ulterior motive.'

'I didn't think for one moment that there was,' she muttered.

They walked unsteadily back to camp. Sean had his gun at the ready but Aris somehow doubted whether he could hit anything in his present state. She decided that any recriminations about earlier could wait until they had both sobered up a little.

Back at the tents, Macker was waiting, a blanket in her hands. She looked anxious. Moving forward, she draped it around Aris's shoulders and guided her over to a crate by the fire.

'Hey, where's my sympathy?' Sean asked.

Macker rounded on him. 'You don't deserve any after the stunt you pulled.'

He gently took hold of her arm and guided her out of earshot. 'Macker, I was only trying to ... '

'I don't care. Thanks to your idiotic idea, two people have ended up in the shit. Have you seen Tor? No? Well, he's not good; in fact I'd say at the moment he's pretty screwed up.'

'Okay, so it went wrong, but at least I gave it a shot. The unit was beginning to fall apart ... I had to do something.'

'So you decided to mess about with something you don't understand. When will you learn that you just can't barge into other people's lives and try to fix their problems for them?'

Sean threw back his head and gave a mirthless laugh. 'Oh, now I get it: we're not just talking about tonight are we?'

She glared at him. 'Stop being so fucking juvenile Sean. Whatever problems we may have had together pale into insignificance after tonight.'

Aris unsteadily got to her feet, hearing the raised voices at the edge of the encampment. She stepped between them. 'What's going on?'

They stopped, both looking rather sheepish. Sean took a deep breath: 'It's okay Aris. I've just realised how bloody stupid I've been, that's all.'

The words did not come easy to him; he was not used to having to apologise for making mistakes. Macker nodded, a small smile on her face and placed her hand on his shoulder.

'Yeah,' she said, 'I'm sorry too, I shouldn't have snapped. It's just that Tor ... well... I'm worried about him.'

'Why?' asked Aris.

'It's like he's in shock. He's just lying in his tent with his eyes open, refusing to speak to anyone.'

'I'll go and talk to him,' said Sean.

Aris grabbed hold of his arm. 'No, wait, leave this to me.'

She got to her feet and went over to Tor and Jak's tent. Tor was lying on his back, staring at the ceiling. She gently touched his hand.

'Tor?'

He slowly turned his head and looked at her.

'Aris ... I'm sorry. I'm so sorry.'

'It's okay Tor—what's done is done.'

'But ... ' he stopped as the memory took hold of him again. She squeezed his fingers.

'What you felt—it wasn't nice, was it?'

He shook his head. 'I've never felt such fear, such pain. It just filled my head. I thought I was going to die.'

Aris nodded. 'What else? Did you see anything? Did you see my memories?'

'No. I only felt the pain. And then you screamed. At that point I lost contact. It was as if your mind attacked mine.'

'Thank goodness you didn't see anything,' she breathed. At least Tor had not seen what had happened to her; somehow she couldn't bear anyone to have witnessed that. Tor suddenly struggled to sit up. 'Why, what would I have seen?'

Aris looked away; her throat was so tight she was unable to speak. Tor watched her, not knowing how to help her, or even how to help himself.

'How can I make up for this?' he finally asked.

She shrugged. 'Some things are best forgotten, including this. Whatever you felt tonight, they're not your memories, so don't let them screw you up.'

'Shutting them out is not the way, Aris; you need a healing.'

'What, from you? No thanks,' she said sarcastically, then saw the expression on his face and softened her tone. 'I'll deal with this in my own way and my own time, Tor. But I want you to promise me something.'

'What?'

'That you'll never pull a stunt like that on me again.'

Tor managed a tight smile. 'That's a deal.'

Cold, tired and hungry, Jak and Fenim returned to the encampment in the early hours of the morning. Jak had forgotten to take his warmer jacket with him and his muscles ached. He felt old; much too old to be doing this any more.

No-one seemed to be up. Bloody typical, he thought, someone could at least have had a brew on for us. Grumbling to himself, he walked over to the cooking block, intent on getting it started up and kicked something lying on the ground. It was an empty bottle of kotch.

The bastards! While he and Fen had been freezing their balls off on patrol, the others had been busy getting off their heads. Well, at least he could make them suffer for it this morning.

He strode over to Sean's tent, just as Fenim was coming out, a puzzled look on his face.

'What's up?' asked Jak.

'I ... er ... seem to have been evicted.'

'What do you mean?'

'There's someone else in my bed.'

Jak raised a knowing eyebrow. 'Oh yeah, who's Sean got in there this time?'

Fenim hesitated for a second before answering, but couldn't see any other way around it. 'Aris.'

Jak pushed past Fen into the tent, his head filling with anger. Aris was stretched out on Fen's bed, asleep. Turning to Sean's bed, he threw the blanket off the sleeping man and shook him awake.

'Outside, now!' he hissed. 'I want some explanations.'

Grey-faced, confused and barely awake, Sean dragged his body off the bed and staggered outside. 'What the ... ? Aren't I supposed to give you the orders?' he protested, rubbing at his eyes.

'Stop messing around Hess. What's she doing in there, or is that a stupid question considering it's you I'm talking to?'

Sean shook his head, trying to clear it. 'Hold on Jak, it's not what you think ... '

'So enlighten me.'

I moved her in with me for her own safety: someone tried to kill her last night, and I thought they might come back to finish off the job.'

'You're in no state to protect anyone at the moment. Look at yourself — you're wrecked!'

'Will you please stop shouting. My head's splitting!'

'Serve you bloody well right for drinking that kotch.'

'Ah ... yes, well, I was going to ... '

'Save me some? I don't think so.'

'Look Jak, I needed it to loosen her up.'

'For what? Getting her into your bed?'

'No, for the mind to mind,' Sean mumbled and looked away.

Jak threw his hands in the air. 'You don't mean you really went ahead with it?'

'We were going to, then I changed my mind...'

'And?' Jak demanded.

'It all got fucked up Jak, really fucked up.'

'Tor?'

'He was going to use the energy he'd raised to give her a healing but somehow he still connected to her mind. I don't know what he saw or felt but it freaked him pretty bad. Aris certainly didn't take it too well and ended up walking out of camp on her own ... and I let her.'

'So? She can look after herself.'

'You didn't see her, Jak. Anyway, while she was out there, someone took a shot at her.' Sean shook his head. 'I couldn't have messed it up any worse if I'd tried, could I?'

'You stupid bastard,' Jak mumbled, but his tone had softened; he could see the other man was in a state and he couldn't help a kind of satisfaction at Sean's discomfort. After all, as far as most people were concerned, he was the perfect captain, the one who never made mistakes.

Fenim had been keeping his distance, but now sauntered over from the cooking block with a mug of char.

'Any idea who fired the shot?' he asked.

Jak smirked. 'Well, it wasn't me. Unfortunately I wasn't in the right place.'

Sean gave him a black look before answering. 'We don't know. Only Aris saw him and she couldn't really give much of a description.'

'So you only have her word that she was shot at?'

'Everyone this side of camp heard the shot, Jak.'

'Couldn't she have fired it herself and made up the story?'

'Oh, come on; that's stretching it a little far. Besides, when she went off she had no weapon on her at all.'

'Not one that you saw,' Jak mumbled under his breath.

Tor emerged from the tent, his face pinched. There were dark circles under his eyes. Sean beckoned him over.

'So what actually happened to you last night?'

Tor shook his head. 'I'm not really sure. I must have prepared myself so well for doing the mind to mind that I couldn't switch off. So when I did the healing, it all just happened anyway. I couldn't control it Sean, I'm sorry.'

'I told you not to mess with things you don't understand, didn't I?' Jak rounded on Sean. 'Maybe you'll listen to me in future.'

Sean ignored him and turned again to Tor. 'Out of interest, when you got into her mind, did you see anything, learn anything?'

Tor shook his head 'No. Well, not exactly.'

'What do you mean?'

Tor shook his head. 'It's hard to explain. I hadn't planned on being there in the first place, but when I entered her mind I had the strangest feeling of walking down a long corridor. Then there was a door, a closed door. I felt compelled to open it but when I did, all these 'things' came out.'

'Things?'

'Look, I know it sounds strange. These 'things'... I couldn't actually see them — they were vague, grey shapes — but I could feel them. They gave off these emotions and they were so strong.'

'What kind of emotions?'

'Mostly fear. And pain too. I know pain isn't an emotion but when those things came out, the most terrible pain went through my body. I thought I was going to die. Then there was a loud scream and a bright light from behind me seemed to tear me away. That was when the vision ended.'

Jak snorted. 'I'd say you'd had too much kotch, myself.'

Fen turned to Tor. 'And that's it? You can't remember anything else?'

Tor hesitated a second. 'Well, there was another emotion. It wasn't strong and didn't make a lot of sense at the time. But there was also guilt. Whatever happened to her, and I'd say it was something terrible, it also caused her a sense of guilt.'

'So,' said Sean, 'I guess the other important question is, how are these things going to affect her now?'

'I don't know.' Tor slowly shook his head, trying to evaluate his experience. 'However, the door was closed on those 'things' for a reason. She had somehow locked them away, along with her memories.'

'Which is why she's never elaborated about Balaat,' Sean cut in.

'Exactly. But now I've opened the door to them.'

'And her demons are walking free,' Fenim said softly. 'That is not good — for any of us.'

Jak raised an eyebrow. 'I still think she's got you all fooled.'

Tor turned to him. 'Back off Jak. She'd have to be very clever to fake what happened last night.'

Jak's voice was cutting, cynical. 'Clever? She's already in Sean's tent, isn't she?'

The sun was beginning to heat the air to an unbearable temperature when Aris finally awoke. She cautiously stuck her head out of the tent. The encampment seemed empty which was strange, considering Sean had been so concerned for her safety last night. Still, she wasn't concerned; she really didn't feel like seeing anybody at the moment. She supposed they had volunteered to help out with engineering duties, seeing as most of the experienced mechanics were already working on fixing the filtration plants. Standing in the sunshine, she stretched her aching body.

'So you're awake then?' said a voice over her shoulder.

She spun around to see Jak. 'God, Jak you made me jump. I thought everyone was out.'

'You hoped, you mean. No, Sean wanted someone to watch over you while they were away and naturally I volunteered.'

'How kind of you,' she retorted sarcastically.

'So how did you do it?'

'Do what?'

'Get them to believe all that crap about what was in your head. You might be able to play mind games with them but don't think you can do it with me.'

She shook her head in disbelief and turned to go back into the tent. He blocked her way.

'You can't fool me Desun. I know what you are.'

She turned on him. 'What I am at the moment is in need of the latrine and shower block. You are welcome to come with me if you feel the need, but be warned, it won't be very exciting.'

He gave her a cold look. 'Do what the hell you like. As if I care anyway.'

She took her personal kit from her tent and headed out of the circle of tents, feeling Jak's eyes bore into her back as she went.

Fifteen minutes later, her ablutions over, she exited from the shower block and began to walk back to the encampment. Then she stopped. She couldn't get last night out of her head. She needed to know who had been watching her every move until he'd had the chance to take her. She knew that he would be even more desperate now, although it was likely he'd lie low for a few days until she was off her guard again. To feel safe she had to find him, and fast. Her hand slipped to her belt; she had her knife with her this time. It wasn't as good as a rifle, but Jak would probably notice if she returned to pick that up. No, she couldn't risk that.

She walked on a bit further, varying her route and occasionally looking back to check she wasn't being followed. It all seemed clear. Then she headed towards the watchtower she went out of last night. She cleared her exit with the guards by saying she was looking for a knife she'd lost on the last patrol. Security was nowhere near as tight as City's had been, she noted as they let her through without question, just as they had the previous night.

The track looked different in daylight: the ditch not so deep now that she was sober. Walking slowly, she looked for footprints but the ground was so hard and dry there was no sign at all. Soon she came to the crushed greenery where she had fallen into the ditch. Stopping, she looked toward the direction where the man had run off — surely if he'd gone off the path, he would have broken some of the vegetation as well. With a new determination, she continued walking, her senses alert in case he was still around. She was no great scout, but if he had left any sign, she was sure she would find it.

A cracking noise, like dead plant stems being broken, abruptly broke the silence behind her. She dived for cover behind the nearest tree and waited, her eyes trained on the direction of the sound, heart beating fast.

A small deer with its fawn broke cover and trotted across the path, completely oblivious to her presence. Breathing a sigh of relief, Aris stepped back onto the track and continued her search.

Jak, too, froze at the noise. When the deer crossed in front of him, he thanked his luck that they had done so before his presence disturbed them. If they'd startled from cover, it would have given his position away.

Up ahead, Aris stopped, examined an area of bracken and then disappeared into it. He waited for a minute and then followed, making his way along what looked like a wood-rat run. On either side the bracken rose to chest height, giving him good cover as he stalked his prey. She was wary though: every now and again she stopped to listen, looking around her and Jak stopped too, until she relaxed and walked on again.

At one point she seemed to have disappeared and he thought he'd lost her. Cursing himself, he carried on anyway knowing she couldn't have gone far. A little bit further on, a larger track opened onto the wood-rat path from the left. It looked man-made by its width and character, the undergrowth beaten down on both sides. Maybe she'd gone that way. Keeping low, he peered along it but found his view obscured by a thick scrub of thorny saplings. He cautiously made his way forward, his nerves all the more on the raw for not knowing where she was.

Beyond the saplings, the track opened out on a small clearing, again manmade. In the middle stood a crude wooden shack with a tin roof — not exactly ideal home material, but practical enough for shelter. Of Aris there was still no sign, but he felt sure she was inside.

Gotcha! he thought. Now I can get my evidence, and afterwards ... well, I won't be dragging her body back, that's for sure. He removed the safety catch from his RD10 slowly so as not to make any noise and moved forward. There were no openings on this side of the shack, so she would not see his approach. Reaching it, he crept around it until he came to the canvas-covered doorway. Readying himself for whatever he might find, he brought his weapon up and burst through.

Apart from some basic furniture, the room was empty.

Shit, you fool! he cursed himself, but it was too late. He felt the blade of a knife press up under his ribs from behind.

'Drop the gun, Jak,' Aris ordered.

Jak had no choice but to comply. She kept the pressure on the metal blade as she bent down and picked it up.

'Now, put your hands on top of your head, walk over to the wall and turn around.'

Was she going to shoot him? If so, no-one would know — it would be a long time before anyone found his body. And in the meantime she could continue wreaking chaos around the camp.

'Now,' she said, ' Tell me why the fuck you were following me.'

Jak shrugged. 'Do you really need an answer? Anyway, looks like you've led me straight to your hiding place.'

She gave a short laugh. 'Is that so? For God's sake, Jak, I was following the tracks of the man who attacked me last night. They led to this place. Now if you're half the soldier you think you are, you'll help me find out who the bastard is instead of carrying on this vendetta of yours.'

Jak was silent, thinking. On closer inspection, the hut seemed to contain items that pointed to a male occupant rather than Aris: an oversized jacket and boots as well as some shaving equipment in the corner. When he was following her, it certainly looked as though she was following a track left by someone else rather than heading straight for somewhere she knew. Yet he still didn't want to believe that he had been wrong. She was an infiltrator, he was sure of that. Maybe the man who lived here was her accomplice, in which case the quicker he could escape from the gun pointed at his head, the better.

'Okay,' he said, 'maybe I'll believe you.'

'Just like that?' she said sarcastically. 'I think it's time we sorted things, don't you?'

'Do I have a choice?'

'Not at the moment.'

'Let's get started then.'

'Not here—it's too risky; our man might decide to come back.'

'Maybe you'd appreciate some help.'

In answer she prodded him out of the door with the gun. 'Get moving Jak, and no sudden moves.' He muttered an obscenity in reply and began to trudge back along the track. She trained the weapon on his back and followed.

The situation was bleak, Jak could see that. She had him where she wanted him and at the moment there was nothing he could do about it. And yet, in a way, he was glad it had come to this: at least now he might find out the truth, even if he didn't live to celebrate being right. There again, he wasn't dead yet.

Back on the main path again, Aris directed him northwards, their footsteps taking them to the ruins of an old house raised up on a small hill. Once, before the troubles, it would have been a pretty little cottage with a hedged in garden, but now it stood with the roof sagging and walls crumbling, the garden overtaken by brambles. Checking for signs of any recent visitors and finding none, she motioned Jak inside first.

The room they entered was dingy, the few fittings that remained showed it had once been a kitchen. A small number of blue tiles still lined the wall where the sink had been and rotting linoleum covered the floor. Everywhere was layered in dirt and plaster dust.

Jak slowly turned and nodded towards the RD10. 'Don't you

think this is going to be a bit of an unequal conversation?'

She regarded him for a moment. 'You didn't worry about equality that day when you took me prisoner.'

He didn't answer. She was right. Why should she trust him enough to throw her weapon away? He knew he certainly wouldn't have trusted her if the tables were turned.

'So tell me, why all the bad attitude when I've done nothing to you?' she asked.

'Got all afternoon? Maybe it's because I know you're lying about something. Maybe it's because I think you're here to cause trouble for Hellyon. Maybe it's because I'm not going to let a bitch like you cause good men to die. Pick any of the above. Or maybe it's because there's something about you I just don't like.'

'There's something about you I don't like either, but that is probably to do with the way you've treated me ever since I got here. So come on, why do you think I'm so dangerous, so bad for Hellyon. Do you think I'm a spy sent by Tiern?'

'You said it.'

'Well, you're wrong Jak.' She sighed, and to his surprise walked over to the corner of the room, laid down the weapon and walked away from it.

'There,' she said. 'With you causing me so much trouble, don't you think that if I was the infiltrator you think I am I'd have taken the opportunity and killed you here and now? Instead I've just thrown away the advantage.'

Jak narrowed his eyes, trying to see the trap, but there didn't seem to be one. Why was she doing this? Of course there were answers, rational answers that he didn't want to contemplate for they made him to be in the wrong. Instead he let other images dance before his eyes: another dark haired girl protesting her innocence; faces laughing at him for being so wrong, so misled. He had seen those dark eyes goad him before; the fact that they now belonged to another person didn't matter. They still represented all that had broken him.

He dragged his thoughts back to the present. 'Nice trick, Desun, but you haven't changed my mind. I still say you're hiding something.'

She shook her head. 'I'm not hiding anything that concerns you.'

There was something in her voice, her face that gave her away. He studied her for a moment, then he knew what had been bothering him since he'd first interrogated her.

'You were at Berryn's Crossing, weren't you? You lied to save your ass that day in the watchtower.'

He saw her pale for a second. She had obviously not expected him to have found her out. Then she composed herself again. 'So what. You would have lied in the same situation.'

'We're not talking about me. So, how did it feel to be responsible for the deaths of thousands of men and women? How did it feel to mow them down in cold blood?'

'It wasn't like that.'

'No? Well it was from where I was on the field. I saw them die.'

'I meant that I had no part in the fighting. I was only a junior officer back then and was placed with a rear support unit — out of the front line. But we were all there because those were our orders that day. It was our job. No-one from City, except Tiern and his unit commanders, knew that the plan was to turn on Hellyon.'

'Why the hell should I believe you?'

'Because it's the honest truth. What City did was wrong, was more than wrong. But that doesn't make individuals like me guilty when they were just doing what they were told. On the other hand, I can assure you that if they had known what was about to happen, many City soldiers would probably have refused their orders that day.'

'You included?'

She shrugged. 'Honestly?'

He nodded.

'I don't know. I was very ambitious then and wanted to have command of my own unit. Just because I didn't agree with an order would not necessarily have stopped me from carrying it out.'

'So you're the sort who doesn't give a shit about who gets hurt along the way just as long as you get your reward in the end.'

'If I was like that I would have been a commander by now, instead of just sergeant. And, more to the point I'd still be in City'

'You're just like her, full of lies and deceit. Why do you think I never was fooled by you?'

'I see,' she replied, 'so I am to be the scapegoat for your past.'

His face blackened.

'Oh yes,' she continued, 'I know all about Ardaya. Got that one very wrong didn't you? You missed the signs there. So are you trying to make up for lost time with me?'

He stared at her, trying to control his own anger. How much of the story did she know? Did she realise what it had done to him?

'What happened between me and Ardaya is none of your business, or anyone else's. As far as I'm concerned, I'm only interested in looking after the people I care about.'

'But you're not very good at it are you? What about your family, Jak? You didn't look after them very well. Why didn't you move them to a safer settlement when you had the chance? Instead you let them get killed.'

Her words stabbed at him, pricking those ancient wells of guilt that he thought he'd locked up long ago. The floodgates finally opened as outrage turned to fury and he launched himself at her, knocking her to the ground. This was it, she wasn't going to get out of this one.

He began to fumble for his knife. By now Aris had recovered her breath and began to struggle, freeing her arms. She swung upwards with her right fist, trying to catch him in the throat, but he was too quick. Catching hold of her arm, he pinned it above her head, his breath ragged, his mind black with rage. Fighting for her life now, she went for his face with her left hand but within seconds he had that pinned down too. For all her combat skills she was no match for his strength. Changing position slightly, he held both her wrists firm with one hand, leaving the other free to go for his knife. Now, at last, here on the dusty floor he would make an end of it.

He pressed the blade against the soft flesh of her throat. All he had to do—all he wanted to do—was to press a little harder, let the sharp metal bite through skin and blood vessel. But the something broke through his anger, staying his hand.

For all her taunting he realised that she was right. He had been using her as a scapegoat for his past. She had come from City, had been from a force responsible for the massacre of some of his greatest friends. Worse than that, her resemblance to Ardaya was such that he found himself confused, haunted by a ghost that wouldn't lie quiet. Yet, for all his wild anger, his need to kill the past, there was still a part of him that knew right from wrong. And this was wrong. He was wrong.

He frowned, his anger dissipating. Abruptly he let her go and got up. She still lay there, her eyes wide, trying to gauge his next move, tensed for a new assault. But he just stared at her, seeing her now as if for the first time.

'I believe you,' he said gruffly. 'Now go … please.'

She stared back at him for a few seconds, then silently got up and left.

Trying to gather his thoughts, he moved over to the window. A few minutes ago he'd hated the woman, wanted to kill her. But he now knew that even if he'd had Ardaya herself in this building this afternoon, he could not have found it in himself to kill her any more than he had Aris. Fen had said earlier that Aris's demons were now out and walking. If that was the case his had been running wild for years. He had to lay them to rest, before he ended up doing something he would regret.

7

Jak arrived back at CU11's encampment just as Sean was rebuking Aris for leaving camp without his permission. She just stood there, taking it without any of her usual rejoinders and afterwards just walked off to her tent.

'Go easy on her,' said Jak.

'What?' Sean turned to face him.

'I said go easy; she's had a bit of a rough time in the past twenty-four hours.'

Sean looked at him puzzled. 'Hang on a minute, usually I have to defend her against you, not the other way around.'

'Yeah, well, things have changed a bit since this morning.'

'How come?'

'We sorted a few things out.'

Sean's eyes widened in surprise and then narrowed. 'You two didn't have a fight did you?'

'We're both in one piece, aren't we? As I said, things are sorted.' Jak's voice brooked no further inquisition. Sean decided to carry on anyway.

'So you went out of camp together?'

Jak hesitated for a minute. 'Yes, sort of. She wanted to find where her attacker ran off to last night and I thought I'd better follow her.'

'Did you find anything?'

'Yeah, just off the side of the track there was a hut with a few basic pieces of equipment in it. I've already been to see the Intel guys and they're going to put an observation team on it.'

Sean nodded. 'Good. Well at least Aris was in no danger then, if you were with her.'

Jak smiled. 'What do you think.'

That evening Sean came into camp whistling.

'Message from Felson,' he called to them. 'The unit's got a week's stand-down for its troubles, so you're free to go and have some fun.'

'That's all right if you know where to find it,' Jak grumbled.

'Even if you did, it would probably take one look at you and run in the opposite direction,' Tor smiled. 'I think I'll go and see if Macker's off duty; she owes me a game of Rafts. Anyone else coming?'

Sean nodded. 'Yeah, why not. Fen?'

'No. I think I'll get an early night and head off to see my family first thing tomorrow; they've probably forgotten who I am by now.'

'Aris? Jak?'

Aris shook her head. 'I think I'll head for an early night too: I haven't exactly had much sleep lately.'

'The same for me,' Jak said.

Sean shrugged. 'What a boring bunch—give them time off and all they want to do is sleep. Come on Tor, looks like Macker will have to make do with just us two.'

Aris felt herself being shaken awake. She opened her eyes and saw Jak standing above her.

'What the ... ?' she said and looked at her watch. She was irritated to find that she'd only been asleep for an hour.

'I've just had a strange message from Felson,' he said.

'Felson?'

'Vallen was here just now and said that Felson wants to meet you up at Weapon Store 2 at eight o'clock — that's in ten minutes.'

'Vallen?'

'Yeah, he said that there was a problem with one of the PN3s that you might know how to fix.'

'Okay Jak, you might as well get back to bed; no use both of us looking like the undead in the morning.'

'I look like the undead anyway, so it won't make much difference,' he grinned. 'Still, I think I will head back to bed.'

Within minutes she was dressed and heading for the weapons store. She was almost there when she heard footsteps running behind her. Turning, she saw Jak running to catch up with her.

'What's up?' she asked.

He shook his head. 'The more I thought about it, the more I felt that something wasn't quite right about Vallen when he spoke to me. He seemed sort of ... twitchy. Not obviously so, but I've been around long enough to know when someone's trying not to be nervous.'

'I know. He was lying to get me there.'

'And you're going?'

'Well, I wouldn't want to disappoint him.'

'Oh, I see, I didn't realise ... '

Aris laughed. 'No Jak, it's certainly not a romantic rendezvous. I recognise him from somewhere and he knows that. In fact he looked terrified when he first set eyes on me. I just wish I could remember ... ' She looked thoughtful. 'Just a minute, did he actually say what was wrong with the gun?'

Jak frowned trying to recall. 'Yes, I think he did, but I was only half awake when he said it. Something about a blockage at B something or other. B7, does that make sense to you? He said you'd know how to free it.'

The memories started to slot back into her head bit by bit: the firearms training school at City, her first introduction to the workings of the PN3. She'd been in charge of a small group looking at how the B7 firing mechanism worked. She tried to recall the faces of those who were in her group.

'Oh, shit,' she said quietly.

'What is it?'

'I think we've found our saboteur — and the man who tried to kill me. He was on a weapons course with me during basic training in City.'

'Vallen? Oh come on, he's been here for years and is one of the most harmless people you're likely to meet.'

'Exactly — no-one's going to suspect him of anything, are they?'

'So how come you didn't remember him before?'

'He wasn't particularly memorable back then, either. He kept himself to himself and from what I can recall most people thought him a bit of a loser. In fact he dropped out of the course before it got to half way.' She smiled. 'And he had more hair when I knew him.'

'So what do we do?'

Aris smiled. 'Like I said, I'd hate to disappoint him.'

Jak glanced at his watch. 'It's nearly eight o'clock now. Why don't we just wait around the corner and see what he does when you don't turn up?'

'No Jak, I'm going after him. Some backup would be appreciated, but if you'd rather not be involved ... '

Not waiting for a response, she turned and marched off in the direction of the weapons store. The squat building seemed eerily still.

She heard Jak running after her. 'Aris!' he called and grabbed her wrist, bringing her to a halt.

'What?'

'Have you noticed that no-one's on guard duty? A bit unusual don't you think?'

'So? He's probably dealt with them the way he did the others.'

'Well you may have a death wish, but I certainly don't. Why are you walking into what is so obviously a trap?'

'Because I know I can handle him. Once a failure, always a failure, and he doesn't have the element of surprise that he thinks he has.'

'Never underestimate the opposition Aris, surely you were taught that.'

'Look, if I hadn't been the worse for drink the other night, I could have taken him out.'

'Maybe, but now you're the worse for being over-confident; you're not thinking straight. Why don't you just go and explain things to Felson, get Vallen brought in for questioning?'

'Because Felson would never believe me.'

'You don't know that until you try. Anyway, Vallen will be a lot more use to us alive than dead.'

She was quiet for a minute and then gave a resigned shrug. 'Okay, you win, but if Felson doesn't bite, then we go after Vallen my way.'

'Agreed.' Jak let go of her wrist and they began to walk back into the centre of the camp.

Behind them the world exploded.

Aris felt herself spinning through the air before the ground knocked the breath from her body. Burning debris began to rain down on either side as further explosions rocked the camp. She felt Jak grab her arm and pull her in the direction of the nearby latrine block. They half-crawled, half ran until they reached the relative safety of the back wall and then they turned and looked back at the chaos.

'He's blown it up,' Aris whispered.

'At eight o'clock — and you were meant to be in there,' Jak said softly. 'He must have had a timer. So much for your man being a failure.'

'He's failed to kill me so far ...'

In the gathering darkness of the night, the flames lit the surroundings like a ghastly torch, illuminating the growing number of figures running towards the scene of the explosion. Jak staggered to his feet to get a better look at the devastation.

'Oh, no. Please God, no!'

'What?' asked Aris struggling up beside him.

'The blast took out the nearest encampments too.'

Aris looked closer and suddenly realised that where an area of tents should have been there was nothing but scorched earth and twisted, blackened objects, some of them still on fire. With a jolt she realised that they were bodies. The enormity of the situation sunk in and she stood transfixed, almost detached, watching people running towards the scene.

'Come on,' said Jak. 'Let's find Felson.'

She shook off his hand and began to move forward, towards the scene of carnage. 'No Jak, first I need to see what the bastard's done so that I can remember it.'

The walk towards the fire seemed to take forever. A few metres out she stopped, faced with something that had once been human, that not so long ago had been alive as she was now. By rights that should have been her. Anger began to grow in her, cutting through the anaesthesia of shock. She turned on her heel, almost walking into Jak who had been following quietly behind. He put his hand out to steady her, slow her down.

All of her anger, all her frustration emerged as she pushed him aside. 'I've got to find Vallen,' she shouted. 'That bastard's not going to get away with this one.'

'Whoa, you're not thinking straight. He must have been watching and he would have seen you escape. Do you really think he's going to be hanging around for you to find him?'

'I'll find him wherever he's hiding. You saw what he did Jak, those people ... '

Jak nodded. 'Believe me Aris, I want to get him as much as you, but if we rush into it we could lose any advantage we may have.'

'So what are you suggesting?'

'We go and see Felson now — tell him what we know.'

They marched over to the Command Tent just in time to catch Felson coming out with the other commanders.

'Sir ... ' Aris stepped in front of him. He looked at her and a flicker of irritation crossed his face.

'What is it?' he demanded. 'Is it anything to do with fire control?'

'No sir, it's ... '

'Well, it can wait until morning.'

'Sir ... ' Jak stepped in.

'Look, Merron, Desun, I've got a fire that's out of control and spreading towards the other stores. That's my number one priority — anything else can wait.' He swept past them.

'Stupid bastard,' Jak whispered under his breath.

Aris threw her hands in the air. 'So what do we do now?' she asked.

'Well there are enough people here to sort this out so I suggest we go back to the encampment and get some rest. Intel will be at that hut we found by now so if Vallen's gone back there, they'll get him. We'll see Felson first thing tomorrow.'

CU11's tents were empty by the time they got back: obviously the others had gone to help at the scene.

'And left the place unguarded ... ' Jak mumbled.

Aris sank down on a crate and leaned her head forward into her arms. Jak looked at her. 'You're exhausted,' he said. 'Go and get some sleep. I'll keep watch until the others come back.'

'You'll tell them — about Vallen?'

'Tomorrow. I don't think anyone's going to take it in tonight.'

She nodded, got up and headed for Sean's tent. Jak watched as she went and then settled himself down in front of the cooking block — its bricks still warm from supper. His head ached with tiredness but he was determined to stay awake. He hadn't wanted to say anything to Aris but he was worried that if Vallen knew she was still alive then he would come after her again tonight. Wrapping himself in a blanket he gazed at the orange glow lighting the sky over the camp to the north.

Within five minutes he was asleep.

At first Aris thought she was dreaming, or back in Balaat. Her bed seemed to have been pulled out from under her but the hardness of the ground was real enough. She had began to turn over onto her back when a heavy boot connected with her side and she instinctively curled up into a ball.

'Get up Desun!' a gruff voice ordered.

She risked a glance upwards, blinking to clear her vision. It was already morning. Two armed men were in the tent, their guns pointed at her head, their faces stern, unyielding.

'What the hell's going on?' she asked, confused.

'You're not at liberty to ask questions, just do as you're told,' the older man shouted into her face.

She began to get to her feet as Sean came in through the flap.

'Captain, is this really necessary?' he began.

The older man rounded on him. 'Get out Hess, this is nothing to do with you ... at the moment.'

Sean must have read the warning in the man's eyes for he exited quickly without even throwing Aris a glance. She began to shake with shock, bewildered at the sudden hostility against her. What had she done? Unsteadily she pulled on her shirt and trousers and allowed herself to be roughly escorted into the middle of the encampment. The others were already out there: Sean, Fen and Tor stood off to one side, arguing with a man she hadn't seen before. Jak, who was also being held under armed guard stood next to Fen's tent. She was pushed towards him.

'Jak, what's happening?' she asked anxiously.

He shook his head. 'I don't know. They want to search the tents.'

'What for?'

He shrugged. 'All I know is that they are from Internal Security, the biggest bunch of sadists you're ever likely to meet outside of Balaat. They're investigating the explosion.'

'Oh God, they don't think we're involved do they?'

He frowned. 'It looks like it. Someone must have reported seeing us by the weapons store last night. It's probably only routine; they're hardly likely to find anything incriminating are they?'

Aris was silent. She hoped Jak was right, but she couldn't help a dreadful coldness stealing over her. It didn't take a great deal of imagination to put a name to that someone. Even so, Jak was right, there was no evidence to implicate them here.

Sean sauntered over to them, throwing his hands in the air in a gesture of exasperation.

'Sorry guys, I can't seem to talk sense into any of them. He insists that Felson never gave any orders for anyone to meet him at the store yesterday. I even told him what you told me about Vallen, Jak ... '

'And?'

'He just laughed.'

'I'm not surprised,' said Jak resignedly. 'I would have laughed a couple of days ago as well.'

'Well, I shouldn't worry about it. When this drama is all over and they realise there's nothing to be found here, they'll just go away and hopefully that will be an end to it.'

Behind him, a shout went up from his and Aris's tent. The captain of Internal Security rushed in to investigate. Sean swore, turned on his heel and followed.

Jak and Aris looked at each other, a terrible realisation dawning.

'We've been set up,' Aris said.

Jak said nothing; he seemed stunned. And then she saw him clench his fists.

'Not now Jak,' she whispered. 'Keep calm, let's see what they've got.'

The captain came out carrying something small in his hands. He walked towards them and held the object in front of Aris.

'Do you know what this is?' he asked, his voice curt.

She glanced at the device. 'Of course, it's a Mark Two Howden detonator.'

'Well, well, I thought you would have denied all knowledge.'

'Why should I? Its common enough.'

'In City, maybe. But not here.'

'So?'

'It was found, along with two others and a timer in your kit box. Funnily enough a fragment of a similar device was found at the scene of last night's explosion.' The sheer hatred in his voice was unmistakable.

'They must have been placed in my box when the camp was empty last night, just after the explosion.'

He glared at her. 'And you were both seen at the weapons store last night, just prior to the explosion'

'By whom?' Jak asked, his voice had that edge of coldness that Aris had come to know so well.

'Never mind who. It's enough for you to know that they are regarded as a reliable source.'

'It was Vallen wasn't it?' Jak spat. 'In which case, he's won.'

The man gave him a long hard stare and then turned to his soldiers either side. 'Secure them,' he ordered.

Aris felt her arms being forced behind her back and restrainers being put on.

Sean came marching up, flanked by Tor and Fen. 'Hang on,' he said angrily. 'There must be some other explanation. I know these two and I know that Jak certainly wouldn't get involved in anything like this.'

Aris turned to look at him. Jak. What about her? Did that mean that he thought she could be responsible for the explosion?

The captain held up his hands, trying to placate the Sean. 'I'm sorry, Hess, but as of now Desun and Merron are under arrest and are therefore my responsibility, not yours.'

'But ... ' Sean protested and began to move towards them. Fen held onto him and whispered something in his ear. Sean nodded.

'Okay,' he said. 'But this isn't the end of it, not by a long way.

And when I've finished you guys are going to look pretty stupid.' He looked at Jak and Aris. 'Just go with them for now; I'll sort this.'

The Headquarters of Internal Security was brick built like the weapons store and was far better guarded. Inside the place was like any other prison—grim, grey and smelling of damp and dirt. Every fitting was functional and basic as though the idea of anything pleasant was seen as abhorrent, distasteful. The soldiers serving in the unit also all looked grim, grey and functional.

In fact the whole place unsettled her; more than unsettled her. As she was marched through the first entrance, the sights and sounds reminded her all too clearly of the women's detention block in Balaat Fort. For a moment she stopped dead, resisting her captors, only to be forcibly dragged in front of the sergeant in charge. She willed herself to breathe slowly. Get a grip, she told herself, this is Hellyon, not Balaat—you'll be treated okay here.

After being checked in, she was separated from Jak and taken to a small, grubby cell. The only light came from a row of tiny square openings high in the wall, and the only furniture was a low, long bed with a bucket beneath it. As the metal door clanged shut behind her, she turned and sat on the bed and considered her position.

The only person who could fully back up her story on what had happened was Jak but he was a suspect himself and hardly likely to be in a position to help her. She had seen the doubt in Sean's eyes when he looked at her and somehow that look had injured her far more than anything Vallen could have dreamed up. Surely he would realise that she had had nothing to do with it and would find a way to prove it. But what if he really did think she was guilty? And how about Tor and Fen, did they think that she'd betrayed them all?

She felt very alone.

Lying down, she stared up at the ceiling. The light from the small windows picked out a mass of cobwebs, matted with grey filth hanging in great clumps above her head. She stared at them, closing her mind to all else. If it was one thing Balaat had taught her, it was how to wait with fear.

What seemed like hours later, the door opened and she was taken into another room. This one was twice the size of hers and lit by a flickering electric lamp. As she entered, a man got up from a desk by the back wall and came towards her. He was older than the other guards and carried an air of authority.

'I am Captain Najik,' he said warmly and she was suddenly reminded of her grandfather.

She began to relax.

'Sit down,' he said and pointed to a chair positioned to one side of the desk. He didn't bother to introduce the other two men in the room, both of lower rank.

Aris sat down and gave him a smile. He smiled back. A good sign.

'I am just going to ask a few questions.' His voice was soft, calm. 'I'm sure you'll want to co-operate fully with us so that this whole matter can be cleared up.'

Aris nodded.

'Good,' he continued. 'So first why don't you tell me how you came to be in Hellyon?'

'I'm sure you already know the details, sir.'

'Hmm,' he looked thoughtful. 'Well, yes, I am quite aware of your original story but I was rather hoping that you would give me the truth.'

'The truth?' Aris was stunned for a moment. 'That is the truth, sir,' she said as steadily as she could.

'Oh it was a very good story, I'll give you that; very convincing. But in the light of the new evidence I'd say it's lost its appeal, wouldn't you?' His face lost its smile.

'It is the truth, sir,' she repeated firmly.

'Don't lie to me Desun!' he suddenly shouted, his face inches from hers. 'Stand up!'

She had no sooner done so than the fist in her stomach made her double up again, retching. Another blow to the head sent her to the floor where she lay for a few seconds trying to gather her wits. She felt herself being picked up and waited for another blow, but it never came. She stood head down, not daring eye contact—a rule of self-preservation she'd learnt from Balaat. For a long time there was silence, but then the captain spoke, his voice once again soft, cajoling.

'So, tell me, who sent you to Hellyon?'

'No-one, it was as I said.' Her voice was quiet, but still steady. 'Why can't you believe me?'

This time all three men gave their share of punches and kicks until once more she found herself on the floor, half-conscious.

'Oh Aris, Aris, we'd like to believe you—very much,' said a soft voice from what seemed like far away. She felt herself being hauled upright again and made a determined effort to stand by herself. The room seemed to be spinning. She could taste blood.

The soft voice continued: 'Do you think we like having to get the truth out of you this way? Where did you get the explosives from?'

'They're nothing to do with me,' she said through rapidly swelling lips.

'They were in your kit box. Don't you think that's rather incriminating?'

'I was set up, sir.'

He laughed. 'Set up? Really? Who on earth would want to do that?'

The name of Vallen was on her lips but she bit it back — the guy would never believe her. She remained silent.

'What's this Desun? Run out of stories? What a shame, I thought you were a bit more inventive than that. Perhaps we ought to give you time to think up some more. Unless of course you feel its in your best interests to tell the truth.'

'I am telling you the truth.'

'So you keep saying. To be honest Aris I am getting a bit bored listening to that particular fairy tale.'

He snapped his fingers and the two other men grabbed her arms, spun her around and marched her to the wall. She stared at the whitewashed bricks and swallowed hard. Did he mean to shoot her here and now, without waiting for the trial? No, surely not; Hellyon had a system of justice, although as she was finding out, it wasn't exactly just. She stood as straight as her injuries would allow. If she was feeling fear, she wasn't going to show it to him.

He spoke. 'Now get on your knees with your hands behind your head.'

She did so. The room seemed suddenly silent. There was a click behind her and she felt the muzzle of a pistol placed against her head. She closed her eyes and prepared for death.

It never came. In the next moment she was yanked to her feet again and dragged from the room back to her cell.

The light also flickered in the room where Jak was being questioned. Jak's interrogator, a sergeant who'd introduced himself as Claris, seemed very young to him but he more than made up for that by his arrogance. Jak had been restraining his natural instincts to deck the guy but it hadn't been easy.

Claris stood in front of him, arms folded across his chest. 'Come on Merron, I don't believe that you were the brains behind this. She did all the planning didn't she? She was the one with the mission to cause trouble here. Her motives are clear. But why would you want to betray your own country? It doesn't make sense, unless of course she made you an offer you couldn't refuse.'

'Don't be so bloody stupid,' Jak said through gritted teeth.

'Oh I'm not stupid Jak. I've been doing some checking and I found out that up until a couple of days ago you and she were at each other's throats. Now you seem to be the best of friends and I have to ask myself, what changed things?'

'That's none of your business.'

'Oh but it is. You see, I think she saw you as an obstacle to her plans and so she made sure that you might be a little more ... well-disposed to her.'

Jak took a deep breath. 'What are you getting at?'

'Bear with me Jak, bear with me. Tell me, why were you so against her in the first place?'

Jak stayed silent. The other man considered him for a moment then bent down to whisper in his ear. 'You thought she was an infiltrator, didn't you? Like that other girlfriend of yours — Ardaya wasn't it? You were arrested after that too, weren't you?'

'And cleared!' Jak snarled, not liking the direction in which the conversation was heading.

The man straightened up. 'Yes, you were cleared of any involvement, except with Ardaya; you could hardly deny that, could you? After all, you were in love with her, had plans to make her your wife as I understand. It must have hurt like hell when you found out the truth.'

Jak glared at the man, trying to control his anger. To lose

control now was what Claris wanted him to do. He wasn't going to give him the satisfaction.

'Still no words of wisdom Jak? Well, let me try and work it out for you. I've heard whispers that Aris looks a bit like Ardaya. What must that feel like — to have a constant reminder of that pain? Is that why you hated her so much at the beginning?'

'Aris is nothing like Ardaya — there's no point in comparisons.'

'No? So what changed your mind? You say there's no comparison — are you sure about that?'

Jak frowned. 'What do you mean?'

'Well, they were certainly alike in looks — were they alike in other ways ... shall we say, more intimate ways?'

Jak looked at him with contempt. 'Piss off Claris, you're way off the mark.'

Claris smiled. 'I don't think so. Oh come on Jak, let me spell it out for you seeing as you're having so much trouble. At your age and, lets face it, with your looks, you're not exactly overwhelmed with female companions are you? Aris probably saw that as a weak point, especially when she found out about Ardaya, and made a play for you. Who could blame you for falling for it, for being so blinded as to her true motives?' He gave a sickly smile. 'That's what changed, isn't it? You and she became lovers.'

Despite himself, Jak could have laughed, what a joke. Instead he gave a wry smile. 'Some things would take a miracle, sergeant.'

Claris had not been expecting this sudden change of mood and regarded his prisoner with sour suspicion. 'Well, if you're lying we shall soon know. I don't think Desun will hold out for long under Captain Najik.'

'Najik!' Jak exclaimed, remembering the man from his first arrest.

Claris smiled. 'Yes, not known for his caring nature, is he? Just be thankful you've got me: you're having a much easier time of it than she is.'

'What's he doing to her?' Jak's jaw tightened.

Claris shrugged. 'How should I know? But I'm sure she won't look too pretty afterwards.'

'You bastards!' Jak jumped up but was immediately pushed down again by his guards. 'Don't you know what she went through in Balaat? '

'Balaat? Oh that story's worn a bit thin hasn't it? She's clever Jak, very clever — much more so than Ardaya and she'll be hard to crack. But Najik will do it, he's never been known to fail. Why don't you save her a bit of pain and tell us yourself?'

'She's not your saboteur!'

'Oh Jak, why don't you just accept you were conned — again. Just tell us the truth. I would hate to have to hand you over to Najik as well.'

'She is innocent and so am I!'

Claris regarded him for a moment. 'Personally, I believe you, on the last part anyway.'

'What?'

'I think you were duped into getting involved with something you had no idea of. I don't think you meant to betray Hellyon at all. It's not your fault and if you think hard, you'll see how clever she's been. All you have to do is to tell us of what you know of her involvement and I'll find some way of dropping the charges against you.'

'No way!' Jak shook his head. 'Do you really think I'm so shallow that I would drop an innocent person in it just to save my own skin?'

'You're loyalty is commendable, Jak, but as far as I am concerned, she was still very much the outsider and therefore able to get away with things under the cover of a respected unit. However, if, as you're implying, she's become such an accepted member of your little group, then that puts an entirely different light on it, doesn't it?'

Jak raised a suspicious eyebrow. 'Does it?'

'Look at it this way: she hasn't been here long enough for her trial and execution to have much effect, except perhaps to boost morale. If you were also found guilty and executed, that would be a different matter: too many people know and respect, if not exactly like, you. Even so, they would get over it. However, if the whole of CU11 were to be convicted of involvement in this, the effect on camp morale would be disastrous.'

Jak stared at him. 'What the fuck are you getting at?'

The sergeant shrugged. If Aris is so close to you all, then there's no way she could have pulled any of this off without you, your captain, Fenim and Torassin being aware that something was going on. Therefore meaning that the whole of the unit is implicated. Unless of course you retract all your earlier statements and are prepared to testify against Desun at her trial.'

Jak slowly shook his head, unable to believe that he'd been put in this corner so easily. 'You fucking bastard,' he whispered.

Claris smirked and walked to the door. 'I'll leave you to make up your mind Jak as to where your loyalties lie: either you tell us all you know about Desun, or we'll have to — unfortunately — bring the rest of your friends in.'

8

'Come in Sean.' Macker turned from the window as the captain of CU11 came through the door.

'What is it?' he asked, slinging himself comfortably onto her bed.

'I've just had word from Jak.'

Sean suddenly sat bolt upright. 'Jak? How?'

One of my girls was called into the detention centre to make a routine check on the prisoners. One of them was Jak and when he recognised her, he asked her to get a message to me.'

'What did he say?'

'They're trying to get him to testify against Aris. So far he's refused, so they're trying nastier tactics.'

'Like what?'

'Like threatening that the whole of your unit will be brought in for questioning and maybe charged with aiding sabotage.'

'Shit! They can't do that!'

'According to Jak they can. He also said to watch out for Vallen.'

'Vallen. I'm beginning to hear that name a little too often for it to be a coincidence.'

'Me too. When she was here, Aris mentioned that he seemed

familiar to her but she just couldn't place him.'

'So what am I going to do now?'

'It might be an idea to make yourselves scarce unless you want to get arrested.'

'Then we'd really look guilty!' Sean stood up and began to pace the room, thinking. 'This girl of yours, the one who saw Jak ... '

'Wiltsch.'

'Whatever. You can trust her can't you? This couldn't just be another game that security is trying to play with us?'

Macker smiled. 'No her loyalty to me is absolute, I can guarantee it.'

Sean gave her a hard stare that turned into a grin. 'Like that is it?'

'Like what?' Macker said with some irritation. 'I don't need to sleep with someone to guarantee their loyalty. Do you? Is there something about your unit I should know?'

'Okay, Okay, I'm sorry.' He held up his hands, trying to placate her. 'I really need to think of something quick.'

'Go and see Felson, try and get his support. I can't see him turning his back on the whole unit.'

'But if I start accusing Vallen, he won't want to listen without proof. What on earth do I say?'

'You'll think of something, Sean—you always do.' Macker took hold of his hands and brushed his cheek with her lips. 'Now just promise me that you will all take care. I would hate to lose my favourite men.'

Fen and Tor sat under the great oak tree at the edge of camp, looking at the scene of devastation from the explosion.

Finally, Tor broke the silence between them. 'What's up Fen? You've been quiet all day.'

Fenim shrugged. 'I should be with my family at this moment, not stuck here.'

'There's nothing to stop you going.'

Fenim gave him a sour look. 'Do you really think I'd take a holiday while Jak's still being held?'

'I'm sure he'd understand. Anyway there's not much we can do for him at the moment.'

'Except hope that Aris confesses and leaves him out of it.'

Tor looked at him sharply. 'You don't really think she ... '

'I don't know what to think. She's been strange ever since she got here.'

'That doesn't automatically make her guilty.'

'And she's from City.'

'You also spent a lot of time in City before coming to Hellyon and no-one's ever thought of you as being a potential spy or saboteur.'

Fenim looked poised to say something else but then became silent again, staring at the camp below. He shook his head. 'No, you're right. Everything points to a set up, and I suppose that she is as much part of the unit as Jak. We're all going to have to stick together on this one.'

Tor nodded. 'I know it's not easy, especially when the curious come asking questions. I really thought that Sean was going to deck that bloke last night for asking when the next explosion was going to happen.'

Fenim gave a half smile at the memory, and then looked thoughtful. 'Tor, is there any way you could ghost into the internal security building and have a word with Jak?'

Tor shook his head. 'I'd already thought of that. Unfortunately I can't hold the ability long enough to get in and out.'

'Can you use far sight?'

'No. I haven't developed that well enough yet either.'

Fenim sighed. 'Sometimes I really wish that you'd completed your Sharm-singer training before you left home.'

'I don't.'

'You don't miss it then?'

'Home? No, I'm not a family man like you, Fen: I don't miss it at all.'

Something in his voice made Fen look at him. The tone had almost been wistful. A sudden shout from below distracted their attention. Sean was running towards them.

'At last!' he declared, panting. 'I've been looking for you both everywhere.'

'So it sounds,' smiled Tor. 'Either that or you're becoming very unfit. What's the urgency?'

'We've got a problem.'

'What?' Fenim looked up, alarm in his eyes.

'I've had a message from Jak—no, don't ask how. He says we all are about to be implicated in this business, and therefore arrested.'

'How come?' Tor asked.

'He's refusing to point the finger at Aris at her trial. Internal security need his co-operation and are making threats to try and get it.'

'Against the rest of us,' said Tor in a monotone.

'Well, well,' said Fen softly. 'Whoever would have guessed Jak would stick up for Aris and put the rest of us in danger at the same time.'

'So what do we do?' asked Tor.

'For the time being you two are to stay up here, out of sight. Don't go back to the encampment in case security comes looking.'

'What about you?' questioned Fenim.

'I'm going to try and have one last word with Felson, see if I can sort something out.'

'And get yourself arrested?'

Sean shook his head. 'No, I can trust him for a certain amount of safe conduct; I'll be alright. Maybe I can persuade him to get us out of the camp on a false mission until something better is sorted out.'

'Run away, you mean,' said Fen sarcastically. 'What about Jak and Aris? We can't just leave them behind.'

'Who said anything about running away?' Sean answered firmly. 'Just stay put up here until I get back. If anything does happen to me then Macker will get a message to you.'

'Just make sure that isn't necessary,' mumbled Fenim, his face grim.

Felson didn't seem in the least surprised by Sean's arrival in his quarters. Sean cautiously looked around him, but no one else seemed to be in the tent.

'Vallen's out, if that's what you're worried about,' said Felson. 'So what have you come to tell me?'

'I've heard that there may be a warrant out for CU11's arrest. I wondered if you knew about it.'

Felson frowned. 'Actually, no. That's a surprise for me. How did you hear?'

'I can't tell you that sir, but trust me, it comes from an extremely reliable source.'

'Well, we can't be having that. So, the whole of CU11's going to be implicated, are they? Internal Security seem to be enjoying themselves a little too much at the moment.'

'I'd say they're living in fantasy-land.' Sean paused, took a deep breath. 'Sir, if I may speak freely ... '

'Go ahead, you usually do.'

'You've known me a long time, and you've known Jak too—you must know that he'd never get mixed up in something like this.'

'Go on ... '

'And he fully supports Aris's innocence as well. Look, I know he made a bad mistake once, but if anything that's made him more cautious about who he trusts. That's why it's so significant that he believes Aris didn't do it.'

'I see. So if they didn't blow the weapons stores, who did?'

Sean hesitated for a second. 'Vallen.'

Felson raised an eyebrow. 'What? The man who has served me so faithfully all these years?'

Sean looked away, feeling that he'd lost the battle early. 'Yes sir.'

'Well, it may be a surprise to you, but I've also been having suspicions.'

Sean looked up sharply.

'Yesterday I caught him trying to open the locked drawer in my desk. He bluffed his way out of it of course, but he couldn't hide the guilt on his face. And then I recalled other things: the way Jak and Aris tried to talk to me at the fire—unfortunately I sent them away. Then Vallen cornered me and asked if I had seen them; when I said no, he said he'd seen them at the stores earlier, acting suspiciously. I said I'd deal with it, but he'd already informed his friend, Claris, in Internal Security by then. Even for Vallen that was being rather efficient.'

'When's Vallen due back?'

'Oh not for a while yet.'

'Then why don't we have a quick search of his belongings, see what he's hiding.'

Felson paused for a second, then nodded and led the way into Vallen's quarter's within the tent.

The small space was immaculately kept with everything stored away tidily. No spare area was wasted or muddled. Sean took a mental note of the position of everything: a man like Vallen would surely notice if something had been moved.

Felson tried the lid of Vallen's kit box. 'It's locked.'

'Surprise, surprise. Never mind, let me get at it.'

Sean took a small piece of metal from his pocket and bent down to inspect the lock. It was simple enough, and in just a couple of twists it clicked open.

He lifted the lid.

Clothes. Vallen's spare kit was all that seemed to be in here. But if so, why keep it locked? Carefully, Sean lifted the first layer off and felt his fingers connect with something solid and cold.

Metal.

Pulling aside a shirt, he smiled. At last. He looked up at Felson, who stared at the objects in disbelief. 'A Howden detonator, sir and a radio set—both of City origin.'

Felson's expression of shock turned to sadness. 'Okay Sean, looks like you've proved your point.'

'So, are you going to arrest him?'

Felson was silent, thinking. 'No, not yet. We need to know who he's been contacting, and I think I know just the man for the job. In the meantime, we can't have you getting arrested.'

'No sir. I was hoping you could find an outside job to put us on.'

'You mean one that doesn't exist?'

'Something like that.'

'Good idea. At least then it doesn't look like you're running away. But stay close enough in case I need you for this operation to get Vallen.'

Sean nodded. 'Sir?'

'Yes?'

'Who is this other man you mentioned?'

Felson smiled. 'I can't say at the moment until I know he's available ... but be assured, he's one of the best Hellyon's got.'

Kris Varelli lay back in the cool grass by the side of his tent and pondered his life. He loved his work: the more dangerous the better. He was good at it ... the best. No one could survive behind enemy lines and gather intelligence like he could. He was also 46 and well aware that his active days could soon be over. In the past 15 years, he had barely lived a normal life, even for a soldier: his skills were always in great demand, and the Hellyon Commanders would send him on a mission before choosing anyone else. In the last year alone, he'd been chosen for three long term and very dangerous operations in Balaat and Jerregish, including a harrowing episode undercover at Balaat Fort. That was one he'd rather forget: if he hadn't been instructed to gather intel, he would most certainly have enjoyed sending a few souls to hell, even if it meant joining them himself.

His whole life had been spent in secrecy — different identities, hiding out. He used to work within a team, the only men he ever trusted. They were all dead now, killed in one action or another and now he preferred to work alone. That way you didn't have to watch the people you care about die next to you. Ah, what the hell, he chided himself, death was death: he'd seen enough of it — caused a lot of it. At the end of the day there was never time to mourn a loss, only to concentrate on living. But what now? What of the future? He had never had time to form any relationships ... except for one, a long long time ago ... but that was another loss, best forgotten. No, the girls he'd been with were nice enough and served his purposes, but they never lasted long. Sometimes it seemed like he went through women like most men changed their shoes.

Long years of survival had honed his instincts and he felt the person's presence even before he heard their footsteps. He opened his eyes and sat up. The man in front of him was a stranger, and a subordinate.

'Yes?' he asked.

'Message from Commander Felson, sir. He needs to see you.'

'Oh he does, does he?' Kris grinned. Maybe his active days weren't over just yet. 'Okay, soldier, tell him I'm on my way.'

'Yes sir.' The man turned and left. Kris watched him go, a smile still on his face. As long as he was still useful, anything — or anyone — else would have to wait.

Felson's tent was just as Kris remembered it: well ordered. Felson hadn't changed much either, except that he looked older, almost shrunken. Kris didn't bother with salutes or formalities, just pulled up a chair and waited for the older man to speak.

'Good to see you, Kris,' Felson said.

'Thank you sir.'

'You just got back?'

'Last night. Had a bit of trouble getting in through the gate — the password had changed, so I had to get through the perimeter fence.'

Felson raised an eyebrow. 'Let me know where, won't you? Obviously we have a bit of a security problem.'

Kris smiled his wide, slow smile. 'No more than usual, I'm just good at getting into places.'

'Hmm.' Felson cleared his throat. 'I've got a little job for you.'

'I guessed that sir. What is it?'

'We have a saboteur in camp — they blew the explosives dump the other night, caused terrible casualties.'

Kris sat up straight, suddenly concerned. 'Do you know who?'

'We thought we did. Jak Merron and Aris Desun were accused and imprisoned, but now I have some evidence to show they were set up.'

'Merron? Is he still around? Well, I can see why he might have been implicated ... after the last time. And who else did you say?'

'Aris Desun. You would have been away when she joined us. Ex City special ops, escaped from Balaat Fort a few months ago. She's with CU11 now.'

Kris's breath caught in his throat. He'd been at Balaat Fort around that time and had heard the rumours that a woman had escaped but he'd also heard she'd been shot and killed by the pursuit party.

'And you say she's innocent?'

'That is my belief based on the evidence I have.'

'Which is?'

'Certain equipment has been found in Vallen's personal possessions which point to his being the saboteur.'

'Vallen? You're kidding. I though that old fusspot was the model of loyalty.'

Felson suddenly looked very tired. 'Yes, so did I. It appears that I was wrong.'

'So where is he now?'

'I sent him to help over in quartermasters. They're a bit short-handed, so I thought it was the ideal opportunity to keep him out of my way.'

'So what do you want me to do, take him out?'

'No. He must be meeting a contact somewhere, and I want to find out who and where.'

'No problem.'

Felson paused for a second. 'When Vallen meets with his contact, I want both of them—alive.'

Kris frowned. 'I don't think that even I can manage to capture two people on my own, not without constructing a trap. And to do that I will need to know where they'll be.'

'Yes, I know. You will have help.' Felson noticed the sudden tightening of the man's jaw.

'Who?' Kris asked. His voice had suddenly lost some of its friendliness.

'CU11—Sean Hess's men. They're due to be arrested as well, but I've sent them out of camp, so they're out of danger. If I can find out when and where Vallen's meeting his contact, an ambush can be set up.'

'Then why not let them do the whole job?' Kris shrugged.

'Because your reputation is beyond doubt and if you are there with them, it helps to support their case that Vallen wasn't set up in any way on this arrest. Also, four of you will be better than three, especially with your experience.'

Kris nodded, understanding, but he still didn't like the idea. On the other hand, there was no alternative. 'Okay,' he said. 'I'll do it. But understand that I will be in command.'

Sean's sense of irritation burned within him, but he concealed it as he listened to Varelli planning the operation. Although he could understand Felson's reasoning, he resented having another man in charge of his unit, especially when that other man was Kris Varelli.

It wasn't that he had anything personal against the man, but Varelli had always got the missions he wanted, and the accolades he craved. In short, Varelli was the one man who made Sean feel inadequate.

Fenim and Tor seemed okay with it: Sean noted with some

distaste that Tor hung on Varelli's every word. So the guy had a reputation as a hero. So what? He knew of many men who had done braver things in battle but never received the same admiration. Fenim was wiser and less impressed; he'd seen it all before as well.

Felson found it difficult to look Vallen in the eye as he handed him the document, but he forced himself to do so. 'Take this to Commander Leet for approval, then make sure it's destroyed.'

'Sir.' Vallen nodded. He gave the paper only a quick glance as he placed it in his pocket.

Would he take the bait? Felson wondered. The information on that paper was interesting enough — the target co-ordinates of the next behind lines mission. Of course, it was false, but Vallen wasn't to know that. Moving to the tent door he peered after his treacherous valet. Already, moving stealthily behind him, some of Macker's unit began to track his movements within the camp. So far, so good.

Aris sat in her cell, trying to will away the pain in her head. Gingerly she touched her fingers to the source and found a tender swelling caked with blood. Her whole face felt rearranged and she knew without looking in a mirror that she was a mess. The door opened. Najik stood there staring down at her and she couldn't stop herself from cringing into the wall. It was a reflex action, a product of sustained brutality, but she still hated herself for it. Surely he hadn't come to deal out another beating — not so soon after the last.

'I thought your friend would have learnt after the last time,' Najik said, shaking his head. 'But he is very loyal to you. Too loyal for his own good.'

'That is because we haven't done anything wrong,' she answered, wishing she had more strength in her voice.

'So you keep saying. But consider this Desun—his life, and that of CU11 depend on you.'

What the hell was he on about? she wondered. What sort of new trick was this?

He saw her puzzlement. 'I personally believe you worked alone, but others believe that you can't have done ... that CU11 are involved. Which means, unless you confess your part in all this, they will go down with you.' He came closer to her. 'Now I don't think you possess any moral code or integrity, so you probably don't give a damn. However, just in case I'm wrong, I'm going to allow just one visit from Merron. Maybe he'll get you to change your plea.'

Her confused mind tried desperately to take in the full meaning of what he was saying. If she confessed to blowing the ammo dump, Jak and the rest of CU11 would go free. If she didn't ...

She sagged back on the bed. What choice did she have?

Footsteps echoed down the corridor and her door opened again.

'Aris?' Jak's voice sounded so good after Najik's.

She looked up at him.

'Dear God, Aris—what the fuck has that bastard done to you?' Jak exclaimed, seeing the bruising on her face.

She shook her head. 'It doesn't matter Jak, it's over.'

'What do you mean, it's over?'

'He told me what would happen to you and the unit if I didn't confess.'

Jak took hold of her by the shoulders. 'Forget it. No one's confessing to anything they didn't do. The guys can look out for themselves—I've managed to get a warning to them. So sit tight. We'll find a way out of this somehow.'

'Do you really think I have any option Jak?' she asked, her voice sounding suddenly weary. 'I'm tired of the fear I feel waiting for Najik's footsteps to come along that corridor. I'm tired of waiting for each blow to land — or not, depending on what he decides. That man's taking my soul away, Jak, and I just can't fight it anymore.'

Jak swallowed hard and pulled her to him gently, wrapping his arms around her shaking body. If I ever get out of here, he vowed silently, whether that bastard's supposed to be on my side or not, I'm going to kill him.

Kris lay in the darkness of the bush and grinned to himself. The plan had worked perfectly: Vallen had been extremely careless and that was going to lead to his downfall. Not only had he accepted Felson's false information unquestioningly, he had also allowed himself to be overheard using his radio to his contact. So now they were all in place at the contact point, Codie Mound, a tak south east of Hellyon Camp. The whole operation had been quickly cleared and detailed by Felson as arresting a spy and his contact. No actual mention was made of any names.

The light from the moon provided just enough illumination to see the area around the entrance to the cave. He knew it wouldn't be long before Vallen arrived, although to be sure, he'd had Tor follow him from the camp. He didn't like leaving anything to chance. The rest of CU11 were spread out strategically around the area to prevent their targets escaping.

A movement and the soft sound of footfalls brought his attention into sharp focus. A twig cracked underfoot ... one of the many Kris had placed along the path as a warning measure. A dark shape now appeared in the clearing in front of him, paused for a quick look around and then entered the cave.

Vallen, thought Kris. One down and one to go.

The wait was longer than he expected. Maybe the contact had been delayed or was just being extra cautious. Whatever, the moon had already begun to dip in the sky and there was still no sign of the other man. Kris shifted position slightly, the stiffness in his bones giving him an unpleasant reminder that he was getting too old for this. Another cracking twig made him freeze. He listened, but heard nothing else. An animal?

Then another shape appeared in the clearing before it, too, entered the cave.

Kris tensed and readied himself, knowing that the others, too, would be doing the same. Keeping his body low, he moved closer to the cave, getting himself into position just outside the opening. As planned, the others, including Tor, came out of hiding and moved in too.

Inside the cave, they could hear urgent whispers and then the sound of shoes on crushed rock as their targets moved nearer to the opening. These contact meetings never were long affairs so he knew he had to act quickly. One appeared at the opening and both Kris and Sean made a sudden lunge, bringing him crashing to the ground, his face pushed into the gravel. One look told them it was Vallen. The second man was not short on fast reflexes and opened fire from inside the cave.

Fenim, drawing on his own quick instincts, hit the dirt, but Tor was less lucky. With a shout he dropped to the floor hit by one of the bullets.

'Shit,' Kris hissed. Making sure Sean had Vallen safe, he brought his own weapon up, but the man was well hidden by a piece of rock that blocked his line of fire. Kris looked over at where Fenim was, expecting him to let loose, but there was nothing. Fenim was still, his weapon up but his face frozen by ... what? No time to philosophise. Kris crawled on his hands and knees to the cave opening, preparing to blast anything that moved.

Nothing. The stranger had gone. Disappeared into the cave. He could catch the faint sound of running footsteps retreating, even above the noise of Vallen's pleading. Straining his eyes he looked into the darkness. How far did this cave go back? Without light, he was not going to risk going in. The other man obviously knew where he was going, which meant that it was not just a single cave but a whole system, probably with other escape routes. They would be wasting time staying here, and time was something that Tor didn't have at the moment. Shit, he thought. Why hadn't they been told more about this cave? He was going to wring someone's neck in intelligence when he got back.

Fen ran over to where Tor lay on the ground, his breathing ragged as blood flowed from a leg wound. 'Tor, it's okay. I'm here. You're going to be okay.' He pulled his medical pack from his belt kit and pulled out a field dressing. He had nearly finished the bandaging when Kris walked over. He was still curious as to why Fen hadn't acted a few moments before, but decided that this wasn't the time to ask.

'Can he be moved?' he asked Fen.

Fen nodded.

Kris looked back at Vallen's mewling form, easily subdued by Sean. Next to him was a large bag. Making a quick inspection, he smiled: plastic explosive — all the evidence they needed.

Aris shivered under her thin blanket. It wasn't just the coldness of the night: she could hear the cries of an interrogation going on. Did she sound like that, she wondered? Did others lie awake with the strange mixture of relief and pity that she felt? It was a new prisoner, that much she knew. She heard begging and sobbing as he was brought in, but she hadn't bothered to peer through the grille in her door. New prisoners were brought in all the time, although most weren't interrogated to the same degree as this one.

The noises suddenly stopped, a door opened and she heard the sound of footsteps, of something dragging on the floor. Poor bastard had lost consciousness and was being put back into his cell for a while. Surely enough a cell door clanged shut further down the corridor. Voices mumbled quietly and then the footsteps started again, brisk, coming her way. She prayed they would go past.

They stopped and she heard the sickening sound of the key in the lock. Not again …. She had had enough. If it was her turn, she was just going to confess, get it over with. Death was a lot less painful than this fear.

The door opened. It wasn't Najik, but one of his junior officers. This wasn't his usual game.

'Okay, you're free to go,' he said.

Aris just sat there, hearing the words but somehow not believing them. This was a new ploy, a new form of torture. It had to be.

'Come on, Desun, get your ass out of here.' The man was becoming impatient.

Slowly, she stood up and walked to the door, half expecting a blow to knock her down any minute. She walked past him and into the corridor. Nothing happened. Dazed, she started to walk down the corridor towards the exit door. Still no one rushed to restrain her. But experience told her she shouldn't get her hopes up yet — this could still be some sort of cruel joke. Her steps slowed as she reached the last barrier between herself and the outside world and she almost hesitated to push through the last door. Surely now, she thought.

The night air on her face made her gasp as she walked outside. She kept walking, still half expecting footsteps behind her at any minute. The guards at the gate of the detention compound opened it without a word as she stepped past them. As she walked through, a figure sitting by the gate suddenly jumped up.

'Aris, thank God!' Jak said, throwing his arms around her and hugging her tight. She held onto him, her mind still confused.

'Are we really free?' she asked.

'Yes ... hell, didn't they say? They caught Vallen and he confessed to everything.'

'Vallen,' she repeated, her voice sounding dead. Somehow she seemed incapable of any feelings, even of elation.

'I told you the others would come through for us.' Jak suddenly pulled back and took a look at her. 'I think though, instead of celebrating, we ought to get you to the medical centre.'

'They're free!' Sean yelled as he came back into CU11's encampment, breaking the uneasy silence. 'We did it.'

'We screwed up, you mean,' Kris growled.

'We achieved what we wanted — getting Jak and Aris off that charge.' Sean's voice held a challenge.

Kris grabbed him by the arm and took him a distance away, where Tor and Fen couldn't hear them. 'If that was all you wanted, then yeah, you achieved it,' he said. 'On the other hand, we also lost the other guy and got a man wounded in the process. Considering we had the advantage of numbers, surprise and a plan, that is a bad result. I shouldn't have to tell a unit captain that.'

Sean rounded on him, his pent up anger now given full release. 'Don't tell me my job, Varelli. That was just bad luck on top of bad intelligence. None of us knew that cave system could be used as an escape route.'

Kris took a deep breath. 'Okay then, tell me this: why did Fenim hesitate to fire when he had the perfect opportunity? Now, I know that Fenim is a sharp-shooter and has enough combat experience not to freeze when the shit hits. So, why did he? Because that's what lost it.'

Sean walked up to Kris and stood face to face, cold hate now in his eyes. 'You better be careful of what you're accusing my men of, Varelli. Just because others see you as some big hero does not give you the right to be judge and jury. What you are implying is that either he is a coward, or he is a traitor. I don't like that sort of slur being put on this unit. That's what got us into this mess in the first place.'

Varelli shrugged. 'I'm not saying he's either. But you can't deny he hesitated ... for whatever reason. Don't you think you ought to find out why?'

'You were the commander of this unit for that mission only, remember that. It's over now, and what happens within this unit is no longer a matter for your concern.'

Kris half laughed and shook his head. 'Okay, okay, have it your way. But you know it as well as I—we screwed up.' He began to walk away. 'It happens,' he said under his breath.

9

With a grin, Tor placed his gaming piece on the exit square and sat back.

He'd won.

Again.

'You bastard!' Jak exclaimed, glaring.

'That's another fifty dashats you owe me,' Tor smiled.

'The hell I do!'

'Ah well, if you can't afford to pay right now, I can always take it in instalments.'

'You cheated ... used bloody Sharm trickery to confuse me, or something.'

'Nope, just superior playing skills.'

'Superior playing skills my ... '

'Hey, whoa ... what's up?' Sean came over from his tent, drawn by the argument.

Tor looked up at him. 'Jak won't accept that he's just lousy at playing Impasse.'

Sean grinned. 'Well, he should do—I've told him enough times.'

'What's that?' asked Jak, changing the subject and pointing to the mug in Sean's hand. 'That doesn't look like a brew in there.'

'Just getting into the spirit of things for tonight.'

'It's only a camp social,' Jak muttered.

'Don't let Felson hear you say that. The powers that be have decreed it to be a morale raising effort after the crisis of the explosion.'

'More likely they're about to send us all on an offensive into Balaat,' Jak said.

'Mr Cynical as ever I see, although I must admit I tend to agree with you. Still, all the more reason for enjoying tonight.'

Jak grimaced. 'I think I'd rather have an early night.'

'Oh, that's a pity. Saskia will be disappointed.'

Jak shot out of his chair. 'Saskia?'

Sean winked at Tor. 'Oh, didn't you know? Her unit's been reposted from the Jerregish border. She said she'd see you later.'

Jak's face suddenly grew guarded. 'Hang on, you're not messing me around ... '

Sean shook his head. 'Would I lie about a thing like that?'

'And she really wants to see me?'

'You mean, after what happened last time?' Tor said, smirking.

'That was between me and her!' Jak snapped at him. He turned back to Sean: 'She really wants to see me?'

Sean raised his eyebrows. 'Well, if you don't have an early night, you might find out.'

'I heard some girls from Soran were going to be arriving tonight. Is that true?' Tor asked.

Sean grinned. 'Yeah, so looks like we're set up for later.'

'Good job Fen's gone home then — keep him out of temptation,' said Tor.

Jak snorted. 'Whenever have you known Fen to give in to temptation — his middle name's integrity.'

Tor shrugged. 'Well, you never know ... he has been acting a little odd lately.'

'Something's on his mind, ' Sean agreed. 'Still, if he wants to tell us, he will.'

Tor looked over at Aris's tent. The door flap was still closed. She was probably asleep. 'Do you think tonight will take Aris's mind off things?' he asked.

Sean shook his head. 'I don't know. I wish I knew what we could do; her nightmares are getting worse—nearly every night now.'

'Maybe her time in the cell set them off,' Tor ventured.

'Maybe. I'm just worried in case she has some sort of breakdown.'

'She won't crack,' mumbled Jak.

'How do you know?'

'I had nightmares too—after Berryn's Crossing—don't you remember? I didn't crack.'

'No, you just drank.'

'Even so, I coped—and so will she.'

Sean considered him for a moment: 'You know, I still can't understand this radical change of attitude about Aris. Come on, tell me ... what really did happen that day you both went out of camp?'

'Like I said, we just sorted things out.' Jak began to look irritated; he didn't like Sean's tone of voice.

'You didn't ... '

'Get stuffed Hess, I'm not you.'

'Thank goodness, or else I'd have even more competition around here. It's bad enough with the Sharm: he's beginning to make me look old.'

Tor laughed. 'Never mind, I'm sure some young lady will take your mind off your age later on.'

Sean's smile was rueful: 'That and a bottle of kotch.'

'Well, save some for me this time,' said Jak. 'If Saskia's still pissed off with me, I might need it.'

'And if she isn't?' asked Tor

'I'll still need it.'

The day's light was fading fast.

Aris wandered through Hellyon Camp on her own, watching the festivities carrying on without her. She ought to pity the poor sods on sentry duty, but really she envied them. She had even volunteered for the job, but Felson had refused — he obviously thought she needed some fun.

She didn't.

She needed sleep, sleep without the demons that seemed to surround her every time she closed her eyes. Even when awake, memories invaded her vision, so that often she couldn't tell the difference between the nightmarish hell and reality. Maybe it was the mind to mind or else the beatings in the cell that had opened the gates, but now her head was flooded with images from Balaat: the fear, the blood, the pain ... faces of the women she had promised to go back to free, the faces of her captors, her torturers. And then there were the other images, the ones that mixed up her life here with that other time. The worst recurring dream was being back in the arena again, waiting for the fight to begin as she was hobbled by a long rope. Her eyes were closed but she could sense one of those ... things ... getting closer, could feel its breath on her face. However when she opened her eyes, it wasn't Dirik she saw, it was Najik. It was as if they had become inseparable in her head, irrational though she knew it to be.

She knew she had to fight her ghosts alone — no one could help her on this one. She'd hidden the worst of it from the unit

—not the nightmares of course: there was no way she could hide those. At first, when she'd woken up screaming, the guys had come running to her, dragged her back to reality, but now they left her to get on with it. She couldn't really blame them. After all, it was she who'd told them not to bother, that she was alright.

But she wasn't. She knew she was starting to lose control of reality. Maybe it would be better if she was signed off duty; after all, she didn't want to put the unit in any danger.

Lost in her thoughts, she didn't notice a group of drunken men stagger out from an encampment behind her. One, a bit faster than the rest, caught up with her and gripped her arm.

'Hey gorgeous, you out on your own?'

Turning furiously, she wrenched her wrist from his hand and glared at him. 'Do yourself a favour and piss off.'

'Ooh, a bit cross tonight, aren't we? I know a good cure for that.'

She glared at him again, turned and started to walk away. Suddenly she felt an arm around her shoulders.

'Oh come on,' the man said. 'We've been away on the borders for a long time; I think we deserve a little fun. I heard you Soran girls were up for a bit of that tonight.'

She stopped suddenly, realising that she didn't exactly look like a soldier in the loose trousers and sleeveless top Macker had lent her. She held her hands up. 'I'm not from Soran I'm with CU11 ... '

The man was looking at her with renewed interest, as were his companions. 'CU11? That's Merron's unit, isn't it?'

She nodded, hoping that would be an end to it. Instead, they started to close in.

'Looks like it's payback time then,' said the leader. 'Only it'll be a lot more fun with you than it ever would be with him.'

He grabbed her wrist again and pulled her close to him; she could smell the alcohol on his breath. Within a second her knee connected with his groin and she wrenched her hand out of his grip to bring her fist crashing down on his collarbone. He yelled, clutching at his shoulder and fell to the floor. Arms gripped her from behind, as another man closed in front.

In her head ... in the arena, the crowds screamed out ... blood and sand ... the flash of a blade coming her way ... .

Using the man holding her from behind as a counter-balance, she kicked out with both her legs and the one in front went down, winded. That was all she remembered as her reality became blurred with another time and another place.

The next thing she knew, she was standing over a pile of bodies, staring at the damage. Two others from the unit, drunker than the rest, staggered off to a safe distance.

'Shit', she exclaimed, looking at the four lying on the ground around her. Making a quick check, she ascertained that they were all still alive. Silently thanking the powers that be, she turned and quickly made off, trying to get as much distance between them and her as possible.

With nowhere else to go, she headed back to the unit's encampment. At least there she could feel safe and get smashed out of her head.

The encampment was almost in sight when a man stepped out from the shadows to her left. She immediately stepped back and took up a defensive pose. Had those bastards followed her?

'It's okay,' said a calm voice. 'I'm not going to hurt you.'

'Who the hell are you?' she demanded.

He stepped from the darkness so that she could see his face. 'Kris Varelli. No particular unit — I think Felson likes to share me around.'

The name was familiar but it was a few seconds before she

remembered where she'd heard it. 'You're the one who helped Sean catch Vallen.'

He extended a hand. 'I'd rather think of it as him helping me. And you're the one who escaped Balaat Fort — I never believed that was possible.'

She took his hand, feeling the strength in it.

'Were you heading back?' he asked. She nodded. 'Well, I'd leave it a while. Jak's there on his own after downing a bottle of kotch and he doesn't seem in the best of moods. I don't think Saskia turned up.'

'Who?' Aris was confused that this stranger seemed to know so many intimate details about her unit.

'Never mind. Listen, I've got some drink in my tent. Would you like some?'

Aris hesitated. On one hand he seemed friendly enough and from the little she'd heard about him he would have some interesting tales to tell. On the other hand, did she really want to be alone with a stranger?

He must have read her thoughts. 'It's okay. I swear I'll behave like a gentleman... for tonight anyway,' he grinned.

There was something in his grin that made up her mind for her. She nodded.

Following his retreating back she realised that he must have been waiting for her to return all this time. But why? What interest did he have in her?

Kris's tent was pitched close to Felson's but in a space of its own. Backed by other units' encampments it even seemed to acquire an air of that rarest of things in Hellyon Camp — privacy. He dived into it and emerged a minute or so later carrying a bottle and a lantern. Pulling up a couple of nearby crates he lit the lantern and gestured for her to sit down.

For the first time he was able to see her face properly. He

frowned. 'That looks like a nasty bruise on your cheek.'

Aris raised her hand to her face and noticed how sore it was for the first time. She must have sustained it in the fight without noticing. 'I had a bit of a run in with a unit back from Jerregish. They were looking for Jak but found me instead.'

'And...?'

'I don't think they'll be bothering Jak. Not tonight anyway.'

'You took them on on your own?' Kris sounded incredulous.

'I had no choice. Anyway they were very drunk; I could have pushed most of them over — luckily for me.'

Kris frowned again. 'Lucky indeed. I expect that was Saskia's brother you encountered. He has a score to settle with Jak over the way he treated her last year. You shouldn't have been targeted as a payback though. That unit has a nasty reputation for violence.'

She shrugged, trying to cover the fact she still felt shaken by the attack. 'So why?' she asked.

'Why what?'

'Why were you waiting for me?'

He smiled. 'Was it that obvious? I suppose it must have been. To be honest I just had to meet the woman who not only escaped from Circus with her life but also escaped from Pock.'

There was something in the tone of his voice that indicated his interest was not just mere curiosity.'

'What do you know about Circus?'

He took a swig from the bottle and handed it to her. She noticed that it was best quality Jerregishan wine. 'I know enough to say it's not a good place.'

He didn't offer any more and she didn't push him. Maybe she had it wrong. Maybe it was just curiosity.

'So how are you settling in with the unit?'

'They're a solid team. Good people to work with.'

'Hmmm.' He rested his chin on his hand and gave her a searching look. 'But not yet your friends.'

It was a statement rather than a question and for a minute it threw her into confusion. 'Friends? Of course they are.'

'As much as you'll let them anyway.'

Indignation arose in her. How dare this man, to whom she had only talked to for less than an hour, dictate how she was feeling about the unit. 'And what do you mean by that?' she asked acidly.

He held up his hands. 'I'm sorry. I'm not very good at this talking shit — I was just trying to get to know you a bit better.'

She stood up, suddenly feeling too tired to be sociable with the man. 'Well, now you do. And now I'm going to head back.'

He smiled and shrugged but didn't attempt to persuade her to stay. As she marched back to her own encampment she didn't know what bothered her more — the fact that he had been right or that he hadn't tried to stop her leaving.

When she got back, it was as Kris had said. Jak was sitting at the fire, a bottle in his hand. By the one empty bottle of kotch on the ground, he had already been drinking quite heavily. She hesitated at first, remembering Kris's warning, but then forced herself to move forward.

Jak was staring into the fire, looking more miserable than usual.

'Mind if I join you?' she asked.

He shrugged and offered her the bottle. She took a small swig, still mindful of her last experience with kotch.

'The others not here?'

He shook his head. 'They've gone to chase women.'

Something in the tone of his voice made her look at him. He looked completely miserable.

'Are you sure you don't mind me being here?' she asked.

He shrugged. 'You're as entitled to sit by the fire as I am.'

She decided to risk the question: 'What's wrong?'

'I'm trying to avoid someone.'

'By sitting next to your tent? I'd say you're not trying very hard.'

'I didn't say I was trying very hard.'

Aris smiled as she suddenly understood. 'It's a woman, isn't it? That Saskia I've been hearing about. So why are you not trying very hard to avoid her?'

'It's a long story.'

'It always is with you.'

'Let's just say she's after more than I want to give.'

'Love and marriage?'

'Something like that. And she's got her big brother to back her up—a big brother that I had a disagreement with last year. I broke his nose in front of her. As you can imagine she wasn't particularly impressed.'

Aris raised an eyebrow. 'Is he a tall, ugly fellow with cropped blond hair and a scar running under his chin?'

Jak nodded, his interest raised.

'Well, he's nursing another broken nose now.'

Jak nearly shot out of his chair. 'What? How come?'

'I met him and his unit on the walk back—nearly ended up as your payback.'

'Bastards!' Jak exclaimed. 'Did they hurt you?'

She shook her head. 'They didn't really get a chance.' She decided not to mention what she'd been seeing at the time.

'I'll make sure this is settled once and for all.' He started to rise, the misery on his face now replaced by anger.

Aris gripped his arm. 'Whoa, wait a minute. I don't think the opposition are up to a return match right now.'

Jak stared at her. 'You took them all down — by yourself?'

Aris smiled. 'It wasn't so hard: they were all pretty drunk—too drunk to cause me much of a problem.'

He looked hard at her. 'But it does mean that they'll be after you as well as me now. Luckily they're only back for a couple of days, but you will need to keep out of their way from now on.'

Aris shrugged and gave a lopsided smile. 'Don't worry. I don't think they'll come looking for me for a while.'

He offered her some kotch but she waved it aside. 'I've had enough for one night. I think I'll turn in.'

'Aris,' he caught her arm. 'I can only imagine what you've been through, and I certainly didn't help when you first arrived. I know you have stuff that is still in your head but I want you to know that I am always here if you need to talk. You are not without friends.'

Friends, Aris thought. Maybe it was time to prove Kris wrong. Jak had put his past aside, maybe she should too. But was it that easy? She turned and clapped him on the shoulder. 'Thanks Jak. I'll work on it, okay?'

But that night, as with every other, the nightmares still came.

10

'No sir, I cannot.' Aris stood her ground in front of Felson. Not that it was doing any good.

'We need someone on the inside, Aris. You are the only one who can do it. Hellyon ... '

'Needs me? With all due respect, commander, no it doesn't. There are plenty of women you can pick from who would be far more suited to the job. I ... I'm not sure how I would hold up in there.'

Felson cleared his throat. 'You have good reason to feel like you do, and I wouldn't be asking you unless I had to. But Balaat has been getting too sure of itself lately: the raiding on our northern border has reached intolerable levels. We need to hit back a little, go on the offensive for once instead of the defensive.'

Aris shook her head. 'Isn't there some other way?'

'No, in order to successfully make an attack on Balaat Fort, we need people on the inside, in all the areas, including the women's compound. You know how things work there and will be able to blend in easier.'

'I can't go back in that place again, sir ... not after last time.'

Felson looked long and hard at her and then shrugged.

'Alright, I won't force you and your refusal won't be held against you. But I am surprised.'

'Why?'

'Because I remember a young woman standing in front of me not so long ago with defiance in her eyes. Despite all she'd been through she was still determined one day to go back and get the other women out of that hell-hole. Now she has the chance, she's lost all her fight.'

He was right. When she had first found sanctuary in Hellyon Camp she had vowed that she would do all she could to save her friends from the sure fate that awaited them. But that was before her memories started living in the present. That was before the nightmares. Damn you, she thought, why did you have to bring that up and try and guilt trip me? Now I have no choice.

She took a deep breath. 'Okay, I'll go in. But if things go badly, if I'm recognised by the wrong people, I might not even last long enough to do what you want.'

Jak strolled into the camp, a worried frown on his face. 'Has anyone seen Aris?' he asked the others.

Sean stood up and shook his head. 'Come to think of it I haven't seen her since yesterday. I assumed she was in her tent, as usual.'

'That's what I thought too, but she isn't there.'

'You don't think she's left?' asked Fen

Jak considered it for a second and then shook his head. 'Nah. Not without saying something to one of us.'

'Do you think she's in some sort of trouble?' said Sean. 'That other unit Jak mentioned ... might they have taken her somewhere?'

'I doubt it. We'd have heard the fight from here,' said Jak.

'Her kit is still here, so she can't have gone far.'

Sean frowned. 'Well if she's gone out of camp without permission again, I shall bloody well put her on hard labour for a week. I know she's going through some shit at the moment but that does not mean she can come and go from this unit as she pleases.'

'There is another possibility...' Fenim butted in. 'Maybe Felson has sent her on an op somewhere ....

'Without consulting me first?' Sean's voice was calm but the others noted the anger in his eyes.

Torassin spoke for the first time in the conversation. 'Wait, my mate Bulson was on the main gate last night; he might have seen something.'

'Well go and ask him then,' Jak growled. 'And let's hope this is all a false alarm.'

The insertion into Balaat Fort had been easier than Aris expected. Two Hellyon agents, already well infiltrated into the fort had rendezvoused with her escorting unit RU6, as planned. Now, as their 'prisoner' she had been taken back there, ostensibly as a transfer slave from Dengis Fort. No one asked questions, even though the transfer papers hadn't come through, nor were they ever likely to. For the sake of realism, her 'captors' treated her as rough as they dared without causing injury, but at least she knew she was safe while in their presence.

The gates of the women's compound loomed up ahead. She had felt sick with fear right from the point she had agreed to the mission but now the terror threatened to overwhelm her. She stopped, unable to move any further. '

I can't go in there', she whispered.

The man on the right took her arm roughly and pulled her

forwards at the same time bringing his face close enough to hers to whisper: 'Steady, Aris. It's only for 24 hours. They've changed around the guards since you were here, so no-one's going to recognise you.'

Except for the girls, she thought grimly. Those that were still alive anyway. It would take just one to blow the whistle and she would be dead. But most of them had been her friends ... most of them. She took a deep breath and forced herself to carry on.

The man on her left muttered under his breath: 'Okay we're nearly there. Good luck Aris. I'll make sure someone gets you out when the shit hits.'

The guard on the gate of the compound came out to meet them. 'Not another one?' he said. Then looked Aris over. 'Well, at least she's in bit better a shape than most of them around here.'

'Transfer from Dengis,' said the man on Aris's right. 'The paper's have been delayed but there's no problem. If you could just allocate her a bunk and a duty for now, the papers should be here in a couple of days.'

The gate guard grinned. 'What sort of duty might we put you on then?' he said, leering.

The man on her left came to the rescue. 'No, as the papers will say, she is to be put on yard duties for a while to punish her for stealing food in Dengis.'

The gate guard shrugged. 'Just can't trust 'em can you? Alright, leave her with me.'

She was taken into the small square block of the Compound Administration Centre. It hadn't changed much, still smelt of mildew and sweat. The guard on the desk, after being informed of the paperwork delay looked up at her.

'What's your name?'

'Ana Kalaat,' she answered, remembering the false details

she'd been given. 'Let's see your number.' She pulled aside her baggy shirt to reveal the branded number above her breast. He noted it down beside her name.'

'I'm putting you in Bunkroom Five — that's the building you can see on the right over there. Bunk number 32. I'm sure you'll find it — if not, ask someone. Your duties until otherwise notified will be sweeping the yard.'

Aris gave an involuntary gasp: Bunkroom Five had been her old bunkroom. Too much was the same as before: it was like she had never escaped. She closed her eyes and knew that now she had no choice: she had to shut down her emotions again if she was going to have any chance not only of completing this operation but also of survival. When she opened them again, they were harder, less readable.

Just as Tor expected, Bulsan was still asleep after last night's shift. He shook him awake. A frowning, freckled face appeared from beneath the blanket.

'Torassin, you son of a bitch! What the hell do you think...'

'Listen to me, Bul, I need your help.'

'And I need my sleep — piss off!' He turned over and buried his face under the blankets again. Tor grabbed the cover and pulled it off.

'It's urgent. I wouldn't ask otherwise. I need to know something.'

Bulsan sat up and rubbed at his eyes. 'Alright, what?'

'Last night, while you were on duty, did you happen to see a woman leave the encampment? About this high...,' he demonstrated with his hand, 'short black hair, somewhat skinny?'

'Yeah, but what's that to you?'

'Never mind that now. Was she on her own?'

'No, she left with RU6. It looked like they were off on some sort of operation.'

'RU6? They're strictly long range reconnaissance? Do you know where they were going?'

Bulson snorted. 'They're not exactly likely to tell me, are they? Those guys are always on something hush-hush. In fact I'm not even sure whether I should be telling you I saw them.'

Tor smiled at him. 'Oh believe me, it is totally the right thing to do.'

'And another thing ... '

'What?'

'This woman ... she's not a soldier, is she?'

'Why do you say that?'

'She was wearing this strange clothing—baggy trousers and a baggy shirt—rough material, dirty white colour—a bit like those women in Balaat have to wear.'

Tor suddenly felt his blood run cold. 'Thanks Bul, that's all I need to know.'

'So ... are you going to tell me what's going on?' Bul asked, suddenly very awake.

Tor shook his head. 'No, sorry friend. In fact I'm not sure what's going on myself yet.'

Tor started to walk back to CU11's encampment. The implications of what Bul told him were grave and not only for Aris. When the others found out, Felson might need some sort of protection too.

When Aris opened the door, the bunkroom was almost empty—it was probably time for slop—the only word that could be use to describe the food here. She made her way towards bunk 32, finding it halfway down the aisle and up on the second tier of the wooden platforming that made up the bunks. She was about to haul herself up into it when she felt a hand on her shoulder spin her around. She found herself looking at an unfamiliar sharp-faced young woman.

'Who the fuck are you?' the woman asked, her tone decidedly unfriendly.

'I've just arrived.' Aris took the equivalent of a mental deep breath and reminded herself of where she was and of who she was meant to be. 'They transferred me from Dengis.'

'Troublemaker were you? Well, don't make any damn trouble round here, do you understand me?'

Aris shook her head and started to climb up to her bunk again but the woman grabbed her wrist. 'Hey, don't turn away while I'm still talking to you. I haven't finished yet.'

Aris pretended to look suitably cowed; she didn't want a scene.

'What's your name?'

'Ana ... Ana Kalaat.'

The girl grabbed hold of Aris's shirt and pulled it aside, looking at the number. She looked up at Aris, suspicion on her face. 'That's an old number. You're in pretty good condition for the time you've done in Dengis. How did you manage that then?'

'I ... . I had certain privileged duties. I was well looked after.'

The woman snorted and then gave her a hard stare. 'You were one of their whores, you mean. You're the sort who tells tales on us to the men to earn yourself some extra food. Well, let me warn you now—collaborators don't last long here. I'll be watching you, Kalaat, every step of the way.' She smiled like a reptile and then stalked off to her bunk further down the row.

Shit, thought Aris as she watched her go, that's all I need.

'Aris?'

She jumped at the sound of her name and turned. This time

the woman in front of her was one she knew.

'Merys,' Aris glanced anxiously over her shoulder but the first woman was seated with her back to them and hadn't appeared to hear. She raised her finger to her lips and drew Merys to a space where the bunks cut off the other girl's vision of them. 'Please, you mustn't use my name, or look like you know me. I'm Ana Kalaat as far as anyone here is concerned.'

'Ana Kalaat? But why?'

'Long story ... I can't say at the moment.'

'So you did get caught again then?'

Aris hated to lie to her friend but decided it was the best option at the moment. 'Yes, but only after they said I'd been shot and killed. That's why I have the new identity and also why I ended up in Dengis.'

'So why are you back here again then?'

Aris shrugged. 'Administrative cock-up I suppose. Whatever, I'd better keep a low profile in case I bump into any of the guards who knew me, or else you know where I'll end up.'

Merys nodded. 'They'd put you in Circus as soon as blink. Don't worry, your secret's safe with me.'

'What's up with her?' Aris thumbed in the direction of the sharp-faced woman further down the bunkroom.'

'That's just Dita. She thinks too much of herself, thinks she owns the place. I shouldn't worry too much; I heard she's due for Circus herself pretty soon.'

Aris shuddered. Not that she would normally feel any compassion for such a woman as Dita, but she wouldn't wish the horrific experience of Circus on anyone. She changed the subject.

'How about the others?'

Merys shrugged and suddenly Aris noticed for the first time

how lifeless her friend's eyes seemed. 'Faye is around somewhere. She's on kitchen duties so she'll probably be back a little later. Barr's dead — they put her in Circus a couple of months back.'

'Terri?'

'I don't know. She got taken away one night and we never saw her again.'

Aris slowly nodded, suddenly understanding why she had really agreed to this mission. These women knew, as she had known, what it was like to suffer, to feel fear, to despair of ever knowing freedom again. If she succeeded, and now she knew she must whatever the cost, she would be giving these women some sort of life back again. If only she could also take away their memories.

Sean grabbed Tor as he came back into the camp.

'I've just told the others that there will be an all out attack on Balaat Fort tomorrow at dawn. I know it's short notice but we have to have the element of surprise on this one. The recce forces have been in place for days and everything's prepared ...'

Tor stopped him. 'Where are Jak and Fen? I need to talk to you all.'

'They're in their tents, getting ready for later.' Sean frowned, puzzled at Tor's urgency.

Tor ran over to the tents, calling for them to come out. They did, looking just as confused as Sean.

'This is urgent,' Tor said. 'I just talked to Bulsan about whether he's seen Aris.'

'And?' asked Jak.

'She left camp with RU6 last night, dressed in Balaatan clothes — the ones the women wear.'

There was silence as Tor's remarks sunk in.

'Shit,' said Jak quietly. 'She's gone back in on a mission. Felson had better have a good reason for this.'

'It's the assault on the fort,' said Sean. 'She must be in there to sabotage something in the women's compound.'

'That's practically a damn suicide mission!'

'It had better not be or else Hellyon may need some new commanders,' Sean said, his jaw set.

Kris Varelli was on edge, but he knew he couldn't let it show. The drinkhouse in Balaat Fort was crowded with men who had always walked on the rougher side of life, preferring to fight rather than talk. He'd got into enough rumbles in this place in his time, but today he didn't want to draw any attention to himself. He had five explosive devices to plant before dawn tomorrow, and as far as he was concerned nothing was going to go wrong.

'Buy you a beer, Mik?' He heard a familiar voice use his codename and turned. It was Goss, another Hellyon undercover operative. Kris relaxed; by drinking in company he was less likely to get into trouble. He nodded. Goss called over the bartender and ordered a couple of beers, spinning him some coins in payment. He then motioned Kris over to a corner where they could not easily be overheard.

'What is it?' Kris asked.

'You're covering D sector aren't you?'

'Yes, but you're not supposed to know.'

'Call it a guess. Look, this is important ... '

'Okay, fire away.'

'There's another of us in the women's compound — I brought her in earlier. I want to make sure she gets out alright.'

Kris shrugged. 'I'm sure she can look after herself.'

'Probably she can. There's more to it though: she was in here before and I'm not sure how she'll deal with being on the inside again.'

'You're not talking about Desun, the girl with CU11 are you?'

Goss nodded.

Kris's answer was immediate. 'No problem, I'll get her out. She should never have been sent here again in the first place.'

'My thoughts exactly. Still Felson had his reasons I'm sure.'

Kris snorted derisively. Just because a commander had reasons didn't mean they were the right ones.

A group of men came and stood next to them, arguing excitedly.

'We'd better go,' said Goss.

Kris nodded. 'See you tomorrow then.'

Without another word the two men parted company and strode off in different directions down the main street. Great, thought Kris, as if my job wasn't hard enough, now I'm going to have to get into the women's compound when it all hits tomorrow. He considered Desun. He'd only talked to her for a short while, but he felt he'd known her all his life. He certainly knew her history and had some idea of her experiences in Circus. He also knew the bravery it must have taken her to have walked back inside these walls. A plan began to form in his mind.

Yard sweeping was as boring as it was pointless. To make matters worse the morning was getting hotter and there was going to be no respite from the heat of the sun. She was all too aware of the special harness strapped around her waist which carried the explosives. Only two devices — one for each watchtower — but they still felt heavy and awkward. She knew she would have to move carefully and not draw any attention to herself until her task had been completed. She kept her head down and swept slowly, like the two other girls on duty. Now and again she would glance up to check the position of the guards, but mostly they stood in a little group and took no notice of the women — after all, women were hardly considered a threat to the men of Balaat. She was more wary of the guards in the watchtowers within the compound: she couldn't see them from here. She could only hope that they weren't too bothered about their duty either.

She took a route that brought her directly beneath the southern watchtower. Like the others it was built of reclaimed steel, its scaffolded structure stretching high above to support a wooden sentry box. Looking around she saw that the guards had vanished from sight completely. This was her chance. Quickly she darted under the tower and headed for the leg that stood against the perimeter wall. It was in deep shadow. Unhooking the explosives from her harness, she took a thin piece of wire and attached it to the leg, activating the timer and synchronising it with the one Felson had given her before she left. The job done, she darted back out into the sunlight again, just as the guards came back to check that she was still working.

Satisfied that she was, they settled down again to play cards. Aris kept sweeping. The morning dragged on and became hotter. The harness with the remaining explosive became increasingly uncomfortable and the other watchtower still seemed far away, but she knew she couldn't rush the sweeping — it would only draw attention.

Another hour and she was nearly there. Head down, her mind focussed on her task, she didn't hear the guard coming up behind her.

'Oi, you!' he shouted and kicked the broom out of her hands. Startled, Aris looked up and stared at her assailant. Almost instantly she cursed herself for forgetting where she was as a stinging slap landed across her face.

'What are you looking at, bitch?' he demanded, pushing his face close to hers.

She kept her head down. 'I'm sorry, sir. You startled me.'

'You must have been daydreaming then, not working.' He waved a cup of water under her nose and she suddenly realised how dry her throat was. 'I was going to give you this,' he said, 'but I'm not sure you deserve it.'

Laughing, he pulled the cup back and drank it himself, watching her.

'What's your number?' he asked.

She answered him, her nerves stretched to breaking point. She could almost feel the remaining bomb burning a hole in her ribs.

'I haven't seen you around before,' he stated, walking around her. 'You must be new; you're in better shape than most of them.'

Oh God, don't let him touch me, she thought, he'll find the harness. She held her breath as he continued his orbit.

'I think I'll put in a request for you tonight. I'm owed some relief.' Laughing, he walked away.

She let out her breath, grateful that he hadn't tried to molest her — that would have messed everything up. She wasn't worried about what he'd said — a guard wouldn't be given a girl who hadn't been health-checked and classified to be used for pleasure. Renewing her sweeping efforts, her throat was now unbelievably parched and the sweat dripped from her forehead and rolled down her body underneath her tunic and harness. She was practically there now, but she knew she couldn't risk planting the bomb. The sounds of laughter and the catcalls behind her indicated that the guards were now watching her. She would somehow have to find a way of sneaking out tonight to prime the second tower, as well as the inner compound fence.

The day passed in a monotonous rhythm of sweeping and the heat and the dehydration made her feel like passing out. Eventually the claxon sounded and she wearily put her broom away and headed back to the bunkroom, ignoring the obscenities shouted by the guards.

After satisfying her thirst, she climbed into her bunk, and making sure that no-one could see her, took off the harness, hiding it under her blankets with the third explosive device. Then she lay back in the coolness, closed her eyes and waited for the other girls to return from their duties. Despite being exhausted she couldn't sleep — she found herself worrying about how the hell she was going to set the other charges. There was no way she could do it without help.

A light tap on her shoulder made her jump and she sat up straight, suddenly alert again. Then she saw that Merys had climbed up to her bunk and was sat beside her.

'You okay?' she asked.

Aris nodded. 'Just tired, that's all.' She looked at Merys's concerned face. This woman had always helped out in the past; she could be trusted. But would she be capable of doing what Aris needed without putting herself into danger? Hell, Merys was already in danger just through being here. At least by tomorrow it should all be over. And she had to make sure it would be by completing her mission. There weren't so many options now.

She placed her hand on Merys's. 'I need you to help me,' she said.

Merys frowned. 'Of course. What's wrong?'

'Look, what I'm about to say mustn't get out beyond you

and Faye—not until later anyway.'

'Okay,' Merys shrugged.

Aris took a deep breath and told her all that had happened since the escape. She finished by explaining the reason for her return.

Merys listened open mouthed. Obviously whatever she had expected Aris to say, it wasn't this. 'So ... what can I do?' she asked at last.

Aris raised the blanket for a second and showed her the remaining two explosives. 'I have got to plant these some time between now and dawn,' she explained. 'I've got one watchtower, but I had a little trouble with a guard earlier and couldn't do the other. So that leaves me with only tonight to get them rigged up. Trouble is, I need to be able to get away without being seen.'

Merys nodded, suddenly understanding. 'You need me and Faye to create a diversion for you?'

'I know it's asking a lot, but...'

Merys shook her head and smiled. 'Well, if it all works, I don't think we'll be on punishment tomorrow anyway, so what does it matter?' She took another look at Aris's tired features. 'You rest up a while. I'll talk to Faye and we'll come up with the best plan. Which watchtower?'

'The north one.'

'Good, that's next to the slophouse. That's where we'll do it. Slop up should be in about an hour and it will be dark by then.'

Aris smiled. In another situation, Merys would have made one hell of a good tactician.

The slophouse was, as usual, noisy in the extreme and smelled of the revolting slops and guards' leftovers that served as food. Aris noted that Faye and Merys were already seated, as planned, and that Merys was waiting for her signal. Aris wandered over to one of the slop serving outlets next to the generator lead that powered the lighting. Everything was in position now. She reached up and scratched her head: the signal. At once Faye pushed her slops over Merys, eliciting a noisy screech from the other girl. Everyone in the eathouse stopped what they were doing and turned to watch as the two girls began to fight in earnest—pulling each other's hair, punching and scratching. With everyone's attention diverted, including the guards, Aris pulled on the wire hard. The lights went out and there were several screams and curses in the sudden darkness. Wasting no time, Aris ducked out through the nearest door and into the shadows of the night.

Any guards who may have been patrolling the immediate vicinity had rushed into the slophouse, and, for a short while at least, she had a window of opportunity. First of all, she had to get to the inner perimeter fence of the compound: that was the most dangerous task as she was fairly exposed. She dashed through the shadows to the nearest point of the fence and then dropped onto her belly and crawled the rest of the way, her harness digging into her ribs. A couple of minutes later, she was crawling back, her job done. Now it was just the watchtower.

It wasn't long before the guards had the lights back on in the slophouse behind her. Aris hoped that Merys and Faye also had the good sense to have disappeared in the blackout. Luckily the yard was full of shadows and it was a territory she knew well. She reached the watchtower without incident and immediately set to work on fastening the last device to the far leg. Everything was working to plan. Her job done she realised that it was too risky to try and get back among the girls at the slophouse; instead she scooted in the opposite direction, running through the shadows back to the bunkhouse.

As she neared it, her sense of calm returned. She could at

least walk in openly, as she could see that the girls were now returning from their interrupted meal. The lights were on inside and she felt sure that no-one had noticed her absence. All in all, the job had been well done and easier than she had expected. Seeing no guards in the immediate vicinity, she stepped out of the shadows and walked up to the bunkhouse door.

As soon as she opened it she knew something to be wrong. All the girls were stood by their beds, quiet and clearly frightened. Even Dita's eyes held a modicum of pity as she passed by her. A sudden cold fear spread over her as she realised she'd been caught. A noise behind her made her spin around to see two armed guards, and between them a face she knew only too well.

'Couldn't stay away from the place then?' said Tall't—his voice as smooth and calm as ever. 'I somehow can't believe you came back here because you liked the food. Perhaps we shall have to find out, won't we?'

11

Her hands secured behind her back, Aris knew that there would be no way out of this. The important thing now was that they never discovered the true reason for her being here. Even so, she knew they would interrogate her and that she would have to find some plausible reason for her presence. As far as she knew, her captors had not connected her with Merys and Faye so hopefully they would not become involved. If they, too, were brought for questioning then it could not be guaranteed that they would keep their silence under extreme pressure.

Tall't sat at his desk and stared at her for a long time. She did not stare back but kept her eyes to the floor.

'I see you're in better condition than the last time we met,' he said. 'So where have you been, Desun? Did you get back to City?'

'Maybe,' she answered, her voice flat. Let him guess.

He laughed. 'I don't think so. Last time I spoke to Tiern he was still very concerned that you had not been recaptured. Looks like you saved us some embarrassment by turning yourself in.'

Aris looked up sharply at Tiern's name. Tall't raised his eyebrows mockingly. 'You know, he's quite scared of you. Can't see why: you're just a woman—flesh and blood like all of us and quite easily exterminated. I can assure you that you won't be escaping again. Now, why don't you save us all some bother and tell us why you're here. Obviously it's not for the good of your health.'

Aris stayed silent and looked at her feet. She wondered how far away dawn was.

'I see. We will have to get it out of you some other way.'

Suddenly the door behind her sprang open. Tall't shot to his feet, surprised that his office had been invaded.

'She's mine, Tall't!' a voice called out—a voice that turned Aris's blood to ice.

'Did I give you permission to enter, Dirik?' demanded Tall't. The two men stood facing each other, staring each other down. Eventually Dirik looked away.

'I'm sorry, commander,' he said. 'I heard she was here. Her death was promised to me last time and I was cheated. I still have to avenge my son before his soul can rest.'

Tall't looked at the sorry, dirty figure of the man in front of him. 'I understand. First I need to question her but then she will be all yours. Would you like to execute her in Circus?'

Dirik nodded his head vigourously, a smile spreading over his misformed features. 'Oh yes! And I can assure you that her death will be both slow and painful and … entertaining.'

Tall't sniffed and then gave a curt nod. He had no regard for the disgusting man in front of him and he did not share in his extreme sadism, but he had to agree that Dirik and his family had been loyal enough supporters of Pock. And if this stupid girl had to suffer to maintain that loyalty then so be it. However, he could guarantee that he would not be attending Circus that night. There was no honour in watching certain kinds of death.

Aris felt Dirik move closer, could smell him. In spite of

herself she started to shake. He took hold of her chin and forced her eyes to meet his and she suddenly found herself staring into the face that had haunted her nightmares in the past year.

'The time will come soon enough,' he said, half to her and half to Tall't as he squeezed her jaw painfully between his fingers.

Tall't brought his baton crashing down on his desk, making Aris jump. 'That's enough Dirik. I suggest you leave before you try my patience any further.'

Dirik jumped away from her as if struck, gave Tall't a dirty look and stalked off. Tall't sat down again. 'So where were we? Oh yes, you were about to tell me about your mission here...'

Before he could go any further there was another knock at the door. 'What the hell now?' he shouted, exasperated. An aide rushed in and gasped out, between breaths: 'My Lord, there is rioting in the town. Your presence is needed immediately.'

'A riot?' Tall't threw up his hands. 'What on earth is going on tonight? Just as well Lord Pock isn't here.'

Even through her fear, Aris caught the last sentence. Pock not here? But Hellyon Intelligence had been certain that he was present in Balaat Fort and would remain so for the next week or more. And a riot? Surely that had to be other Hellyon operatives stirring things up ready for the attack. She hoped harder than she'd ever done before that that was the case.

'Damn it! I'll be there as soon as I can.' He turned his attention to the guards either side of Aris. 'Take her to a holding cell: I'll have to continue this later.'

As the key turned in the lock of her cell she allowed herself a small glimmer of optimism. Surely it was close to dawn now and the assault would begin. As long as no shells landed on the building and killed her, Hellyon would over-run the camp and someone would get her out.

HELLYON'S STAND

Under cover of darkness two Hellyon brigades, complete with heavy artillery support, surrounded Balaat Fort. Any perimeter patrols had easily been taken care of by the reconnaissance forces.

CU11 were positioned a short distance from the women's compound. After finding out about Aris's mission, Sean had marched straight to Felson's tent and demanded that the unit be put in a front line position outside the compound so that they could be the first to go in. Felson had agreed, albeit reluctantly, and now the time had come. The men were all silent; the battle plans had been gone over time and time again. All they had to do now was to wait for the assault to begin so they could locate and rescue Aris.

Kris settled back into the shadows of the Old Town, listening to the sounds of the men rioting three streets away. He and Goss had started the riot but then slipped away quietly and left the native Balaatans to get on with it. Such was the nature of many of the men here that they needed little excuse for anarchy. The rioting and looting had at least drawn the town's security forces into the one small area, leaving Kris and the other Hellyon agents free to plant their explosives at the targeted points. Now that had been achieved, all he could do was to sit back and wait until the bombs all went off in unison at the allotted time. He stretched and looked up towards the night sky. The orange glow from some of the rioters' fires blocked out most of it but he could still make out one or two of the brighter stars. It had become a ritual of his before any battle or dangerous mission to gaze at the stars and to wonder whether it might be the last time that he would be seeing them. He shrugged and smiled. So what if it was, he'd had a better life than most; he couldn't complain.

Time passed slowly for Aris in her cell. Her shoulders and back were aching from the day's sweeping and although she yearned for sleep, she knew that she would find none here. Every now and again she heard the staccato tap of boots the other side of her door. Each time she prayed for them to keep on walking, her heart in her mouth. The fear inside her just would not go away — her every breath was filled with it. Seeing Dirik again had brought back so much. She tried to quiet her thoughts: it would soon be dawn and she would soon be free. Dirik and Tall't would probably die in the fighting anyway. She had no need to fear.

Suddenly she heard several loud explosions some distance away. Almost simultaneously there was the sound of Hellyon's artillery, pounding the outer walls with their shells. Aris breathed a silent prayer of thanks. This time someone must have been looking out for her up there. The noise of the bombardment was added to by the catcalls and cheers of the inmates in the other holding cells around her.

Above the noise, she heard the outer door clank open and footsteps run down the corridor. She stood up, expecting to to be freed any minute, but the face that appeared at the door hatch was not from Hellyon. As the door opened, she felt herself shrink against the wall.

Dirik stood in the open doorway and grinned at her, a gun in his hand. 'I'm not going to let you escape me a second time,' he said, motioning her forwards.

So this was it, she was going to die after all at this man's hands. Her legs felt weak as she walked towards him. Perhaps she should just run: rather a bullet than a knife. But no, he'd just fire to disable her, and then what? But she knew she couldn't just allow this monster to take her without a fight. As she got level with him she suddenly struck out with her arm, knocking the weapon away into a corner of the cell. Following up with her other fist, she hit out at his neck, but he was faster than she had anticipated and managed to avoid the blow. Instead he caught her arm, swinging her around. His foot caught her in the small of her back and she went sprawling onto her face. As she landed, the breath was knocked out of her and she spent a precious second trying to just to get air back into her lungs. That second was enough for Dirik to start pulling her up by the back of her shirt. Struggling through the pain of the kick to her back, she reached round and tried to grab at his hair, his clothing — anything she could possibly reach and cause pain to. Her fingers closed on the security badge on his shirt. He twisted upwards and the badge ripped off, falling to the floor as he backswiped her across the face, and then again across the temple. Aris blacked out.

When she came to again, her hands and feet were shackled and she was being dragged by the wrists down the corridor of the prison block. At the end of it was a door she hadn't seen before. When it opened it revealed another corridor, this one dark and caked in the grime of years. The floor was rough and uneven and she felt every bump and loose stone jar her body. It seemed to go on forever. Finally another door approached and Dirik dropped her to open it. She lay, listening, as he went into whatever room was beyond and started to move objects within. Strange noises — wood and metal scraping over stone, a bag of metal tools being thrown on the floor. Aris listened and suddenly realised where she was. These were Dirik's interrogation rooms.

Dirik returned and dragged her into the room. Looping a rope around her wrist shackles, he passed the end through a metal ring in the ceiling and began to pull. Aris was no heavyweight and he was a strong man: soon she was suspended upright by her wrists, her feet dangling just above the floor. He turned to a table where Aris could just see a range of instruments laid out as if for surgery. He picked up an evil-looking serrated blade.

'We don't have much time,' he grinned. 'But it's enough for me to collect my dues. Bit by bit.'

Kris raced into the women's compound as soon as the internal fence had been blown. Although most of the guards had either fled or been taken care of, the women were huddled inside their barrack rooms, too scared to come out. Some had erected barricades across the doors against this new aggressor into their world. After all they had no way of knowing that the attacking force would be any friendlier to them than Pock's brutes. Already Kris could see that Hellyon representatives, mostly women, were trying to allay fears and get the women out to a place of safety.

He had to find Aris, but where the hell to start? He ran to the nearest bunkhouse where two female soldiers were talking to the women inside through a small hole in the barricade. One of the women swung around at his approach and levelled her gun at him.

'Whoa, whoa—I'm friendly.' He gave the pre-arranged password and they waved him forward.

He gestured towards the barrier. 'Could you ask them if they know where I can find the new girl who was brought in yesterday?'

One of the women stuck her head through the hole and engaged in conversation with an unseen person the other side for a short while. Then she withdrew.

'She says you could try Bunkhouse Five. A new girl was put in there yesterday.'

Kris looked around him and quickly located the building he wanted. Unlike the others, the door was not barricaded and there was no-one to stop him entering. Inside, the first thing he noticed was the quietness. All the girls here were sat patiently in their bunks, as if awaiting further instructions. Their eyes turned on him.

'Aris, I'm looking for Aris ... you know, the new girl?'

A figure jumped down from her bunk and ran towards him. 'Aris was taken last night. Can you help her?'

'Where?'

The girl shrugged. 'T'allt took her away. I expect he's holding her in the prison block down there.' She pointed out of the door towards a low building at the other end of the compound. 'The others went there too, so I expect she'll be okay by now.'

'Others? What others?'

'They said they were her unit. CU something. Seemed pretty desperate to find her.'

Kris swore under his breath: he'd wanted to be the first to find her. He muttered a hurried thanks and ran off in the direction of the building. Fenim stood outside, on guard. Recognising Kris, he gave a barely perceptible nod and stepped aside to let him pass. He found the rest of the unit in heated argument in an empty cell halfway down the corridor.

'Well how the fuck should I know what to do now?' Sean threw up his hands. 'I'm as much at a loss as you, Jak.'

'Well we can't stay here all night, we need to keep looking!' Jak said.

Kris strode up to them and took in the empty cell, the

bloodstain on the wall. 'Don't tell me you've lost her,' he said.

'Us?' Sean turned on him. 'Do you have any better ideas?'

Kris said nothing but kept looking around. Something caught his eye in the corner of one of the other cells and he moved towards it. It was a piece of ripped material — part of a security badge. He could just make out three letters: DIR. Dirik, he said under his breath and his blood turned cold.

The others were suddenly silent. 'What did you say?' asked Jak.

'Dirik has her — Balaat's chief interrogator.'

'He was the one ... ' Jak started.

Kris nodded curtly and strode out of the cell, looking along the corridor to the door at the end of it. 'She's through there!'

He ran towards it, closely followed by the others, and tried the latch. It was open. Racing down the next corridor, the men steeled themselves against what they might see.

At the next door they stopped and Kris cautiously tried the handle. Again, it was open, and he signalled to the others to ready themselves. Counting quietly to three, he threw the door open with a crash and quickly took in what was before him. He briefly noted Aris on the suspended in the air and Dirik in front starting to cut through the fabric of her clothing with a long, thin knife. At the intrusion Dirik reached for his weapon on the table but not quickly enough. Kris let off two rounds, hitting him in the arm and the leg, disabling him, but not killing him.

Beside him, Sean raised his weapon to finish the job but Kris held his hand up, and, keeping his weapon trained on Dirik, moved closer to the frightened, bleeding man. Jak ran forward to check on Aris — she looked bruised and dazed but otherwise unharmed: thankfully they'd got there just in time. Taking his own knife he reached up and cut the rope that held her, supporting her as she almost fell to the floor.

'You okay?' he asked, his eyes full of deep concern as he undid her shackles.

She nodded, unable to take her eyes off Dirik. He saw an expression in her now that was almost inhuman—full of hate, black hate. Kris saw it too. Stepping forward, he handed her his weapon. Jak, realising his intention, nodded. She needed to do this.

'Go on sweetheart,' Kris said to her, softly. 'His actions have already condemned him. Time for his execution.'

For a moment she looked as if she might back down, walk away. She just stared at her former tormentor, shaking her head as her memories danced in front of her again. And then she was firing, firing and couldn't stop. Each bullet found its mark in his body, mashing it to a bloody pulp on the floor.

'You dirty bastard. Motherfucker! Go to hell!' she yelled, almost incoherent as the bullets continued to fly and the mess that had once been a body in front of her did its little death dance. Then there was silence as she ran out of ammunition, yet she continued pressing the trigger, tears pouring down her face. Gently Kris took the weapon from her and went to hold her. She pulled away and began to walk back along the corridor. The others stared after her, dumbfounded.

Suddenly she stopped and turned, saying in a cracked voice and with a forced smile. 'Come on guys, let's get back to camp. I feel I owe you all a drink.'

12

Two figures leaned hard into the driving rain as they struggled up the mountain path. Dressed from head to toe in traditional Hardaga robes, even that tightly knit material couldn't stop the water from reaching their cold skins. The Hardaga were a tough mountain people related to the Sharm, but even they headed for shelter and a warm fire in conditions such as these. Climbing higher, the rain began to turn to snow, rushing past their faces in a white blinding torrent of hell.

The taller figure turned to his companion. 'Nearly there. The shelter is not far now.'

Aris nodded with difficulty, already aware that she was beginning to feel numb and tired: not a good sign. The short distance to the little mountain shelter hut seemed to take forever, and she began to think they wouldn't make it. How ironic, she thought, if we died within crawling distance of the door.

Then, through the confusion of the blizzard, a shape loomed up just feet away and they summoned up their last bit of energy to reach it. Inside, the contrast couldn't be greater: all seemed at peace. No winds, no swirling snow. They both collapsed on the floor, regaining their breath and looked around. The old stone structure had withstood many years on the mountain, its sturdiness a testimony to the skill of the tribal people who had built it. In the corner stood a stone fireplace, a fire ready to be lit in its grate. A pile of dusty but dry robes was stacked next to it. Aris smiled: Hardaga hospitality was legendary, even going so far as to regularly clean and restock these rarely used huts. She looked over at her companion.

Kris pulled back his hood to reveal his hair wet against his head as he headed toward the fireplace. Finding the flint and tinder box, he crouched over it, willing the little flame to become stronger, to light the fire and give them some warmth. Within a short while the fire was dancing in the hearth and starting to heat the small room.

'Best get out of these wet robes and into some dry ones,' he said, gesturing to the pile next to him. 'It's okay,' he smiled, 'I promise I won't look.'

Aris smiled back. 'You must think I was born yesterday, Kris Varelli.' But even if he did look, somehow she wouldn't mind. She had spent much time in his company in the couple of weeks after the attack on Balaat and found him to be a person of great charm and interesting conversation. As she had on the first night she talked to him, she felt there was some strange connection between them – something she couldn't quite define. And now that Dirik was dead, she felt like a different person. Gone were the nightmares and the spring-tight tension: instead she felt more open and happy than she had for a long time. The only thing that still brought her any grief was the separation from her daughter.

Kris shook the dust off the top robe and threw it to her. Smiling, he turned his back and began to strip off his own wet gear, hardly caring whether she saw him naked or not. Aris knew that she should show him the same respect that that he had given her, and turn away, but she found herself staring at the play of the firelight on the muscles of his back. He may have been 46, but he still carried a young man's body. Swallowing hard, she forced herself to pull her own wet robes over her head and put on the dry ones. Was he was taking his time on purpose, she wondered, allowing her to watch him as he slowly dressed?

'Can I turn around yet?' he asked.

'What? Oh, yes, of course.' Aris, lost in her own daydreams felt herself go red. Maybe he had only been taking his time in order to allow her to get changed.

Kris, obviously familiar with these huts, wandered over to a storage trunk and pulled out the cooking equipment stored inside as well as a small barrel and a box. Pulling the cork from the barrel he sniffed it.

'Water smells okay. We'd better boil it to be on the safe side though.'

'They put water supplies in too?' Aris asked, incredulous.

'Oh yes, all part of the service, as is this.' He shook the box he held in his other hand.

'What's in there?'

'Looks like a dried legume and vegetable mix. Boil it up with a bit of water, add some strips of that dried meat in our packs and we should soon have ourselves a tasty broth.'

Aris grinned. 'This is almost luxury. All we need now is a bottle of wine.'

He raised an eyebrow and gave her a wicked grin. 'Why, would you be trying to get me drunk and have your wicked way with me?.'

Aris felt herself go hot again and changed the subject. 'The negotiations went well, Kris — you have a talent for it.'

'More like years of practice. It hasn't all been guns and gore you know: I've also done my fair share of diplomatic relations for Hellyon.'

'Well, Hellyon could sure use those extra supplies coming in from the Hardaga Tribelands. It's a pity the other tribes don't give us as much support.'

Kris shrugged. 'You can't blame the others for not wanting to be seen as allied with Hellyon. After all, if Hellyon falls they could be next to come under Balaat's or Jerregish's roving territorial eye.'

There was silence for a minute and then Aris said quietly: 'Kris, do you really think that Hellyon could go under?'

Kris took a deep breath before answering. 'If you want my opinion, from all that I've seen and heard, it's a matter of when rather than if. Balaat and Jerregish aren't even really trying — probably because they still fear some sort of reaction from City if they do. But even so, with all the raiding, Hellyon itself is shrinking every year. If both enemies decided, or were encouraged, to make a push on both fronts at once, we wouldn't stand a chance. As you know, City has been dealing with both Balaat and Jerregish of late, for what, we don't yet know. But it's possible that Hellyon could be part of the payment.'

Aris became very silent. She had been caught up in her own problems for so long that she hadn't seen the wider picture of events unfolding in her own backyard. She had thought that somehow, while Hellyon still held ground, she had a chance of getting back into City and putting right all that had gone wrong. She had dreamed of that day; that day when Ani would come running into her arms again and it would all be as if nothing had happened. Now she looked at it again, she saw what a hopeless dream that would be: even if she did get back to City, she would be a fugitive with no hope of getting anywhere near her girl.

'Are you all right?' Kris asked.

'I was just thinking about my daughter.'

'You have a daughter? I never knew ... '

'Yes, in City. She probably thinks I'm dead. I had always hoped to somehow see her again, but I have just realised that that may never be possible. If Hellyon falls, I shall be pushed further away from her than ever.'

'That depends ... .'

Aris looked up sharply. 'What do you mean?'

Kris shifted uncomfortably. 'I'm not sure that I should be telling you.'

'What?'

'Two years ago I was asked to go along with a reconnaissance unit to meet with underground resistance fighters from City — I'm sure you know the people I mean.'

Aris nodded. 'Insurgents. Yes, my unit in special ops often went after them.'

'Insurgents?' Kris raised an eyebrow. 'I suppose you could call them that, depending on what side you're on.'

Aris looked down. 'I don't know what I'd call them now.'

'Friends, maybe?'

'I ... I don't know. To be honest Kris, friends is not the first word that comes to mind — I lost too many people to them.'

'And they lost many good people to City Special Ops.'

'How did the meeting take place? At that time any movement in or out of City was heavily restricted.'

Kris looked at her for a minute, as if he was deciding how much more to tell her. Then: 'There are series of underground tunnels and shelters beneath City - many of them built by the resistance. One such tunnel leads outside.'

Aris shook her head, wondering. 'We had heard that they

had such tunnels but we never managed to discover them. Even the people we managed to send in undercover only heard of rumours.'

Kris nodded. 'Very few 'insurgents' as you call them are ever allowed to know of their location. The same with our Hellyon agents—the group that carried out the meetings was known about only by selected members of Hellyon Command.'

'You said 'carried out', past tense. Does that mean that Hellyon no longer has contact with them.'

'I don't know. I was tasked with going because Hellyon Command had designs on me heading up another follow-up group, but then my orders changed and that was the last I heard of it. For all I know, it may still be going on. Hellyon still needs intelligence and weapons from City after all.'

Aris mused on what she had heard. 'So there is a backdoor into City. I could theoretically get in and get my daughter out.'

Kris shook his finger. 'Hold on, don't start getting too hopeful. First, Hellyon would still have to have a good relationship with the undergrounders and second, Hellyon Command would have to agree to the whole thing. Even if all of that happens, which is a long shot in itself, how happy are the undergrounders going to be to see you again?'

Aris conceded that his last point was also his strongest. The undergrounders would certainly know of her and her unit, and what she had accomplished against them. She couldn't see that they'd be too quick to help her.

Kris reached over and put his hand on top of hers. 'But I'll do all I can when we get back. If I can help you get your daughter out of there, I will.'

His words were sincere enough. Aris looked up at him and found herself locked in his gaze. They both stared at each other for what seemed like forever, until Kris broke the contact.

'We'd better eat,' he said. 'That soup mixture should be ready about now.'

She nodded, grateful for the excuse to move a bit further away from his presence. She hadn't had these sort of feelings for a long time and now she was unsure of herself. What if she had imagined that look in his eyes — she didn't want to make a fool of herself.

They ate in near silence, savouring the simple but tasty meal. The silence in other circumstances could have felt uncomfortable, strained — but between the two of them it was restful. It gave Aris time to collect her thoughts about her future; she wasn't getting any younger and she would soon have to consider how her life would be in 10 years time. That she wanted Ani to be with her was beyond question so it was really a matter of getting her out of City and then maybe finding somewhere far away from Hellyon and far away from this war. She was sure she would find some other sort of work — she was a survivor.

She thought back to all that she had been through so far as Kris cleaned up after the meal. She had survived all that Balaat had thrown at her, and now that Dirik was dead the nightmares had gone, the anger had gone — it was as if the very act of killing him had exorcised her demons. And it was Kris who had put the weapon in her hands that day.

She looked at him intensely as he came to sit down beside her. 'You knew didn't you?' she said softly. 'You knew that by killing Dirik I could heal what he did to me.'

Kris nodded. 'He deserved to die. If you hadn't done it then I certainly would have.'

There was something in his voice that was close to hate, disgust.

'You sound as if you knew him,' she challenged.

Kris shrugged. 'I've seen his handiwork and that is enough.'

'What do you mean?' Aris demanded, suddenly sensing that there was still a great deal she didn't know about this man.

He hesitated briefly before continuing. 'As you know, I was undercover in Balaat Fort for quite a while. When I first arrived I didn't know much about the place. These guys befriended me and invited me to go to Circus with them.' He shook his head at the memories. 'It was the most gruesome, stomach-turning spectacle I have ever seen, and I've seen a few ...' Suddenly he stopped and looked at Aris. 'I'm sorry, you probably don't want to hear all this.'

Aris shook her head, hearing the pain in his words. She guessed that maybe he hadn't told anyone about this before. 'Please Kris, go on.'

'They brought 3 girls out, and just to liven it up they were given weapons, small clubs. Dirik entered the arena, and with him, four or five of Pock's mutant spawn. One of the girls was chained to an A Frame but the other two were let loose.' He paused, gathering strength to go on. 'He raped the girl on the A frame while the mutants did the same thing to the other two girls. Despite the weapons they could offer no resistance at all. Once Dirik had finished, he began to cut the girl on the frame with one of his surgery tools. Shit Aris, I swear if I could have saved her somehow I would. He bled her slowly and then made the two others drink the blood. It was disgusting.'

Aris turned her head away as her own memories and emotions rose to the surface. At least she had survived her one time in Circus, thanks to her skills with the weapons and by the time she'd finished three of the mutants were dead at her feet and even Dirik wouldn't come near her. Pock had obviously enjoyed the entertainment she'd given — enough to let her live to fight at some future point. The other two girls with her though, like the majority of those sent into Circus, had not been so lucky. Their fate had been just as Kris had described.

He continued. 'The crowd was going wild around me. I had to pretend that I was one of them and cheer too. But I wasn't cheering, I was screaming. I'm sorry — I should have done something to help them.'

Aris took hold of his hands. 'It's alright Kris. You couldn't have done anything by yourself.'

Kris shook his head. 'And then he called the mutants out again. This time they had knives too. All the girls were cut up, disembowelled slowly so that they didn't die well. I couldn't watch anymore. That day changed me Aris, and I swore that that monster would die, whatever I had to do to make it happen.'

He looked up at her fully now, his eyes dark. 'I never went to another one after that, but I still heard about them from the other men. They were always boasting and laughing about it. Then I heard one day that this woman had not only survived Circus but had also escaped from the fort.' He smiled at the memory. 'I thought then that if ever I had the chance I would find that woman, not that I knew what I'd do when I found her. I just wanted to see some hope come out of that evil place.'

'Seems like your wish came true.'

'But then I nearly lost you again before I could get to know you.'

'And now?'

'I never want to lose you again.' Gently Kris reached over and took her face between his hands. He kissed her lips softly as if fearing a rejection. At first she held back, unsure of herself, but then, like ice melting, she drew him to her, returning his kiss. Somehow, the feel of his skin, his scent ... it all felt so right. At last she felt safe enough to let go of the soldier within her for a few hours and just be the woman. She looked into the eyes that reflected her image and knew that this night would be a special one for both of them.

13

Hellyon Camp seemed a brighter place to Aris as she walked back to CU11's encampment. Felson had just finished debriefing her and Kris about their mission and they had planned to meet again later, off duty.

'Hey guys!' she shouted as she entered the encampment. The rest of CU11 looked up to see her grinning face.

'Well, the mission must have succeeded then,' Sean said.

'Complete success,' she answered.

'So how come you're two days overdue?' asked Jak. 'Overwhelmed by Hardagan hospitality?'

'No, we got delayed by a mountain blizzard on the way back and had to shelter in one of their huts for a while.'

'I hope Kris didn't try and take advantage,' Sean frowned

Aris laughed. 'He didn't need to.'

Jak raised an eyebrow. 'Well that explains the big smile then.'

Sean opened his mouth as if to say something else and then disappeared into his tent, with a dark look. Tor grinned at Jak, revelling in the unusual sight of his captain's nose being put out of joint.

A moment later, Sean reappeared, seemingly having composed himself. 'Right, time we were back on duty. Felson wants to see us.'

'Looks like we're on another special mission,' Jak mumbled, his mood blackening again.

'Already?' Aris threw her hands up in the air. 'But I've only just got back.'

'Better get used to it if you hang around with the likes of Varelli,' said Sean, a hint of sarcasm in his voice. 'Anyway, sounded more like a holiday to me.'

Aris bit her tongue. It was unlike Sean to let his feelings get the better of him. She wasn't going to make it worse by answering back.

They all walked over to Felson's tent in silence, each lost in their own thoughts. Felson, too, seemed more sombre than ever.

'Sit down,' he motioned, and waited for them to get settled. 'Right, I'll come straight to the point. There is a man in Jerregish called Raul A'dat. He is one of the brothers of the present Shaikyn and an extremely wealthy man with some important contacts. Our Intel informs us that he has been seen in Balaat and City, although who he is meeting with, we don't know. But we must assume that he is an important link with Jerregish in City's future plans. As we know, City is already dealing with Balaat, which can only mean that all three are working together for Hellyon's eventual downfall. A'dat seems like an indispensable figure in these negotiations so to buy us more time we would do well to remove his expertise from the equation. That's where you come in. Your unit is the best I have in terms of the skills and experience needed for this mission — you should have no problem infiltrating into Jerregish and taking him out.'

'Just like that?' questioned Jak. 'If he's as important as you say, he'll be surrounded by bodyguards; we wouldn't get near him.'

'Some of you might. A'dat is to host a diplomatic banquet soon and will need more house servants. Fenim and Aris can easily be placed under cover working in the kitchens or wherever. We already have people in Jerregish who can 'loan' them to him.'

'What about the rest of us?' Sean asked.

'You will act as backup, just in case they get into trouble. There is also a little matter of a new communications tower nearby. Perhaps a little well-timed sabotage wouldn't be out of order either.'

Jak nodded slowly. 'That won't be a problem, but I still can't see how Fen and Aris are going to get near enough to A'dat to do anything.'

Felson took a deep breath. 'That will have to be weighed up when you get there. I'm sure a way will be found — that's why your unit was chosen Jak. If anyone's going to take him out it will be CU11.'

Back at the tents, Kris was waiting. Aris glanced across at Sean.

'Go on,' he scowled, 'but don't be long. We have a lot of preparation to do and I want to be off at first light.'

Aris nodded and strolled across to Kris. He looked quizzical. 'What was that all about? I came across to see whether you were off duty for a while. I gather that you aren't.'

'No.' She took his arm and led him away to one side. 'Look, I'm off on another operation tomorrow. I don't know how long I'll be away for.'

'Where?'

'You know I can't tell you that.'

Kris bit at his lip and smiled. 'Of course. I shouldn't have asked. It's a bit tough though, sending you on another one so soon after coming back.'

She shrugged. 'It's okay, I'll handle it. Just looks like we'll have to hold the romance until I get back.'

He took hold of her shoulders and gave her a playful shake. 'Just make sure you do.'

They heard Sean's voice, calling for her from the other side of the tent.

'Must go,' she said.

He bent down and kissed her lightly on the lips. 'Take care, sweetheart. I'll look forward to your return.'

She gave him a wistful smile and went to join the rest of the unit.

'About time,' Sean commented acidly. 'It's not as if you won't be seeing him again.'

She mumbled an apology and took her place in the meeting, but her mind and her thoughts were on the figure retreating into the distance.

Even with the use of a personnel vehicle, the rough roads of the mountain passes meant that it took a day to get to the border with Jerregish. The walk to their rendezvous point took until mid-morning the following day. When they finally arrived their contacts were already there, waiting for them. They looked worried.

'Thank goodness you've got here,' one said. 'We've promised to hand the new servants over to the housekeeper by noon, so we're cutting it a little fine. Now then, who are the lucky ones destined for domestic servitude?'

Aris and Fen stepped forward and were handed some clothes, obviously the livery of the A'dat household.

'Put these on,' the other contact said, 'and then we'll be on our way. As for the rest of you, we'll show you the best place to hide up next to the palace.'

Two hours later Fenim and Aris stood in the kitchen of the rather large and ornate palace of Raul A'dat, receiving their instructions from the Head of Household. The Head, as they were to address him at all times, was a pompous, plump little man, much given to grandiose gestures with his hands. This house was his domain, his little kingdom, his life and Raul A'dat was the god he worshipped. Any servants therefore were lesser beings apt to undisciplined behaviour, needing to be watched over at all times. He walked, or rather waddled, around the two, making little noises of approval, or disapproval, as the fancy took him.

'Hmph,' he said at last, looking up at Aris. 'You, young lady ... what was your name again?'

'Avala, Head.'

'Hmmm, Avala ... well, I want you to make sure that every bedroom in the east wing is swept and cleaned every morning, preferably after the occupants have vacated. Every bed must be stripped and re-made with clean sheets.'

'Yes, Head.'

'And you?' The Head asked, looking up at Fenim with already a look of distaste.

'My name is Halir, Head.'

'Well, Halir, the head Gardener needs a hand in the water gardens. You can join him there.'

Aris could almost sense Fen's disgust at being placed in the garden. Personally she would have swapped her job with his any day. Never mind, this work wouldn't have to go on forever.

They separated to their individual tasks. Another house-servant called Durra showed Aris where she had to go and what she had to do. Aris let her surprise at all the finery around her show, making herself look like a wide eyed country girl. 'So his lordship A'dat lives here?' she asked.

'Oh no,' replied Durra. 'His lordship lives in the west wing. The east wing is for honoured guests, and we are expecting many this evening at the banquet. From what I've heard a lot of important people will be here. That is why all the bedrooms have to be even more spotless than normal. We'll also be expected to attend at the dinner tonight. If we're lucky we may even get some of the left overs — that is, if the Head doesn't stuff them into that fat belly of his first.'

Aris smiled. 'He's not a favourite of yours then.'

Durra dropped her voice to a whisper. 'He's not a favourite of anyone. I've heard that even his lordship detests him but has to keep him on because he is so efficient.'

'So, if he's not liked, how does he manage to keep such good order around here?'

'Easy. Everyone's afraid of him. The slightest transgression or little mistake and he'll have you flogged. Just about all of the servants here have been flogged at least once, even me. I left a dirty sheet behind in a room by accident and that was it — ten lashes. You don't forget that in a hurry. The rule around here, girl, is keep your head down and don't do anything to get yourself noticed.'

Durra may have painted a black picture of the regime in the household of A'dat, but to Aris it was almost a holiday compared with what she had endured at Balaat Fort. Even so, by the evening she felt tired and ready for bed. But she knew it would be a long time before she would be allowed to retire. Already many guests had arrived and were milling about the great hall, talking and waiting to be seated. From their style of dress, there were representatives from City and Balaat as well as Jerregish. She caught sight of Fen, now dressed in household rather than garden clothes, and made her way over, pretending to deliver a message.

He had been given the task of standing along the wall, like an ornament, along with some of the other gardening staff. The servants were obviously on display as a sign of their owner's wealth.

'Everything okay?' she asked him.

He grimaced. 'If you like pruning. How about you?'

'Fine. I'm in the opposite wing to our target though. I'll have to do something about that.'

Aris passed on by, not wanting to attract the attention of the Head, who was casting a sharp eye over the activities of his servants. He stood at the top of the hall looking fatter than ever in his bright clothing, his eyes not missing a thing. Aris knew she could safely assume that he had seen her talking to Fen; she only hoped that he would be so occupied for the rest of the evening that he would forget all about it. Seeing the rest of her serving group disappearing off to the kitchen to fetch the first course, she joined them, all the time keeping her eyes and ears open in case any information came her way as to how she could get to A'dat.

Fenim stood quietly in his allotted position, casting his eye over the guests as they made their way towards the long dining table arrangement. Hearing the different dialects of Jerregish brought memories of his youth, as did the objects of Jerregishan culture on display everywhere. He realised that a part of him still yearned for the pleasures, sights and sounds of his native land, although he felt more at home in Hellyon now.

Out of the corner of his eye he caught a man walking toward him with a strange loping gait. He knew that walk … but surely not … not here? The man stopped in front of him and he felt a sudden stab of fear. Fenim tried to force himself to keep his eyes lowered, his face hidden under the shadow of his shoomuk, but he could not help himself. He found himself drawn to see the face of the man before him. Their eyes met and the man smiled. Fen felt himself grow cold, all the colour drain from his face.

'Fenim, nice to see you again,' the man smiled before walking slowly away. Fen took a deep breath to control his shaking. What the hell was he meant to do now? Would Massim alert the others to his presence? No, of course he wouldn't, Fen reasoned. He would have more to lose than to gain. All the same, the time of reckoning would happen sooner or later, and when it did it could possibly compromise the whole mission. Damn, why did he have to be here?

The guests were seated, and to Fen's increasing discomfort, the man, Massim, was seated opposite to where he was standing. He tried to avoid his gaze but felt it on him the whole time. Fen wished he could just get out of that room, and out of the clothes which were making him feel increasingly claustrophobic, but he knew that that would be the most fatal move he could make. At least Massim wouldn't know Aris, so she was not in any danger at present. He would have to try and warn her somehow though, to avoid him for now. He caught sight of her now and again as she served the different courses to the guests, and by the eighth and last dish most were the worse for drink. More than once he saw her avoiding a questing hand, or other unwelcome attention. He did not worry on that score though: Aris was more than capable of avoiding unwanted attention. He just hoped she wouldn't hit anybody.

The man he presumed to be A'dat was sat at the opposite end of the room in the middle of the high table. His bodyguards were discreet but their presence was still unmistakable. Maybe he or Aris could reach him at this meal, but as they were both presently unarmed, it wouldn't do much good. And they'd be dead in seconds. No, they would have to wait and hope that a better opportunity presented itself.

Hours later the meal was over and the guests once more milled around in their little groups. A female servant came over and pressed a small piece of paper into Fenim's hand with a little smile. 'From the gentleman over there,' she gestured and winked knowingly. Fen did not need to follow her gaze to know who she was talking about, although her assumption of his intentions was entirely wrong. Fen waited for her to move away and then unrolled the message. It read: Meet me at the water garden in ten minutes.

Fen frowned and scrunched the paper up, putting it into a pocket. He had no choice, he had to go.

Aris stared at the pile of dirty plates in front of her, not relishing the task of cleaning them all. Next to her, Durra struggled with a large stack of dishes, trying to put them down as they began slipping out of her hands. Aris automatically turned and tried to steady them but to no avail as they came crashing down around them. Bits of fine china shattered across the tiled floor, the noise bringing all the conversation in the room to a halt. The Head stalked across from the other side of the room, his thick eyebrows knitted together in impatience.

'What, can't I turn my back for a minute without some disaster? Look at the mess? Have you any idea how much this china is worth? Careless little fools!'

Aris and Durra contritely mumbled their apologies.

'You can clear this mess up, and wash up what's remaining. As for punishment, his lordship asked me to send two servants to attend to him later — so don't think you'll be getting any sleep tonight.'

He turned away, leaving the two young women to start

picking up the debris.

'I suppose it's lucky he didn't flog us, but being on duty outside A'dat's room is hardly fun either,' Durra moaned.

'Why?' asked Aris.

'It means that we have to stay awake, especially if his lordship's got someone with him. We'll be fetching and carrying all night, if not for him then for his bodyguards. And tomorrow we'll have to go straight to our other duties.'

If Durra was in despair, Aris couldn't believe her luck. It was as if fate was smiling on her. Now she had the best chance of all to complete the mission, and if she could get inside A'dat's private rooms there was no reason that she couldn't complete her task and escape before anyone noticed that he was dead. Then all she had to do was get over to Fen's dormitory and get him out too. Maybe this wasn't going to be so hard after all.

Once all the clearing up had been done, Durra led Aris over to the West wing, stuffing some leftovers into her pockets as she went. She stifled a yawn. 'There I go already. I'm so tired, I really don't know how I'm going to get through tonight.'

Aris smiled, but her mind was concentrating on memorising the route to A'dat's quarters. 'What's he like then, this A'dat?' she asked

Durra thought for a minute before answering. 'He's seems alright enough - I've never heard anything bad about him, but it's always hard to tell with those who are in power.'

'Have you been on night duties before, Durra?'

'No, but from what everyone else has said, it is always the same. We never actually see his Lordship, because he is busy with some new lover or other. Instead will have to be running around fetching food or drink for his bodyguards.'

'How many bodyguards does he have?' she asked, trying to appear casual.

'Oh, about six or seven. They're all — big blokes and arrogant with it, and they seem to do nothing but eat. As you'll find out.' Durra turned a corner and headed into a corridor that seemed more richly decorated than those before. 'We're nearly there,' she announced.

Fenim walked quietly through the water gardens, the plants throwing weird shadows in the moonlight. Where was Massim, damn him?! The bubbling of the fountains made it almost impossible to hear anyone's approach, and Fen found himself looking around for the first signs of movement. Then he saw him: Massim was leaning against the walls of the teahouse, making no effort whatsoever to conceal himself. Fenim strode over.

'Well, here I am. What do you want?'

'I wanted to thank you for not shooting me that night when Vallen was caught,' smiled Massim.

'It's more than that. What are you after?'

'Dear boy, I am only having a friendly chat, so why all the unfriendliness? Unless of course you have forgotten what you are?'

'I've not forgotten. But I want none of it. That all happened long ago when I didn't know any better.'

'Oh, I think you knew what you were doing alright. So, Fenim, I suppose you are here on some kind of operation for Hellyon, and that you are not on your own?'

'What I do is none of your business,' Fenim growled.

'Quite the opposite dear boy. Vallen's death left an opening in Hellyon Camp. It's time to consider yourself activated.'

'Go to hell!' Fenim hissed and started to walk away.

Massim caught hold of his arm. 'I wouldn't be so hasty to throw down your duty to City, Fenim.'

'Like I said, go to hell.'

'I hear that you have a nice little family now — two girls isn't it? It would be such a shame if something happened ... '

Fenim swung around, grabbed the man by the throat and threw him against the teahouse wall. For a burning moment he looked hard into the man's face. Massim stared back unperturbed, as if he was used to such treatment. Eventually Fenim let go, resignation on his face.

'Okay, okay ... what do you want me to do?'

'Prove your loyalty to me. Just tell me where the rest of your unit is. I'll do the rest and see that it looks like they were accidentally discovered.'

'Never.'

'Just take a few minutes to think what is most dear to you — your daughters or your companions. It's an easy enough choice Fenim, even for you.'

'Damn you!' Fen looked down at the ground, beaten. 'Alright, but tonight they are all spread out around the grounds so I can't tell you exactly where they are. I'll be told the rendezvous point tomorrow first thing and I shall get a message to you then. Is that good enough?'

Massim smiled. 'I knew you'd see sense: you always were a bright boy.'

'Not bright enough though.'

'What do you mean?'

Fenim pushed his face close to Massim's. 'Because, if I'd had any sense, I would have shot you dead that night.'

Massim laughed. 'Probably, but it wouldn't have done much good. There are others who would have found you eventually.'

He walked away, leaving Fenim alone in the solitude of the gardens. He sat down, trying to think. He had to find Aris and get them all clear of the palace before dawn. And then he had to find a way to get his family away to a place of safety. Now that his past had caught up with him, there was going to be nowhere to hide.

The night duty had not been as busy as Durra had said it would be. In fact A'dat seemed to be asleep alone in his room and his guards, too, were undemanding. After three hours of waiting in the corridors for non-existent orders, Aris felt her eyes growing heavy. Durra had already fallen asleep, curled up on the floor, but Aris could not afford to let her tiredness win.

Aris heard a soft sound from the corridor leading to A'dat's rooms, but couldn't see anything in the darkness down there. She took a deep breath and brought herself to full alertness, ready to kick Durra awake if need be. She listened but heard only silence broken by the snoring of the bodyguards in the next room. A fine bunch of bodyguards they were, she thought and sunk back into her previous position. She didn't relax for long though; something felt wrong. Soldiers accustomed to covert operations seemed to develop a kind of sixth sense, a prickling of their skin when an enemy is near. Aris felt this now and knew that someone was standing in the shadows, watching her. Cautiously she moved forward, her body tensed for any sudden movement in the darkness. As she crept towards it, a shape moved within the shadows and slowly came towards her. She halted, suddenly unsure as to what she, as a mere servant, should do in these circumstances.

She stood her ground. The shadow came closer until it revealed itself in the dim light. It was A'dat. Aris gasped and he smiled as he raised a finger to his lips to warn her to keep quiet. Passing by her to look at the sleeping figures of Durra and his bodyguards, Aris noticed that he walked like a cat, almost gliding over the rich carpet. Turning back he smiled at her again and beckoned her to follow. Aris felt her throat go dry.

There was no sound between them until they were both in A'dat's luxurious apartment. He closed the door.

'I think I'll have to change those guards,' he smiled. 'Anyone could just walk in here and attack me. There again, they'd have to get past you first. Drink?'

Aris nodded, her eyes trying to take in the opulence of the room. A'dat walked over to a polished high wooden table at the far wall where a tall glass decanter full of a burgundy liquid stood. The room was richly decorated in burgundy and gold; large tapestries depicting hunting scenes hung on the walls while golden stencilled shutters covered the windows. A log fire burned in a large grate on the far side of the room, whilst to her left stood the largest bed she'd ever seen.

A'dat handed her a glass of wine and noted her interest in the room. 'I chose the decorations myself,' he commented. 'Although I must admit I like to spend a night out under God's heaven now and again, to remind myself that I am just a man, like any other.'

Aris sipped at her wine slowly, still unsure of what to say or even of what was expected of her. Another part of her mind was working out how best she could kill this man without any weapon and without him making a noise. A'dat was tall and strongly built and she had no doubt that he would be more than a match for her in unarmed combat, especially if she lacked the element of surprise.

He beckoned her to sit down with him on a pile of cushions. 'It has been a long day,' he said. 'You must be tired.'

She nodded.

'I notice though that you managed to keep awake.'

Aris had to think quickly. 'I suffer from insomnia, your Lordship.'

'You can stop calling me your Lordship while we are in here. I get sick sometimes of all the bowing and scraping. Sometimes I just want to talk normally like anyone else.' He hesitated for a second as he regarded her. 'Actually I was watching you for some time before you noticed me. You are very different from the other servants: the way you walk so softly, the way you watch and listen to every sound...' He smiled slowly. 'I almost think you would make a better body guard for me by yourself than all those burly soldiers snoring their heads off out there. But that would be rather fanciful wouldn't it?'

Something in his tone made Aris go cold but she forced herself to remain calm. There was something more to this man than she had anticipated. Did he know what she was there for? It was hard to tell. But there again, if he felt himself to be under threat, why didn't he act to protect himself? She cautioned herself to hold back for a while, to learn more about her quarry before she struck. 'Yes, it would,' she answered.

He turned his head and smiled at her. 'Still, I think that you are capable of intelligent conversation which is definitely more than those guards can manage. What did you think of my little gathering tonight? I noticed how you managed to avoid the reach of some of my more... lascivious guests.'

She swallowed. He had been watching her. Had he somehow set up this meeting? But then he would have had to get Durra to drop those plates.... 'I didn't really see much of it — I was in the kitchens or serving the guests. It seemed like quite a lavish affair.'

'Yes, it was. And like most lavish affairs it was extremely boring. Like my life. You probably wouldn't think that my life was boring, would you? After all I have enough money and authority to do almost anything I want. But there is no challenge to being the Shaikyn's brother, nothing to aim towards — other than peace of course.'

'Peace?' Aris asked, not quite sure she'd heard right.

'Between Jerregish and City, between Jerregish and Balaat, between Jerregish and Hellyon. Stopping this senseless territorial war is the one thing that still drives me; that's why I invited all those people to dinner tonight. Tomorrow I shall try to start some talks.'

Aris felt numb. As far as she had been told, this was the man who was behind Jerregish's negotiations with City and Balaat to carve claims out of Hellyon land. They had never said anything about his striving for peace.

'Talks?'

A'dat motioned for her to sit down on the rug beside him. 'Yes, talks. I was born into warrior stock, was raised as a warrior and given the best of warrior weapons. I have seen much war and commanded many combat units in my youth. But do you know what? War sickens me. It sickens me to my very stomach. There is no dignity in killing just to gain a few inches of land, and there is certainly no glory in dying. Jerregish is a beautiful land, with beautiful people; we should have no need to push Hellyon into oblivion, or to bargain with barbarians like Pock. City, too, should leave well alone.'

'In an ideal world, maybe,' Aris countered, hardly believing what she was hearing, 'but there are other factors involved — political ambition, mineral wealth ... surely you know that? Your own leader and brother, Jessyn, has his agenda just as much as Pock or the City Governors. So how on earth do you think you can change things by talks?'

He smiled at her and she noticed that his eyes had golden glints in them. In a way that she could not explain he reminded her of Kris. Maybe it was the wine.

'Your grasp of politics is very commendable — for a servant

girl,' he said with a wry smile. 'Many of these people here tonight think like I do. Maybe if we can find some way to get our voices heard, we can gain support and eventually oust those who want only war.'

'Jessyn will never let you get that far.'

'It is a risk I have to take. He already has his spies in my court, as has City — not very clever ones though. I know exactly who they are and what misinformation to feed them. I expect there are others here tonight who will also go away and make trouble for me — but it will be worth it in the end. And it is not just a case of ending war or of saving Hellyon: there is much more at stake than you could possibly ever know.'

Aris paused for a moment, noting how much he had emphasised his last sentence. It was a dangerous question, but it was one she felt she had to ask: 'So why are you trusting me with all this information? I might be a spy too.'

He reached out and touched her hair. 'No, you are not a spy. I know exactly what you are and why you are here. I also know that ultimately you believe in peace, as I do. If I die by Jessyn's hand when my campaign is underway then I will become a martyr and my cause will grow. However if I die tonight, by your hand, it will all be for nothing.'

Aris felt frozen to the spot. How had she given herself away so easily to this man? She started to get up, planning to make a run for it but A'dat gently took hold of her arm and pulled her back down again.

'You have nothing to fear from me,' he said. 'Our meeting was meant to happen. And now you must return to Hellyon and let your commanders know that they have my full support. We are alike, you and I — both searching for our own kind of peace.'

Aris felt herself relaxing again. Instinct told her to trust this man; a small, irrational part of her felt like she had known him all her life. 'But how did you know ... ? she asked.

He pulled back his sleeve, revealing a small, delicate bracelet. The markings were not Jerregishan. 'This was my mother's — she was a Sharmsinger. My father met her on his travels and fell in love with her. Because of her race she was not allowed to become his wife, but she stayed as his most beloved concubine for all of his life. She had the Sharm powers, although she rarely used them. I must have inherited them because I have been dreaming about you for a long time. When I saw you in the hall tonight, I knew that the dream had come into being.'

Aris shook her head in disbelief. 'You're part Sharm? But you look so Jerregishan.'

He laughed, deep and low, as sweet as honey. 'Maybe that's just as well: the Jerregishan nobility would not have been so prepared to accept me if I had the golden hair and light eyes.'

He closed his eyes for a moment. 'You must go now. I also dreamed about your companion. He is in trouble and needs you. You will find him in the water gardens. But first, please take this ... ' He struggled to pull a ring from his finger. 'It is called a bond ring. It will identify you as one I trust... and protect. Show it to any of my people and they will give you whatever assistance you need. After tonight we may never meet again but I hope that you will remember me every time you look at that ring.'

He placed it on her trembling forefinger. She looked up at him, still overwhelmed by events. He released her hand. 'Now you must go.'

He turned his back, breaking the spell that had been cast between them. She backed away and then ran from the room, her bare feet making no noise as she raced past the still slumbering Durra and guards. Her mind was in a whirl, confused. She had to find Fenim, find out what was happening. But what was happening? She had been close enough to her target to have taken him out, but she had failed in her mission. He had known right from the beginning. A'dat ... his name echoed in her ears with every footfall as she raced through the empty corridors out into the water garden.

Up ahead she could just make out a silhouette in the moonlight. 'Fen?' she whispered.

'Aris!' he spun round and strode over to her, grabbing her by the arm. Where the hell have you been? We've got to get out of here, I've been compromised. Someone recognised me from when I was in City.'

'Has he raised the alarm?'

'No, not yet, but we have to bail out right now. We'll meet the others at the rendezvous point.'

'Fen ... '

'What?'

'I couldn't do it.'

'Couldn't do what?'

'Kill A'dat. I was right next to him, in his room. He isn't what we thought, he wants peace.'

Fen gave her a hard, appraising look. 'Okay. We'll talk about all this when we're back over the border. Right now we've got to get moving.'

14

No one spoke until they had re-crossed the border into Hellyon. It had been a hard tab and all felt tired. Sean radioed in for a personnel vehicle to come and pick them up and then joined the others around a small fire.

'So, what happened?' he asked, directing his gaze at Aris and Fenim, his expression stern.

'Someone recognised me,' said Fenim in a quiet but steady voice. 'I had no choice but to abort the mission.'

'Who was it?'

'Someone from my days in City, when I was at college.'

'Who'

'Just someone I knew.' Fen didn't elaborate and Sean didn't press the issue, there was no point.

'Did you speak to him?'

'I didn't have much choice. He threatened to reveal me, Sean. I felt that my own situation was likely to put everyone else in danger—especially Aris.'

Sean nodded. Fen had done the right thing but it still galled that one of his operations had failed so badly. His unit was known for succeeding.

'What about you, Aris. Did you manage to get anywhere

near the target?'

Aris paused, trying to find a way of saying what she had to say without making it look so bad. 'Yes.'

'So what happened? Is he dead?'

She shook her head. 'Sean, he isn't what Hellyon Command thinks him to be. He's actually trying to hold talks that might mean peace for all sides. I couldn't kill someone who might potentially be on our side.'

She heard Jak's sharp indrawn breath beside her and looked to the ground to avoid the cold fury that now presented itself in Sean's eyes.

'Since when did you take it upon yourself which orders you obey and which you don't? Your were to take out the target the first chance you got. Now I'm hearing that he sweet-talked you into leaving him alone?' Sean's anger was such that he was having trouble getting the words out.

'Killing him would have been against Hellyon's interests in the long run. Anyway, assassinating one man isn't going to have any effect on what is going to happen to Hellyon any day soon. We all know that.'

'But we still carry out orders. For God's sake Desun, Felson will have your head for this!'

'Sean, wait,' Fen interrupted. 'What she says could be right. Most of the people at that meeting were those considered to be liberal in their views and politics. Representatives were there from Balaat and City as well, people who are known to be thorns in the sides of their leaders. Hellyon will not survive an all out assault, we all know that. But if it could gather supporters — vocal supporters in these other countries — we would have a far greater chance of keeping our lands, or getting them back again. I heard many good things said about A'dat last night.'

It was Fenim's turn now to taste Sean's ire. 'Even if half of what you've said is true, I still have to face Felson with some kind of explanation that won't get us all into trouble, as if we haven't had enough of that lately.'

'There was another thing,' Aris said. 'Something that Tor might find especially interesting. A'dat is half Sharm, from his mother's side, and he has inherited some of the powers. He knew why I was there and, to be honest, he could have had me arrested at any point without me even getting near him.'

'Sharm?' questioned Tor. 'Did he say who his mother was?'

'No.'

Tor shook his head. 'I remember hearing stories when I was young of a young Sharm girl who had run off with a Jerregishan lord. Maybe that was her. And he had the powers you say?'

'He told me that he had dreamt of my arrival for years. He also knew that Fen was in danger and sent me off to find him.'

Sean nodded. 'And his Sharm blood would certainly explain his preference towards peace.'

'So what do we say when we get back then?' asked Fen.

Sean sighed. 'The truth. Felson and the other commanders need to hear that we may have the chance of support in foreign quarters. I just hope you're right and that I can explain it well enough to avoid Aris being court-martialled.'

The camp bristled with activity. Along with the other military bases within Hellyon's borders, the personnel were busy fortifying the defences and making sure that all weapons were in good working order. Even so, it seemed that most of the artillery was on the edge of defunct and there were not enough small firearms and ammunition to go around. Everyone was on edge: word had it that Balaat was gearing up for an invasion and that maybe Jerregish was going to push in on the northern side too.

CU11 were put to work strengthening a PN3 position on the western side of the camp. Their failed mission was now three days behind them and so far there had been no come back over Aris's lack of action. Sean felt that he had put the situation over well to the combined command arm of the camp; in fact he had found them most interested in the prospect of such a powerful ally in Jerregish. Only one person was unhappy with the situation: Fenim had asked for leave to go to his family and take them to a safe place but it had been denied on the grounds Hellyon needed every fighter ready to take their place when the invasion came. He worked hard alongside the rest of them but his anger was so obvious that no one dared to speak to him.

The heat of the mid-day sun was becoming oppressive. Aris stood up and stretched her aching back for a second. She looked across the cleared area beyond the fence into the forest and wondered for a moment where Kris was. She had gone searching for him upon their return only to find out that he had been sent on another job. She wasn't surprised: with the increased threat of invasion, any extra intelligence or help would be welcomed, and Kris was still one of their best men.

'Hey, are you CU11?' called out a voice. They all turned to see its source. It was a man that Aris vaguely knew by sight from one of the medical units.

Sean stepped forward. 'We are. What's up?'

'Felson sent me to ask you to get over to his tent as soon as you can.'

'Did he say why?'

'Nope. All he said was that you had to get there as quickly as possible.'

Sean thanked the messenger and turned to the unit. 'Well, down tools people, you heard what the man said.'

Felson smiled as they entered. 'We've just had some good news. As you were the unit that helped bring it about, I thought you should know. We have just received a secret delegation from A'dat offering Hellyon financial support as well as a list of contacts in Balaat and City. It seems that the Sharm tribes are willing to offer our families sanctuary when the invasion begins.'

'That's wonderful sir,' smiled Sean.

'There's something else. A'dat has links within City — important links. He has arranged for a team to get in with the aid of one of City's underground terrorist groups to inspect a new range of weaponry.'

'Are these the same groups Hellyon was in contact with a while ago?' asked Aris.

Felson gave her an appraising look. 'So you know about that, do you? Well, keep it to yourself — it was an experiment at the time and nothing ever really came of it: Hellyon couldn't afford the asking price.'

Aris nodded, aware of her unit's questioning eyes. So that's why Kris never got to go again.

Felson continued: 'If what we find is suitable he will arrange the finance for an arms deal to go through, as well as making sure that we have enough ammunition for the weapons we have already. However, it is all on one condition: he personally requested Desun and her unit to be chosen for the acquisition team.'

Aris took a sharp intake of breath and nearly choked. She was going back to City. Was this her chance?

'So when do we go?' Sean asked.

'Tonight. We can't hang around with Pock building his forces on the border. One thing does worry me though ... '

'Sir?'

'Desun, you were in City Special Ops. Is there any chance that one of this resistance group will recognise you and cause trouble?'

Aris shrugged. 'They might know my name but they won't know my face. We always kept ourselves covered in any operation. Anyway, even if they do remember me, hopefully the fact that I'm with Hellyon now will help.' She paused. 'Although it will seem strange working with them rather than against them.'

'If anything, Aris's knowledge of their structure and even the members may help us,' said Jak.

Felson nodded. 'Alright then, everything seems in order.' He handed Sean a piece of paper. 'Rendezvous with the City group at these co-ordinates at 1am.'

'Sir.'

They turned to go but Felson called Aris back. 'A'dat wanted me to give you this message...' He handed her another piece of paper, fastened with A'dat's personal seal. 'He thinks very highly of you,' Felson smiled.

'Thank you sir.'

Aris slowly walked back to encampment, opening the letter. It read: *Aris, once you are in City, use the time wisely. Get her back.*

Aris stopped in her tracks. She had never mentioned her daughter but obviously he had known, like he had known everything else about her. And now he was giving her the greatest gift she could ever have asked for. In that instance she realised A'dat's powers, compassion and his bravery were not only a blessing for her, or for Hellyon: potentially he held the future of the world they all knew in his hands.

They arrived at the rendezvous point dead on time. The resistance group from City was already there and after an exchange of passwords, their leader, masked and hooded, silently gestured for CU11 to follow them. No weapons were in evidence but Aris felt they were being watched. If the unit had shown any hostility then no doubt they would have been cut down by a swathe of bullets from behind the bushes. Their trail took them through heavy undergrowth to where a trapdoor set into the earth was covered in greenery. Sweeping the branches aside, the leader pulled open the door and two of his members disappeared through it, downwards into the earth. Next, he motioned for Fen to go into the tunnel. Without a second glance Fen headed into the unknown, Sean following. Aris swallowed hard as she swung her legs over the edge and felt her feet hit the wooden rungs of the ladder. Her life in City had been spent searching for tunnels such as these; now she was an invited guest. She wondered whether she would be so welcome if they knew who she was.

The tunnel was low and narrow; they had to walk crouched over for what seemed like forever. Then, just as their backs began to ache with the strain, it opened out into a series of rooms. This had to be the group's operating headquarters. Oil lamps lit the walls, enabling the men to switch off the precious batteries in their torches.

'Please, sit down,' the leader of the group said, removing his face mask. Aris knew him as soon as she saw him: Marko Furnetti, self-styled revolutionary, and commander of the largest terrorist group within City. Her heart missed a beat— what the hell was A'dat doing dealing with such a dangerous man? Then she stopped herself. He was considered dangerous to City because of what he believed, but he was certainly no worse than Tiern and all his double-dealings with Balaat.

Marko looked around their faces and Aris noticed that his eyes lingered the longest on her. She hoped that it was just because she was a woman and not because he knew her past.

Marko handed around a small bottle of kotch. 'Welcome to City, the underground portion anyway. We have been informed why you are here and will assist you in every way we can, although you must be aware that as long as you are in our territory, I shall be in command. It is a matter of safety — for us all.'

'Understood,' said Sean. 'When do we get to see the weapons?'

'Tomorrow. Jano and Lachlan will take you to the factory; we have some business clothes for you to wear so that you won't stand out in the crowd. However, we can only take two of you, for security reasons.'

'What about the rest?'

Marko smiled. 'They won't be idle. A'dat has given me some other details to further the cause and I will need the rest of your group, especially you,' he jabbed a finger at Aris, 'to make the operation a success.'

'Hang on a minute,' said Sean, suddenly wary. 'What other operation? We weren't told that we had to do anything else.'

'That's because your commanding officer would probably never have agreed to it.'

'What makes you think we will?'

'Listen to me and let me explain.' Marko looked at Aris. 'I know who you are — A'dat told me that you were once from City and we did a bit of background research. So, Desun, what's it like to be on the losing side for a change?'

Aris felt herself go cold. She had not expected that A'dat would betray her in such a way.

Marko continued without letting her answer. 'Of course my first instinct was to want to kill you: after all, we were adversaries, albeit indirectly, for some time. Then I thought how much use you could be to us. After all, we both share a common adversary now — Tiern.'

'Wait a minute,' said Sean, 'I want to know exactly what's going on here.' His hand rested on his holster, his face wary of a trap.

'Sean,' Aris interrupted, 'let's hear him out.'

Marko nodded his thanks. 'Please be assured that none of you will come to any harm here—not from anyone in this group anyway. You will get what you came for, and hopefully you will also be able to help us in this little matter too. Aris, I understand that you knew Tiern well before he arranged for you to be disposed of.'

Aris nodded.

'Then I assume you must have done something that threatened him to make him react the way he did.'

'I thought you had all the answers,' she replied coolly.

Marko shook his head. We've heard rumours, that's all. Someone from your ops unit defected to us after your disappearance. He told us that he had a friend who had argued with Tiern over something she found. I suppose that friend was you.'

'Who was it that defected?'

'It doesn't matter—he's dead now — shot by his, and your, former unit. More to the point, do you still remember the layout of Tiern's apartment?'

'Yes, unless things have changed.'

'Well he hasn't moved and I would have thought that getting rid of you would have meant that he didn't need to change much else.'

'So the security number into his apartment should still be the same?'

'We think so.'

'I see. I suppose you want me to find something in his apartment? Something that will help topple him?'

'Not just him, but most of the Governors of City. We know that a lot of corrupt dealing has been going on with Balaat, but we just need the documentation to prove it. We have a man in the Senate, a friend of A'dat's who will be able to publicise anything we find. He's old and very ill so we must get the information to him as soon as we can.'

Aris smiled. 'I think I know exactly what documents you mean. Those are the ones I confronted him with, the ones that caused me all the trouble in the first place.'

'So will you do it?'

'Slow down a bit,' said Jak. 'This is all very well, but none of this has been okayed by our High Command. Aris could get into a hell of a lot of trouble, that's if she comes back alive in the first place.'

'At least she will be avenging what Tiern did to her as well as carrying out an extremely important mission—important for the future of City and all our lands.'

Sean shrugged and threw his hands in the air. 'It's up to you what you do Aris, but the rest of the unit will have no part in this.'

'I'll do it,' she said, 'but on one condition. Marko, I want you to help me find my daughter and get her out of City.'

Marko nodded thoughtfully. 'That shouldn't be too hard. I have contacts in the relevant departments. All I'll need is a name and a few details.'

After a restless night, Aris woke to a breakfast of dried meat and bread. She found herself sitting next to Marko. It appeared that Sean and Fen had already left to make an inspection of the weapons factory and Jak and Tor had gone with Marko's men to see the rest of the set up.

'Sleep well?' he asked her.

'Not particularly.'

'Maybe it was the ghosts of those you killed come back to haunt you,' he said, softening his words with a sardonic grin.

She didn't answer and he shrugged. 'What's past is past now as far as I'm concerned. I only deal with the present ... and the future.'

'Which is?'

'Greater democracy and individual freedom for all the citizens of City, and a fairer share-out of the wealth.'

She leaned back and studied him. 'But surely, City would have even greater wealth and freedom if it struck a peace deal with Balaat and Jerregish. Just think of the extra space the confiscated Hellyon lands would bring.'

'So what exactly was in those documents?'

Aris shook her head. 'To be honest, I didn't really get to see much before Tiern returned. It looked like they were after some land in Balaat, but why, I haven't a clue. All I know is that Tiern seemed to over-react when he saw me with the file. That's what started off the whole argument.'

'In that case, it's even more important that we get those documents: they obviously hold the key to what Tiern is planning.'

Aris nodded. 'I suppose you have Tiern watched by your people?'

'All the time.'

'So when is he due to be at the barracks today?'

Marko looked at his watch. 'In about another half an hour.'

'Okay. That's when I'll go in. I'll need some old clothes though: it will look rather obvious if I go in as a soldier from Hellyon.'

Marko grinned. 'How about you go in as a cleaning lady?'

Aris grimaced. 'If I have to. Now, what about the other part of the deal?'

'Your daughter? Yes, I've already had one of my men pull out some information about her. She was living with your sister after your disappearance. It seems that your sister kicked up a bit of a fuss about what happened, insisting that you would never betray your unit or desert. Unfortunately, she became a bit too much of a thorn in Tiern's side and… and I'm afraid she was found dead just a couple of months ago. The official report is that she hung herself, although in light of everything else I would say that was just a little bit too convenient, wouldn't you?'

'Hanid, dead?' Aris stared at him in disbelief.

Marko put his hand over hers. 'I am sorry. Maybe I should have said that a little more sensitively.'

'And what about my daughter?' asked Aris, a panic rising in her. 'What of Ani?'

'Don't worry, she is safe. She was placed in the City orphanage after your sister's death. One of my people works there and should be able to get her out and to us.'

Aris nodded, biting back tears of both grief and relief.

'I will get you those old clothes you wanted now,' said Marko, getting up from the table. 'It is time for you to go.'

Feigning a limp and with a scarf covering her face, Aris walked through familiar streets to the building where she had once been a regular and welcome visitor. It all looked the same, as if she had never been away at all. Tall, multi-storey blocks of apartments stretched skywards, making the most of City's limited ground space. The odd shop or eating house here and there added to the feeling of being back home again. Except that it wasn't her home any more and never could be again. She felt heavy both with dread and the ghosts of her old life as she stood at the door of Tiern's apartment block and tapped in the entry code. The door opened but she had never expected that door to be the problem. It was the next one.

Her heart was now racing as she walked up the three flights of stairs to his flat, her cleaning tools tightly grasped in one hand. A couple of occupants passed her, but they didn't even seem to see her: cleaning ladies were a necessary evil in such a busy city.

Tiern's personal door loomed in front of her — painted cold white it seemed to forbid her very presence. Muttering a little prayer, she tapped the old security number into the keypad and waited. For a second, nothing happened, and then the door swung open into the room she knew so well. Like everything else, nothing had changed. Tiern was a man of habit, always preferring to keep things the way he was used to. Sloppy security, but at least it made her life easier.

She moved into the hall, shutting the door behind her with a click and quickly made her way to his office. As always, his desk was immaculately tidy which made looking through any documents in his trays all the easier. But there was nothing of interest in them so she turned her attention to the large set of storage drawers under the window. Inside the first drawer was a series of boxes, all labelled with what they contained. One, bigger than the rest, had no label at all. She pulled it out and opened it up.

Inside were documents that she recognised by their blue edging: these were definitely the ones she had come for. Flicking through them just to make sure, she placed them inside the pocket sewn into the inner lining of her cleaner's coat and closed the box. As she replaced the box back into the drawer, she heard a vehicle door slam in the street outside and instinctively looked out of the window.

What she saw gave her a brief moment of panic. Tiern had come back unexpectedly. He seemed to be waiting for something. Suddenly another transporter drew up and from out of it stepped another familiar face: Tarran Moscati, the wife of the Commander in Chief of City's Army and Police Force. But what was Tiern doing here with her? They disappeared from view as they entered the building and Aris knew she had to think fast about what she was going to do. If she moved quickly, she would still have enough time to get out of the door and down the stairs while they came up in the lift. On the other hand, maybe she could profit from staying a little longer and finding out what was going on. Deciding on the second option, she ran into Tiern's living room and hid behind an ornamental screen that stood in the far corner.

The door opened and Aris could hear the soft laugh of a woman. Through the small join in the screen, Aris could just about see Tarran throw down her coat on to the floor and then move out of view. There was more soft laughter followed by the sound of a long, deep kiss. Aris smiled: this was going to be even more interesting than she could have imagined. She heard their voices, the voices of people infatuated with each other:

'We don't have long,' she heard Tiern say. 'I'm expected back at the barracks in an hour.'

'What did you tell them this time?' Tarran asked.

'Same as usual — to mind their own bloody business.'

Laughter.

'I suppose an hour's long enough,' said Tarran, 'for what I want to do to you.'

Another kiss and the sound of clothing being removed.

'Where are you taking me?' asked Tarran.

'Into the bathroom. I've always wanted to screw you in the bath.'

I've heard that one before, Aris thought acidly, remembering a similar scene a long time ago.

Five minutes later and she heard the sound of running water. It brought back memories of Tiern's large white bath, the smoothness of the porcelain. A few more minutes and the water stopped. Now there was the sound of more laughter and splashing, punctuated by the occasional sigh. Satisfied that the living room was now clear, Aris ventured out from behind the screen and crept over to Tiern's gun belt lying on the floor. She removed his pistol from his holster, quietly checked to see if it was loaded and then smiled. Let's see how stiff you stay with one of these pointing at you, she thought. As an afterthought she also took several restraint cuffs and put them in her pocket.

Softly, she approached the bathroom. The sounds now coming out from behind the door told Aris that they were in the middle of love-making. Just perfect.

She entered the bathroom. The couple were lying in the water, Tarran on top and riding Tiern like her life depended on it. Both of them were so wrapped up in their own pleasure that they didn't see her standing there. Aris gave a little cough, feeling it was time she was noticed. The look of horror on their faces as they turned to see her was one she would cherish for the rest of her life.

'Fucking hell!' Tiern mouthed.

Aris waved the pistol—his pistol—at him. 'If I were you, I'd not make any fuss. Just do as I say and I wont have to use this, tempting as it is.'

'Who the hell is she?' Tarran hissed at him.

'A ghost from his past you could say,' Aris answered for him. 'Still like it in the bath then, Tiern?'

Tiern had turned white, fine beads of sweat stood out on his forehead.

'Thought I was dead Tiern? Oh no, you must have known I survived because you ordered Vallen to get me out of the way in Hellyon Camp, didn't you? Bet you didn't think I'd come back for you though.'

'Tiern?' Tarran whined, as if he was somehow meant to jump out of the bath and save her.

'What do you want?' he managed to gasp out at last.

'Well, I came back for my daughter and my sister. The trouble is, I can't find my sister. I was told that she was dead, that you had her killed. Did you think I'd let that go?'

She now read fear in his eyes. He was her prey. She had him.

'Get out of the bath, both of you. Slowly. Any sudden or stupid moves and you're dead.'

They both obeyed her, keeping their hands in the air as they did so. Their wet, naked bodies made them look even more vulnerable and ridiculous.

Aris pointed to Tiern's now limp penis. 'Didn't think you'd be able to keep it up under pressure. But then, you were never much of a man unless you were in control, were you?'

A brief flash of anger passed across his face, but it soon disappeared as Aris produced the restraint cuffs from her pocket and waved them at her captives. 'Remember these? You used to love playing games with these, didn't you, or maybe you and your boss's wife haven't got to that bit yet.' Aris addressed her next comments directly to the woman. 'Allow me to introduce you to a new game. You should enjoy it. Maybe your husband will even want to try it after he finds out what you've been up to.'

With the weapon aimed at their heads, she made them stand facing each other, their arms out straight so that they clasped their hands behind each other's back. Aris then applied the restraint cuffs to both of their wrists and ankles. Pulling some pieces of cleaning cloth from the other pocket, she rolled two long strips up and forced them into the mouths of her captors before binding them in place with two more strips. She stood back to admire her handiwork, but something still didn't seem right: they would still be able to move around too much and raise the alarm. Keeping the gun trained on them, she walked over to her cleaning bag and pulled out three more strips of cloth. She made them shuffle over to a heavy wooden and leather armchair so that Tarran's back was against the back of the seat. Next, she gave the couple a little shove so that Tarran was forced to bend over backwards with Tiern having no choice but to bend over her. Taking the first of the strips of cloth, she tied one end around Tiern's hand restraints and the other around one of the front legs of the chair. With the other two strips, she repeated the process with the ankle restraints and the back legs of the chair. Now she was sure they wouldn't be going anywhere.

However, they had started to struggle. Tarran, in particular, had snapped out of her initial shock and seemed almost hysterical as she shook her head from side to side and made moaning noises. It was a good job she had the gag in her mouth. But no amount of struggling made a difference either to their bonds or the position of the armchair. They were trapped and would remain so until someone came looking for Tiern.

Aris bent over to whisper in her former lover's ear. 'This is just a taster Tiern. Next time you see me, you can be sure that I'll be bringing your death warrant, you bastard.'

She went back into the office to retrieve her stuff. As she was about to leave, she noticed a small, smooth cylindrical paperweight on his desk. It was an empty, lightweight shell casing and it gave her an idea, something that would complete her revenge just nicely. This one was going to be for all the shit she'd suffered in Balaat. Picking it up, she walked back out to the struggling pair.

Walking up to Tiern, she grabbed hold of his buttocks and pushed them apart. Grasping the cylinder in one hand, she pushed it violently inside him, feeling his body suddenly go tense and rigid with the pain.

'Now you have every reason to call me a pain in the ass,' she said, before picking up her bag. 'Have fun.'

When Aris reached the safe house, Marko was already waiting for her. He looked relieved.

'You're late,' he said. 'I was beginning to think something had happened to you.'

'I was busy making something happen to Tiern instead.'

Marko paled. 'Shit, you haven't killed him have you? That could ruin everything.'

She shook her head. 'No, don't worry. He's just going to be a bit tied up for a while?'

'What?'

'I'll explain later.' Aris reached into the lining of her coat and took out the wad of papers from Tiern's file. 'Here, this is what you wanted.'

Marko took it from her hand. 'Thank you. And now follow me... I have someone waiting for you downstairs.'

He took her down into the cellar and through a concealed trap door into the secret tunnel system until they came to the carved out rooms that served as the group's headquarters.

'Mummy!' A small figure, long hair flying as she ran, launched herself at Aris.

'Ani,' Aris swept her daughter up into her arms, holding her tightly as if she were never going to let her go again. Mother and daughter smothered each other in kisses and tears, murmuring words of love and promises. It wasn't until some time later, when Aris finally set Ani back on the earth again, that she noticed the whole of her unit had witnessed the event. They, too, were grinning, infected by the joy of the reunion.

An hour or so later, Ani had curled up in the corner, asleep on some blankets and CU11, Marko and some of his men sat around the table and discussed the day's events.

'So what happened with you?' Aris asked Sean and Fen.

Sean answered. 'We got what we wanted. The dealer will deliver the weapons to a middle man tonight who has arranged false exit papers to get them out of the gates — supposedly to go to Balaat. Jak's radioed for a couple of armaments units from Hellyon to rendezvous with the convoy and pick up the cache just before dawn. I'm pretty sure there won't be any problems.'

'And I hear you have the documents,' said Jak, smiling at Aris. 'I bet Tiern will be mad when he finds out.'

'He's mad already,' said Aris, smiling at the memory of his bound, writhing body. The faces around her looked puzzled, so she explained what had happened.

'You did what?' exclaimed Jak.

'You heard.'

'Hey lads, she's more dangerous than we thought,' joked Sean. 'Better make sure we don't bend over any more when she's around.

They all dissolved into laughter which woke Ani. She merely turned over, caught sight of her mother, smiled and went back to sleep again.

'So when are we leaving?' Aris asked Sean when the laughter and ribald talk had died down.

'In a couple of hours, when it's really dark.'

Aris nodded and looked over at her daughter again. She wanted to get her away from this place as soon as possible.

Marko looked over the documents again and frowned. 'This doesn't make sense. The papers are all here and show that Balaat will give City land in its southern lands in exchange for weapons, but I just can't see what City will get out of it.'

'Let me see,' said Aris, stretching out her hand for the sheaf of papers. She spent some time quietly studying the maps and the agreements while the others talked softly around her. At first she was as puzzled as Marko: the land area shown in the maps wasn't agricultural quality and didn't even have a major port or manufacturing base. Essentially it was an area used and destroyed by the people from the Old World. No one went there anymore. Then she noticed two areas were specifically mentioned in the agreements as being contained within the new territory, and as she looked, something surfaced in her memory. Her history lessons had taught that the Old World people had set down the constitution of City so that what they considered to be harmful technologies would never be developed and used in any way that would cause environmental or social harm. From what she had learned, the old 'home' planet, if you believed in such things, had been subjected to such pollution and harmful inventions. Pictures of the inventions stood out in her mind — there had been a machine that could fly through the air and drop bombs on people below.

'My God,' she said quietly and the conversation around her ceased immediately.

'What have you found?' asked Marko.

'Balaat may just have made the worst deal possible.'

'What do you mean?'

'City isn't planning a long term allegiance with Balaat and Jerregish at all: it wants to wipe them out too and take the lands all for itself.'

Marko frowned. 'But how do you see that? City would need massive resources to manage that. How could they get anything like that from land that's virtually worthless?'

She turned the map around and pointed to what she was talking about. 'There's a place with what looks like a long straight road, running for almost a mile. It was built by the people who lived before us. They used to fly their aircraft from it.'

'Aircraft? You mean like the flying machines in the old legends?'

'Yes, except that they were real. I heard a rumour some time ago that City scientists were interested in developing a prototype aircraft. Of course the Constitution forbade it and the project was stopped. Or maybe that's what the Senate have been allowed to think. From this it looks like others have been secretly funding and encouraging the experiment to go ahead.'

'You mean Tiern and his cronies?'

Aris nodded. 'But to see if it works they will need a long flat strip of land for it to get up enough speed to take off. Obviously there is no room in City so they have had to look outside.'

'And with a fleet of aircraft they would then be able to dominate Balaat and Jerregish. Surely those countries would soon see it too and retaliate?' Marko asked

'Not if Tiern came up with a cover story about what the land was for. Anyway, for most Outlanders the stories of the Old World people have been just that — stories. And that isn't the only piece of land City is interested in: it's also after the wasteland zone to the south west.'

'But that place is contaminated. What the hell would City want that for?' Fen asked.

'You're right: it is contaminated by chemicals from an Old

World factory. Another of these documents mentions making a new weapon — one with chemicals in that would be able to kill hundreds of people at once.'

Marko shook his head 'Shit. This has got to be stopped straight away.'

Aris shook her head. 'It won't be easy, Marko. No matter how repulsive the idea seems to you and me, it will be put to the people of City in such a way to make it sound as if it will bring them all a greater prosperity. They will all be behind such a plan. When they realise what has been done in their name, it will all be too late.'

'Then somehow we are going to have to make sure the aircraft and chemical factories are sabotaged beyond repair,' he said.

Aris shook her head. 'I know from experience that the security around those places will be almost impossible to get through.'

'Maybe but we have to try, for all our sakes, and for the sake of our children.' They all glanced at Ani, asleep with her thumb in her mouth. He was right. City had to be stopped at all costs.

15

Sean and the rest of the unit arrived back at Hellyon camp just before dawn to be met by Macker.

'Everything okay?' she asked, then noticed the sleeping child in Aris's arms and smiled. 'I can see that for one person it is.'

Aris nodded and smiled back at her. 'It couldn't be better. However, I think I'd better get this little lady to a proper bed.' She walked over to her tent and disappeared inside.

Macker turned to Sean. 'Felson will be wanting to see you straight away I expect.'

Sean nodded. 'I was going to go over there anyway. There's quite a bit he needs to know.' He frowned. 'But how come you're here? Is something wrong?'

'No. I just came to let Tor know that he's got a visitor waiting for him over at security.'

'A visitor?' Tor questioned.

'Your sister, Marissa.'

Tor frowned and made off in the direction of the security block.

'I thought he'd be happy to see her,' said Macker.

'He probably is. It's just that any news from home makes him nervous.'

Tor arrived at the security block, took one look at his sleeping sister in her room and confirmed her identity to the sergeant on duty.

The sergeant nodded. 'Just had to be sure. Especially at a time like this, when Balaat and Jerregish are knocking on the door.'

Tor went and stood by her bedside, taking in the features that he had not seen for three years. Marissa was two years younger than he was and in their childhood they had been virtually inseparable. It was only when Tor started to harbour ideas about going away to fight that they began to argue and drift apart. She had called him unnatural. The rest of the family agreed with her. Now he looked at her with new eyes. Her pale blonde hair fell across a face that seemed to have matured since the last time he had seen her. With a shock he realised that she was no longer the little girl he had remembered.

As if aware of his presence, she slowly turned over on to her back and opened up her eyes.

'Tor,' she said. 'You're safe.'

She sat up and he bent down to hug her. Before he could stop himself, he began to cry, the tears flowing down his face. When he pulled back he could see that she was crying too. He hadn't realised how much he had missed her, missed his family.

'It's so good to see you,' he said. 'How long are you staying?'

'This isn't just a social visit, Tor. I wish it were.'

'What's wrong? Is something wrong at home?'

She nodded and bit her lip. 'Father is dying. The medicine people say that he has only got a few weeks to live at the most. We need you back Tor.'

He stared at her, his emotions thrown into sudden turmoil. Despite the arguments at his leaving he still loved his father very much. The old man had seemed so strong, so invincible that Tor had never considered that one day he might die.

'The omens have been cast,' she continued, tears once more flowing down her pale cheeks. 'They all say that the eldest son must take over the leadership of the tribe. That's you Tor.'

'But I can't,' he replied in a whisper.

She shook her head. 'Now is not the time to talk about it, brother. You are tired; you need to rest. I will stay as long as I can, so we will have plenty of time to talk this through.' She swung her legs off the bed and walked over to her travelling pack. 'I suppose I'd better meet the rest of the people you live with.'

It was afternoon before Aris woke up. She immediately turned over to check on Ani but the bed was empty, her daughter had gone. In something approaching a state of panic, she stumbled out of the tent opening, her eyes blinking in the bright sunlight. There, on a crate by the cooking block, sat Ani, playing a game with some woman that she'd never seen before. Relieved that her daughter was safe but curious as to the identity of the woman, she approached the pair.

The woman looked up at her and smiled. There was something in the smile that Aris found familiar: she was sure she had seen it somewhere else before. Ani jumped up when she realised her mother was standing next to her.

'Mummy, this is Marissa. She's been teaching me how to play Three Stones.'

'Hello,' said Marissa. 'You have a wonderful daughter. She learnt to play the game in just a few minutes and she's beating me at it already.'

'I'm sorry,' said Aris, her voice carrying the tone of suspicion, 'but I still don't know who you are.'

'My apologies, I should have introduced myself better. I am

Torassin's sister, I shall be staying for a few days.'

Aris smiled. 'I thought your face seemed familiar. Now I know why; you and he are quite alike.'

'So we've often been told.'

'This is the first time any of his family have visited him, isn't it?'

'Yes. When Torassin decided to go and fight in someone else's war, it was against our ways. We tried to persuade him to change his mind but when he wouldn't we had to let him go. It was as if he'd imposed exile on himself. Our father forbade anyone to see him until he decided for himself to come home.'

'So why are you here now?'

'Our father is dying and Torassin is the only one suitable to replace him as leader. That's what the omens and the medicine people have told us. I was sent to try and persuade him to come back; they thought that he might listen to me.'

Aris sat down and hoisted Ani onto her lap. 'That won't be easy. Tor is very much his own person. He regards himself as part of Hellyon now.' She paused, before adding in a much quieter voice, 'as we all do.'

Ani pulled at Aris's sleeve. 'Mummy, I'm hungry. Can we go and get some food?'

'You'll have to wait a bit, sweetheart. The cookhouse isn't open yet.'

'But I can't wait, I'm starving.' Ani's eyes pleaded with her.

'Listen,' said Marissa, 'I have a few pieces of dried fruit in my bag. Would that be all right until dinner time?'

Ani nodded vigorously and Aris smiled. 'Thank you Marissa. I forgot how hungry children could get. This camp isn't really suited to youngsters, so I guess I'll have to see what I can do about transferring us to some family quarters, maybe be in another camp.'

'And leave the unit?'

Aris shrugged. 'I don't want to, but Ani is my life and I want us to be together no matter what.'

Tor emerged from his tent, a broad smile on his face as he saw Marissa giving her dried food to Ani.

'You didn't tell me your sister was here,' said Aris, walking over to him.

'You were asleep when I got back to the tents and I didn't want to wake you.'

'Marissa tells me she's come to take you back.'

The smile disappeared from Tor's face. 'That's what she may think, but what I do will be another matter.'

'What about your father Tor? Surely you want to see him before he dies.'

'I don't know. Well... yes, I suppose I do, but...'

'But what?'

'I just have this feeling that if I ever go back to the tribe, I'll want to stay.'

'Is that such a bad thing?'

'Hellyon has become my home now, and CU11 my family. I can't leave them either, Aris. I feel torn.'

Marissa rejoined them, a grinning Ani at her side.

'She seems to have taken to you,' Aris observed, not being able to help a twinge of jealousy.

'Well, I have taken to her too. As we say in our tribe, she has a ancient heart and head.' Marissa grinned down at the young girl and Ani giggled back.

'Since when were you so good with children?' Tor asked. 'Last time I saw you, you were still climbing trees with the other boys.'

'After you left I got married to Ronas. I have a daughter, one year old.'

Tor was almost lost for words. 'My sister, married, and with a child?'

'I'm sorry if it comes as such a shock, Tor. Maybe we should have sent you some kind of message. So much has happened since you went.'

'So I am an uncle?'

'Yes.' She looked at him for a second as if she was about to say something else, then seemed to change her mind. She turned to Aris instead.

'Listen, I know you are still going to have to do whatever it is you all do while I'm here, so if you wish, I am only too happy to look after Ani.'

Aris nodded. 'Thank you. That will give me some time to sort out what I am going to do next and where I'm going to go.'

'Go?' said Tor. 'You aren't leaving us are you?'

'If I have to, Tor,' said Aris, pointing at Ani. 'I'm sure you understand why.'

He nodded. Children were the best reason for anything.

When Sean returned from his daily briefing with Felson, his face was serious, no sign of his usual smile. Motioning for the rest of the unit to gather around the crates, he sat down, and the others followed.

'Looks like we're about to face the big one,' he said. 'Balaat has lined up its armour and troops along our border in the last day and the build up is continuing. Jerregish has also started preparations for an attack on the northern border. That means an all-out invasion by hostile forces can be expected at any time from now on, in which case our own defensive preparations will need to be speeded up.'

'What about A'dat's support?' asked Fen. 'Maybe there is something he can do.'

Sean shook his head. 'There isn't much anyone can do at the moment—it's all moving too fast. By the time a message gets to him, it will probably be too late.'

'I suspect he already knows what's happening anyway,' Aris said, 'but Sean's right, there isn't enough time for him to do anything to help us.'

'So what's the plan?' asked Jak.

'Our unit, along with the rest of our division, is being moved to a position along the border with Balaat. We'll be facing two divisions of Balaatan artillery plus their infantry, so it won't be easy...'

'Bloody impossible more like,' grumbled Jak.

Sean gave him a look that was difficult to read. 'Like I said, it won't be easy, but it won't be impossible either. As a unit we will be taking a PN3 with us, and we will have the advantage of terrain: we have the high ground there, don't forget. And we know how to work in that sort of country more than they do.'

'But we'll still be outnumbered,' said Tor.

'Yes.'

'And our chances are still pretty bad,' Jak added.

Sean was silent for a short while. 'Yes. I can't pretend that we are going to win this one. The chances are that some of us here will not make it through the battle, so maybe the first thing for you all to do now is to get your affairs in order. We leave tomorrow at dawn.'

Sean stood up and walked out of camp without another word leaving his unit suddenly pondering their futures. Although this day had been expected, now that it was here things were moving far too fast.

At first, Aris didn't do anything. She stayed sitting on the crate, watching two figures in the distance returning from the cookhouse. Ani and Marissa were obviously unaware of what was about to happen and looked the picture of innocence as they strolled between the tents, making their way back to the encampment. Aris felt that with Sean's announcement, her new-found world with her daughter was about to be taken away again. She had hoped she would be able to leave before the invasion started; take her daughter somewhere safe and start a new life. But now, well, she could hardly leave before the battle. It would look like desertion, feel like desertion, and she wouldn't be able to live with that either.

'Not easy, is it?' Jak's voice broke through her thoughts. He sat down beside her.

'It's like being torn in two,' she replied. 'For Gods sake, Jak, I've just got her back and now I might lose her again, maybe forever. What if I get killed? Not only will she have no family but she's out of any environment that is familiar to her.'

'I know, it's tough. Send her somewhere safe and we'll just have to make sure we look after you so that you can get back to her after.'

Aris smiled at his attempts to make her feel better. 'But where can I send her? I need to be sure that she will be looked after.'

Jak nodded towards Marissa. 'I would say you couldn't get much safer than Tor's family. I'm sure Marissa would only be too happy to look after Ani.'

He gave her shoulder a reassuring squeeze, then got up. Aris stayed sitting, looking at the tall woman holding hands with her daughter. Jak was right, she wouldn't find anyone better for the job.

Tor took Marissa up to his favourite spot by the cliff face. There wasn't nearly enough time for everything that had to be said between them. They were silent for a while, looking out over the view; taking in a sky that would soon be choked by the smoke of battle. Tor was the first to break the silence.

'You need to get out of here tonight,' he said. 'I'll arrange an escort to take you to safe ground.'

'Then you're not coming back with me?' she asked.

'How can I? You know what's about to happen.'

'Yes. Hellyon will be overrun. Lots of people are going to die. And it will happen whether you are here or not.'

'That's not the point Marissa, I'm still needed by the unit.'

'You are also needed by your father.'

Tor fell silent. His father's face appeared in his memory and he suddenly felt a heaviness in his heart.

'What's the matter Tor?' Marissa asked angrily. 'Do I take it that you don't love him any more? The man who gave you life and taught you all he knew about caring, about love? Have you changed so much that those things don't count for anything?'

Tor shook his head. 'I... I don't know.'

'Well, neither do I. I can't believe that this place has turned you into a stranger so easily. You're certainly not the brother that I remember.' She stood up and turned to go.

'Marissa, wait,' he called out after her. She stopped, but did not face him. He could sense her despair as well as her anger.

'Marissa, if what I hear is right, this battle will be over very quickly — maybe a day or two. I promise that once it is over I shall travel back to see you and father... and maybe stay.'

She slowly faced him. Her eyes were full of tears. 'And what if you don't come back? What if you are killed?'

He put his hands on her shoulders and drew her to him. 'Then it's in the hands of the spirits, isn't it? If I am truly intended to take my father's place, as the omens say, then I shall live. If not, then maybe you shouldn't put so much faith in the shamans.'

She sobbed into his shoulder and he held her tight. 'I shall come home, sis, I promise. Now, have I ever broken a promise to you? Have you ever doubted that I meant what I said?'

She shook her head. 'No. Well, I suppose that's all there is to be said now. It's time for me to go. I promised Aris I'd get Ani to safety as soon as possible, so the sooner I leave the better.'

Tor nodded. 'Aris is lucky you were here. I don't think she'd be able to find a better foster mother for her daughter anywhere else.'

Marissa reached up and touched his cheek. 'May the spirits go with all of you.'

Those last words of hers seemed to echo in his mind as he watched her walk back towards the encampment. He placed her face in his thoughts, a talisman to protect him against what was to come.

A'dat let his fingers run across the luxurious silk of his favourite robe. His eyes swept the expensive wallhangings and the soft bed. He sighed. Soon these would be all but a memory. He had seen it all clearly in his dreams: someone was about to betray his intentions to his brother. Once Jessyn knew of A'Dat's support for City and the Tribelands, armed guards would be sent to arrest him and his household. No mercy would be shown. He had to get himself and all those in danger out of Jerregish now if his plans had any chance of succeeding.

The door opened and he spun around, startled out of his thoughts. A tall, blonde girl stood there, her face flushed from running.

'You sent for me Lord?' she said.

He smiled. 'Ah Tass, my dear girl. The time is here. Send a message around to all my faithful servants.' He emphasised the word 'faithful'.

'We are leaving for the Tribelands Lord?'

'Within the hour. And from now on you must call me Raul. After all, exile is a great leveller.'

She nodded and a smile played around her lips, the smile he had grown to love. As she left, he caught a trace of her perfume lingering in the air. She had grown so fast from girl to woman, and grown so strong, too, in the short time he'd known her. One day soon, he knew, she would make her mark in this world. Though how and why, even he couldn't foretell. All he knew was that he had to get her safely back to her people in the Chapter Homelands. Then the story could begin.

Jak, Sean and Fen took a short breather as they packed their kits in preparation for moving to their battle positions. Sean had found an unopened bottle of kotch, but it sat untouched in front of them. No one felt like drinking.

'How about your family, Fen? Did you manage to get a message to them?' Sean asked.

Fen nodded. 'Although I would have preferred to have gone myself. Jeanna's sister has an empty house in the northern Marran Hills. At least they should be out of the front line fighting there, and if the threat gets too much, I'm sure Jeanna will have the good sense to get herself and the girls to safety somewhere in the Tribelands.'

Sean grunted and smiled, trying to give Fen the impression that he thought he'd done the right thing. Privately though, he was not so sure. Neither Pock nor Jessyn were considered to be compassionate rulers. Even if Fen's family were out of the battle area, the aftermath could still bring reprisals on innocent civilian heads. And if Fen got killed, how the hell was Jeanna going to cope with raising two young children?

It was almost as if Fen read his mind. 'Sean,' he started, his voice uncharacteristically unsure, 'I want you to promise me something.'

'Okay.'

'If anything does happen to me, and you come out of it alive, I want you to find Jeanna and the girls and make sure they are safe and well. Will you do that for me?'

'Of course. I'll look after them as if they were my own, you can count on it. But what are you on about? You're going to come out of this fine. It'll probably be me who gets it this time. Or Jak.'

'Cheers,' mumbled Jak. 'Personally I intend to stay alive. I have great ambitions to get to old age and be a pain in the ass to everyone.'

'You've certainly practised long enough,' Sean grinned.

Jak was about to retort when he caught a movement out of the corner of his eye. Something small dashed between the tents. It was his adopted cat. And what would happen to her, he wondered? He certainly couldn't take it with him. It looked as though the animal would have to take its chances in the invasion like everyone else. 'Poor sod,' he mumbled under his breath.

16

CU11 reached their defensive position just before dawn. The division they were with spread out to various strategic points along the ridge just above the enemy. With just 4000 fighters and 20 heavy artillery pieces they were meant to hold off some of Balaat's 10000 strong fighting forces encamped just out of range.

Jak looked through his viewers, trying to make out anything that would give him information, but the enemy camp was dark and silent. They weren't giving anything away.

Aris and Sean checked over the PN3 gun, mounted onto a truck next to their position.

'How much ammunition do we have for this thing?' she whispered.

'Not nearly enough. The City underground did their best in the circumstances but really we just have not had enough time to prepare.'

'Which is what Balaat was counting on,' she said.

'City too. I still can't believe that they're taking an active role against us.'

'Can't you?' Aris said wearily. 'Nothing that place does surprises me anymore. I'm just glad my daughter is away from it.'

She turned to go but Sean laid a hand on her arm. 'Aris, tonight may be the last time that we are all together, alive. Tomorrow, whatever the outcome, will change things forever. I think it's time we made our peace.'

'Peace?'

'Well, I haven't exactly been easy to be around this past month or so and I think it's time I explained.'

'No need, what's done is done.'

'Please hear me out. Even if you don't need an explanation, perhaps I need to give one, to clear my mind.'

Aris nodded, understanding. Many truths often came to light on the eve of battle. It was a time when the barriers dropped from men's' souls.

'I've been jealous, if you must know. Jealous of Kris. He has always had everything I ever craved: the missions, the acclaim, the women. And then he had you. Now I know it's no secret that I've always had a soft spot for you, but I also always knew that while you were in my unit I could do nothing about it. Of course Kris had no such obstacles and just jumped in where I could not. It was like having my nose rubbed in the shit one time too many and that's why I acted like I did.'

Aris laid her hand on his shoulder. 'I know. I've known it all along. Why else did you think I put up with it? But it would never have worked — you and me. My feelings for you are deep, and yes, I would put my life down for you, but I do not feel the same as I do for Kris — that I could spend a lifetime with you.'

Sean bowed his head. 'You're right. If I'm honest, I feel the same. For as long as I can remember, Kris and I have had this rivalry thing and maybe it was my sense of competition that made my feelings seem keener, more real.'

Aris grinned. 'That just sounds like a healthy male ego to

me. Anyway, it doesn't matter what Kris has achieved, you will always be my captain, the best I have ever served under.'

'Thank you. Except that makes it even more difficult to tell you what I have to tell you now.'

'What?'

Sean reached into his jacket pocket and pulled out some paper. 'Here, this is for you. Kris gave it to me to give to you just before he took off on his latest mission. But at the time I just couldn't bring myself to hand it over. I'm sorry. I hope that you'll be able to forgive me.'

The paper lay in her fingers, burning her skin like ice. She was silent for a very long time, trying to wade through the mire in her head. She was about to enter battle, maybe even die; she had regained her daughter, only to perhaps lose here again forever, the same with her soul mate. Sean's deceit would once upon a time have caused an outbreak of righteous anger, but now, in the circumstances, it seemed such a small thing.

'Of course I forgive you,' she said finally. 'There's no harm done. It's best we go into tomorrow with clear consciences and clear minds.'

Sean smiled, looking as if a great weight had been taken off his shoulders.

Aris felt as if a great load had been put onto hers. Finding some cover, she switched on her torch, covering the small illumination as best she could with her hand and body. Unfolding the paper she read Kris's words: If we both come out of this, I'll meet you at Tor's village. I miss you now more than ever. You have my love — Kris. She put it into an inner pocket vowing not to read it again until at least tomorrow evening, when hopefully it would all be over, and, please God, she was still alive.

A short while later, the sound of gunfire below their position threw them into a new state of alertness.

'Sounds like our forward positions have had a contact,' said Jak.

Sean nodded. 'Probably some of the Balaatan pathfinders trying to make their way up to the ridge. Aris, you and I had better get to the gun and be ready to fire off a few rounds in support. Tor, you get on the radio, find out what's happening down there, then inform headquarters that it has begun.'

'Me and Fen are going to go forward, see if we can pick off any of the bastards as they come up,' said Jak.

Sean nodded. 'Just watch your backs, okay? If you get into any trouble we won't be able to see from up here.'

Jak grinned. 'No worries, the only trouble will be what we are causing.'

The battle below continued as Aris and Sean raced for the gun. Other positions further along the ridge also began to fire as they realised the battle had been joined. Aris threw herself into the firing seat as Tor shouted out the co-ordinates to her. She fiddled with the controls that adjusted the range: accuracy was going to be crucial. She needed to get close enough to the enemy to freak them yet not so close that she endangered her own side. Sean stood off to one side, preparing to reload as necessary.

With a huge recoil, the gun fired off its first shell, the muzzle flash lighting the scene around them and giving away the gun's position to those below. It was a risk they knew they had to take. The shell landed a way off from where Aris had intended, so she altered the elevation of the barrel just a little. The next shell landed right on target and she allowed herself a small smile of victory as the gun fight below stopped and Tor confirmed over the radio that the enemy position had been eliminated.

The sky was now becoming lighter by the minute and she

and Sean were able to see the other skirmishes going on in the terrain below. The Balaatan heavy artillery also now began to open up, the shells pounding the ridge, searching for the defensive gun positions that had earlier caused so many casualties amongst its forward troops. The air grew thick with smoke and noise and time seemed lost as Aris fired off shell after shell. Now and again an enemy missile landed a bit too close for comfort but their cover was obviously good enough for now.

Tor came running up to join them. 'Headquarters have also had reports that Jerregish is attacking simultaneously on the northern border and City from the east.'

Sean nodded. 'That's as we thought. Okay Tor, could you position yourself just above us and act as a spotter, just in case any of those bastards get past Jak and Fen?'

Tor nodded and disappeared.

It seemed as if the sky was on fire, as if the earth was constantly shaking as both sides exchanged fire. However, something had changed: the sound of hand to hand battle below was coming closer and Balaat, with its superior numbers, was advancing. It wasn't long before Tor's radio crackled into life. He received the message, grim-faced and then ran to where Sean and Aris were, their faces now streaked with sweat and dirt.

'We've been ordered by High Command to fall back to position two,' he shouted above the noise. All units in position one to the south of us have fallen and any survivors are making their way northwards, to regroup with the units up here.'

Sean stared at him. 'You're saying that South Hellyon's fallen already? So soon?'

Tor nodded. 'It's the least secure area of the border. It'll get harder for them the further north they go.'

Sean nodded. 'Right, we'd better pack this thing up and drive to position two then. But what the fuck are we going to do about Jak and Fen? There's no way they'll know what's going on — they don't have a radio.'

'I'll go forward and see if I can find them.'

'Don't be a fool Tor — you don't have a clue where they are. You'll end up dead.'

Tor stared at him, a strange calm in his eyes. 'I know where they are. Don't worry Sean, it's not my fate to die yet.'

And with that he vanished down the slope.

'Crazy idiot!' Sean muttered across the gun to Aris. 'Some day his Sharm beliefs will be the death of him.

Position two was further to the north and closer to the mountains. Each unit, as before, had been allocated an area to be defended, supported by heavy artillery fire from the PN3s. In their new positions, the guns opened up once more on the enemy, although now at a greater range, hoping that their covering fire would allow their soldiers to pull back safely without making it into a rout. Stragglers from the overwhelmed southern units also began to arrive, battle weary and all with horrific tales.

Macker was one of them. Her unit, along with 20 others had almost been caught in a pincer movement. Many died during the first contact, being unable to escape the hail of fire that came from more than one side. The terrain there had been flatter, harder to defend and Hellyon's forces had crumpled within the first hour of conflict. Macker and one other from her unit had only just managed to escape because they had been situated a little further away from the main attack. Then they had run for their lives, heading north to the new position. Seeing Aris and Sean, a look of relief spread over her face, but it didn't last long.

HELLYON'S STAND

'Where are the others?' she asked, almost fearing to hear the answer.

'Your guess is as good as mine,' Sean shrugged. 'I was hoping they would have got back by now. That is, if they are still alive.'

Jak checked his ammunition pouches and discovered that he had nearly run out. He and Fen were positioned in one of the forward trenches that had been dug and manned a few months earlier, when rumours of the attack had started. A whole series of these trenches had been hastily constructed, stretching across the border and backwards towards the high ground in Hellyon. Things were starting to get desperate. Already, Jak had heard from down the line that Southern Hellyon had fallen and that High Command had ordered a retreat to position two. Slowly he could see the men around him withdrawing backwards, but a few—he and Fen included—had chosen to stay forward and keep the enemies' heads down to allow a few extra minutes. Now, with ammunition running out, there wasn't much point in hanging on.

As if in answer to someone's unspoken prayer, Hellyon's big guns, mostly silent for the past half hour while they moved, once more began firing, giving the last stragglers a chance to get out before the trenches were stormed. Jak grabbed Fen's arm and signalled towards the mountains. Needing no second urging, Fen nodded and they both began to run through the maze cut into the newly pocked earth. As they reached the ground behind the trenches, they saw Tor running towards them.

'What the fuck are you doing here?' yelled Jak. 'You should be at position two by now.'

'So should you. I came to see if you needed any help.'

'We're fine. Now get your ass out of here.'

The three of them started to run up the low slopes towards the safety of the high ground—Tor, with his athletic frame and the advantage of youth, a way in front of them.

They only had seconds to react to the shell as it flew over them, throwing themselves on the ground as it hit the earth ahead. The ground shook, throwing up clods of dirt and rock. Jak slowly got to his feet, seeing Fen doing the same out of the corner of his eye. Tor sat up, his eyes glazed, but got no further. His right arm was a mass of torn flesh, blood and splintered bone where a piece of shrapnel had hit it. The blood began to pool around where he was sitting. Fen and Jak rushed towards him, Fen automatically reaching into his pack for the medical kit.

Jak was no medic, but he could immediately see the obvious: the arm was beyond repair. All that Fen could hope to do now was to stem the bleeding and stop the young man from falling into fatal shock before they reached medical facilities. Tor's initial numbness seemed to have worn off; he looked down at his mangled arm and began to scream.

'Okay, okay, Tor. We're here and we're going to get you out,' said Jak, as soothingly as he could.

'My arm, my fucking arm!' Tor's voice was rising into a panic.

'We'll fix your arm, don't you worry,' Fen lied. 'We've just got to get you to a field hospital. You've got to hang in there.'

Fen's quick, skilled fingers made short work of the dressing and soon they were pulling Tor to his feet, half supporting him, half carrying him, making as much ground as they could with shells and bullets crashing all around them.

Eventually they made it to the higher ground. The enemy fire was falling behind them now, the rate of advance slowed by caution. Nevertheless, it was obvious that Hellyon had no option other than to fight a rearward action, retreating with as much honour as possible.

The men reached position two within the hour and immediately sought out medical assistance for Tor. He was quickly put onto a hospital transport and taken to a field hospital, much further to the north and out of the line of fighting.

'Do you think he'll make it?' asked Jak.

Fen shrugged. 'If he wants to he will.'

The two men headed for CU11's position and relayed what had happened. There were nods, the news was taken in, but for now none of the fighters could allow themselves the luxury of feelings. At least Tor was still alive; by the end of the light there might be many more reasons for grieving.

Jak took out his viewers again and surveyed the enemy's advance onto the higher ground. He shook his head. 'They've never dared pursue us into our own territory before: they must be damn confident of victory.'

'Of course they are,' said Sean. He and Aris had been taking turns behind the gun and both of them ached from the exertion. Yet the flow of adrenaline had given them an underlying strength which kept them going, kept their minds clear, and still gave them hope against what was inevitable.

The Balaatan forces were now close enough again to start a bombardment of their own. This time, though, the shelling was more intense, almost continuous, as if they had suddenly acquired more artillery pieces.

With Tor gone, Macker took over the radio for the unit and called in to find out the latest positions. Listening to the news coming in, her face whitened and she whirled to face CU11. 'They've reinforced from the South,' she yelled above the noise.

They've got treble our numbers now.' She fell silent again, listening intently to some other instructions coming over the headphones. After a minute she tore them off and packed the radio back up in her pack. 'We have to retreat, High Command wants everyone to fall back to the Hester Range and dig in there.'

'What, already?' protested Aris. 'But we've only just got here.'

Jak, still looking through his viewers nodded. 'And we're going to have to get out fast. The Balaatans are coming up quicker than before; at this rate they'll reach and overwhelm our front lines in less than ten minutes. There's no way we can hold back those numbers.'

'Then we had better get moving,' said Fen.

'It'll take more than ten bloody minutes to get this gun packed up and moved,' shouted Sean.

'Then we'll have to leave it. Maybe disable it in some way so that they can't use it.'

'No bloody way. We haven't got enough artillery as it is. Look, the rest of you go on—Aris and I will stay and try and pack up as quick as possible.'

'Don't be a bloody fool, Sean,' yelled Jak. 'We're all going and going now.'

'Do it then, but do it without me.'

Jak shook his head. 'If you insist on staying then we all stay. Agreed?' He looked around at the rest of the unit who nodded their reluctant agreement.

The next few minutes was spent in trying to get the gun ready for travel. A restraining bolt had become jammed which meant that nothing else could be done until it had been fixed.

'It isn't going to shift,' grunted Jak, giving another futile push on the wrench. 'Look, we're running out of time here.

We've tried our best to get this thing moving Sean, so I reckon we ought to put a charge under it and get the hell out.'

Sean nodded and looked back towards the approaching Balaatan lines. 'Okay. As captain I'll place the charge; the rest of you are to withdraw immediately.'

'I'll stay with you, give you some cover,' said Jak.

'No. There's no point in risking two of us—it will only take half a minute. Now go, that's an order.'

Jak shook his head but turned to catch up with the others. Sean knew what he was doing and, as he said, setting a charge wouldn't take long. Shells were landing all around him now and he reckoned that they were going to be very lucky if none of them got hit. Then he heard a familiar sound. He stopped in his tracks and whirled around. The PN3 was firing again.

'The stupid bastard!' Jak swore and began to retrace his steps. This time he would make sure Sean came back with him, even if he had to knock the stupid bastard out and carry him. He hoped the rest of the unit had gone far enough ahead not to hear the gun being fired. The last thing he needed was for all of them to put their lives in danger just for the foolhardy bravery of one man.

He got close enough to see the rear of the gun transport ahead when there was a huge explosion and his world lit up around him. He felt his body being transported through the air and them dumped hard back onto the earth, landing in a depression made by an earlier shell. Dazed, Jak slowly raised his head and checked himself over for serious injury. Amazingly, apart from a few bruises, he seemed untouched. Pushing himself back to his feet, he suddenly realised that the PN3 had fallen silent.

He started to run towards the position, only to come to a sudden stop. There was nothing left of the gun or the lorry. The shell had taken them out, leaving a smouldering mass of twisted metal. There was no use searching for Sean—he knew there would be nothing of him left. Jak shook his head, holding back any emotion until later, when he could afford to drown it in alcohol.

The artillery of the enemy had fallen silent too and Jak suddenly realised that their infantry was about to advance to where he was. Turning on his heel, he ran for his life towards the north.

He caught up with the remainder of CU11 two hours later. They had been making good progress towards their northern rendezvous, jogging for most of the way. Now they had stopped for a short break. Their lying up point was so well concealed that Jak nearly missed then altogether. It was only through Fen's watchfulness that he was spotted and stopped.

'Where the hell did you get to, and where's Sean?' Fen demanded. It was obvious from their faces that they had all been concerned.

'Sean's dead,' said Jak, simply.

There was a shocked silence, broken a short time later by Macker. 'But... how?'

'He lied about setting a charge; he went back to fire the gun to give us more cover. Before I could get to him a shell hit it. He died a hero, just like he would have wanted.'

Fen nodded. 'I think he knew this was his last battle. At least he died well.'

'Amen to that,' Jak concurred.

Macker's radio gave a slight crackle, an indication that a message was about to be sent. Macker grabbed the headphones and sat herself down, adjusting the frequency so that she could get a clear reception. At first she wasn't sure whether it was interference—the background noise was so loud. Then she heard a voice coming through, a voice that contained tones of panic and urgency. 'All units,' it said, 'all units. High command is now being attacked. All northern units have been overwhelmed by Jerregish and City and most western positions have been taken. Orders are to retreat to any place of safety. Repeat, all units to retreat. It's over.'

The message was repeated and Macker upped the volume so that all could hear the message.

'Shit. But how the hell do we know it was genuine? It could be enemy propaganda making us think we should give up,' said Jak.

Macker shook her head. No, the message contained the High Command coding. And if the enemy have got hold of that, then they've already taken the place. Either way, Hellyon's fallen.'

'So where do we go?' asked Jak. 'Or do we keep fighting anyway, like Sean.'

Fen shook his head. 'We can do more if we escape out of Hellyon and regroup. Maybe we can then link up with A'dat's forces and other underground groups and fight back that way.'

Jak nodded. 'I suppose so. I must admit, I've never had any intention of dying a hero. So, where do we go and what do we do?'

'I need to get to my wife and children,' said Fen, 'make sure they got away and if not, find a way of smuggling them out.'

'What about Tor?' Aris asked.

'Do we know where he is?' said Macker

Jak nodded. 'Number Six Field Hospital — just up north of the Marran Range — if it's still there anyway.'

'In that case, it looks like we'll have to split up. Fen needs to get to his family and I want to try and find Tor.'

'I'll come with you,' said Macker quietly.

'And I'll go with Fen,' said Jak. 'Okay, so now that's settled, are we going to have a rendezvous point?'

Aris thought for a moment. 'How about Tor's home village. It's safe and a good place to wait if some of us take longer in getting there. There's bound to be other refugees from Hellyon in the Tribelands too.'

Jak nodded. 'That's settled then. Well, we'd better not stay around here too long. See you all in the Tribelands.'

It seemed that they were hunted animals in their own land. With Hellyon's defences abandoned and enemy forces infiltrating from all directions, every piece of movement had to be calculated and assessed before being put into action. Every now and again there would be a short burst of gunfire as a Balaatan unit came across fleeing Hellyon fighters and shot them down.

Aris and Macker moved from cover to cover, looking and listening for danger, hoping to find a gap through the ever enclosing enemy lines. Aris felt herself sweating fear: all her training told her that she should be lying up during daylight hours and only risk moving at night. However, she wanted to press as far forward as possible before Balaatan troops took too firm a hold on the land. Also, she was not as familiar with the territory as someone born and brought up in Hellyon — travelling in the dark in these mountains could prove just as fatal as an enemy bullet. And then there was the third consideration — Tor. The field hospital was situated far enough north and east for there to be a chance that it hadn't been taken yet. However, it was only a matter of time.

They had been travelling for five hours now. That and the battle were beginning to take a toll: both women were functioning on adrenaline alone. They had abandoned their heavier packs miles back and now carried only survival gear in their belt kit. Finding a small gully, they tracked along it for a bit until it began to peter out, making its way back towards the level ground above. Aris inched her way forward on her stomach until she could just see over the top. A few hundred yards away, to the right, sat a small unit of Balaatan soldiers. To the left was a mixture of scrub and rocks, excellent cover. The only problem was that there was a hell of a lot of open ground between them and it.

She made her way back to Macker. 'There's no way we can do it in daylight. We'll have to hole up here as best as possible until dark.'

Macker looked at the water-carved walls either side of them. 'There's not much cover if someone decides to come over here and have a look.'

'Sure, but what other choice do we have?'

Macker shrugged and sat down, her back against one of the sides. 'At least we can have some time to get our energy back.'

Aris sat down next to her. 'I wish this stream bed wasn't so dry though. I'm thirsty as hell and who knows where we're going to find our next water source.'

Macker grinned at her. 'I see City didn't teach you much in the way of survival.'

'What do you mean?"

Macker got onto her hands and knees and began to scrape away the small stones and rocks that formed the dried up bed of the stream. It was hard work, but Macker had soon created a shallow hole that began to fill up with water.

'It may be dry on top, but usually, if the stream hasn't been dry for too long, there's some water still trapped underneath, where it can't evaporate.'

There wasn't much of the precious fluid, but it was still enough to fill the girls' water bottles.

Aris took a long drink. 'Maybe, after all this is over, you could teach me a few tricks.'

'Glad to. And maybe you could teach me some of that hand to hand combat you were trained in in City.'

'It's a deal.'

The two girls sat silent, side by side for a while. Suddenly a flash of movement, just on the rim of the ravine caught her eye. One of the Balaatan soldiers, desperate to take a piss, had decided to use the ravine as a toilet. Before Aris could warn her to keep still, Macker moved her arm up to wipe the sweat from her forehead. The man caught the movement and began to shout, excitedly.

'Shit,' Macker jumped.

Aris was already on her feet, her weapon aimed at him, but he quickly disappeared. Seconds later she heard men's voices getting nearer.

'Looks like we're going to have to make a break for it after all,' whispered Aris to Macker. 'Good luck.'

The two girls clasped each other's arms in friendship and prepared themselves for what was about to happen.

Above them, a cautious male face peered into the ravine, his weapon ready. However he never got a chance to use it as Macker let off two quick shots, hitting him in the head and neck. At the same time, Aris loosed at another soldier, never knowing whether she hit him or not; all she knew was that he had disappeared.

'Let's go,' she yelled and both of them scrambled up the side, keeping low to the ground when they reached the top. The small unit was now on the alert and a hail of bullets thudded into the ground all around them as they ran towards the cover. Zig-zagging across the open ground, Aris and Macker ran for all they were worth, expecting to feel a bullet at any time.

Miraculously, they escaped unscathed and reached the cover of the scrub just as the soldiers began to make their way forward.

The scrub began to change into woodland as the girls found themselves running downhill. Behind them, the sounds of pursuit were getting nearer, or so it seemed. To Aris, it brought back far too many memories of her first flight from Balaatan troops, the one that had seen her as a prisoner in Balaat Fort. On the other hand that pursuit party had seasoned trackers and runners; this time it seemed that the men were just normal soldiers with no special skills—she was sure she could outwit them.

'Go ahead,' she called to Macker. 'I have a plan to draw them away.'

'Are you mad? You'll be killed.'

Aris shook her head. 'I won't. I'll join up with you again at the hospital if not before. Now go.'

Macker saw the determination in her friend's face and knew she was right. If they were to have any chance of surviving, they had to split up and take their separate chances. If Aris could pull off what she had in mind, it would give them both a chance. If not... Macker didn't like to think of the alternative.

She took off in the direction Aris indicated, veering off on a course 45 degrees from their current one. Aris continued the way they had been going, making sure she kept just enough ahead of the pursuers and making more noise than necessary. Hopefully this would draw all of their attention and allow Macker to get clear.

After a while, once she was sure Macker would be far enough away to be in no danger, Aris increased her speed before suddenly veering off down an animal track. Like before she had to dive onto her knees and crawl quickly through thorns and twigs. Eventually she was holed up in a small thicket, just as the first of the soldiers ran past. She smirked in satisfaction as they kept on running, following a quarry that was no longer there. Now all she had to do was wait until she was certain they were well out of the way before breaking cover and striking out in a new direction, one that would take her to where Tor was.

Macker hadn't got far when a loose rock slipped from under her and she fell, twisting her foot at an awkward angle. Pain shot through her ankle but she forced herself back onto her feet again. She had to keep moving forward. Trying to ignore the sprain, she hobbled as fast as she could. At least there were no sounds of pursuit behind her. She knew she couldn't continue for much longer on her injury; she had to find somewhere safe to hole up for a while so that she could treat herself with some of the morphine she'd kept with her in case of an emergency. She slowed down and looked around. Off to one side was another stream bed, like the one she and Aris had found themselves in earlier. As before, the water had cut deep into the rock of the surrounding land, forming a small ravine. Near to the top was what looked like a large clay outlet pipe, maybe one that had been left over from the Old World settlers. It was probably crumbling away or providing a home to god knows what creature, but it still looked the best chance of cover she would come across for a while. Painfully, she made her way down to it and crawled inside. The interior was dark and damp, and only just big enough for her to kneel up in, but there didn't seem to be any sign of animal occupation, so she set about unpacking her medical kit. The sooner she could get some pain relief the better.

The morphine soon began to work and Macker began strapping the offending joint again, knowing that it was going to be near impossible to get it back into her boot. At this rate she would have to continue with one bare foot.

Suddenly there were voices outside, the sound of men's boots crunching over stone. She froze. It could only be an enemy patrol, out looking for Hellyon fugitives. Still, hopefully they would pass by — there was nothing that would lead them to search this pipe, was there? Her mind worked overtime. In her previous pain-hazed state, she hadn't checked whether or not she had left any sign outside, such as footprints. In the dusty soil around the ravine, it was quite possible. Shit, how could she have been so careless?

The voices and footsteps stopped and Macker began to pray, reaching for her weapon. There was a scrabbling noise and the sound of small stones becoming dislodged as one of them began to clamber down to the pipe. She pressed herself close to the cold clay wall and tried to retreat into the darkness. It was no use; at some point in its history, the pipe had been blocked up by rubble. She could go no further. Her hands, clammy with sweat, grasped her weapon as she focussed on the small circle of daylight that was now her only escape.

The darkness of a body blocked out her light.

Her finger squeezed the trigger. Nothing happened. The gun had jammed. At the most crucial moment the bloody thing had jammed!

A blade of torchlight cut through the darkness to catch her like a rabbit in a trap as she saw the expression on the man's face — saw down the barrel of his gun.

Her body felt suddenly weak and her bladder full. She heard her breath rasping, wanted to beg for her life.

And then a shot rang out — the deafening sound crashing off the walls of the pipe, breaking the clay into small, sharp shards.

And then there was silence, and the smell of death.

17

Aris reached the hospital camp at the edge of the Tribelands in two days. For now it was in safe territory although there was always the threat that Jerregish could overrun it at any moment. On the other hand, both Balaat and Jerregish seemed to be expending all their energies in consolidating their gains further south, before pushing any more troops north. Just as well, thought Aris — it would give the remnants of Hellyon's forces time to flee.

Nevertheless, the camp was in the process of evacuation with every available transport ferrying wounded soldiers to various safe havens within the Tribelands. Aris immediately went to the administration tent and enquired after Tor.

The young man on duty looked down his list before shaking his head. 'Sorry, there's no one of that name here. Are you sure that he came to this camp?'

'That's what we were told. Look, is it possible he was transferred somewhere else on route?'

The man shrugged. 'It's possible, but unlikely. No one else has been transferred.'

Aris shook her head, trying to reign in her frustration. 'Well are there any other casualties from C Division here?'

The young man gave her a look that suggested his own patience was also getting stretched. He looked back at his book again. 'Quite a few actually, even the commander.'

'Felson? Felson is here?'

'Block N, tent 8. Serious head and chest injuries. It might be best if...'

Aris did not hear the rest—she was already searching out the row numbers of the hospital tents. Eventually she found Block N and slowly walked down its line of tents, looking for Felson.

Tent number eight was exactly the same as the others: the same size, the same shape. And yet it seemed somehow quieter and darker inside. Aris walked along the rows of beds, trying to shut her mind's eye to some of the appalling injuries she saw. For the amount of damage these men and women had sustained, they were surprisingly silent: no moans or screams of pain. And then she realised why—most of them were doped up on painkillers. The rest, as Aris found on closer inspection, were dead.

She found Felson at the far end. It looked as if most of his lower jaw had been blown away. The chest injuries were hidden beneath a sheet, already stained with blood. At first she thought he was dead too, until she reached for his pulse and found it still there—weak and thready but still there. He was obviously out of it on morphine and looking at his injuries, she was glad. There wasn't much else that could be done for him here. In fact there wasn't much that could be done for any in this tent—the casualties here had been left to die peacefully and with dignity. She sat down beside Felson's bed: at least she could give him her company, his last few hours needn't be alone. Sitting still made her realise just how exhausted she was. She tried to keep her eyes open, but eventually there was no escaping the gentle sleep that closed her mind to the death and dying around her.

HELLYON'S STAND

She was woken by someone gently shaking her arm. It was one of the medics — a woman she vaguely recognised from Hellyon Camp.

'It's okay; it's all over now,' the woman said gently.

'What?' Aris was still confused from sleep.

'He's gone. He won't be in any more pain.'

Aris looked around at Felson and saw that indeed, the delicate rise and fall of his chest had stopped. She shook her head. 'So much death. So much waste.'

The medic nodded. 'I couldn't agree with you more, we've lost so many. Hellyon has become a killing ground.' She looked tired: she must have been on duty for at least the past 24 hours.

She turned to go, but Aris caught hold of her arm, suddenly recognising her face. 'Wait. You're from Hellyon Camp, do you know Macker?'

'Of course, who wouldn't?'

'Do you know if she's come into this camp? She should have got here a couple of hours ahead of me.'

The medic shook her head. 'No, I haven't seen her, but that doesn't mean anything. This place is pretty big. I could try and find out though.'

'Thank you,' said Aris. She stood up and looked back at Felson. 'Well, at least he wasn't alone at the last.'

The medic smiled. 'No. He seems to have been cared about by his men. There was one here earlier but he said he had to leave. I tried to persuade him to stay and be treated: it was obvious his arm stump needed treatment.'

Aris spun around. 'What did you say?'

'He'd lost an arm — such a shame in one so young. I wanted him to get it treated before a fever set in or else he wouldn't be long for this world.'

'Was he tall?'

'Yes. Pale hair. Strange eyes — very light in colour — like a Sharm.'

'Did he say where he was going?'

'He mentioned something about his father, but that was all.'

Aris nodded and let out a sigh of relief. Tor was alive and had already left for the his village. Bad as his arm was, she had no doubts that he would reach his family and that once there would find some proper healing — the sort he had faith in. She knew, and she was certain that he knew too, that it wasn't just his arm that would have to be healed. Knowing that she could do no more for now, she went in search of some food and a place to sleep. She decided that she would stay until noon tomorrow in case Macker turned up, but after that she would strike out on her own for the Tor's village.

Fen's step lightened as he and Jak approached the mountain village of Lapacre, the place where he would find Jeanna and the children. They had not seen any sign of enemy activity for at least a day now and Fen was relieved that his family had escaped to a place that hadn't been touched by either Balaat or Jerregish.

He flashed Jak a rare smile. 'Looks like we were the lucky ones.'

'Depends what you mean by lucky,' Jak grumped. He was not in such a jubilant mood. The fall of Hellyon had affected him more deeply than he thought it would. He had begun to question the entire purpose of his life: what had it all been for, if all it took was just a concerted and co-operative effort by enemy forces to overtake their land? Why the hell couldn't they have done it sooner — at least then he might have had some sort of life, maybe even had another family. There again, who was he kidding? He was a fighter. Farming land or carving wood would have turned him mad in no time. No, he was made to carry on a conflict, and if he couldn't be miserable about that, well, life wouldn't be worth it anyway.

Fen estimated that the village should be about a mile ahead, just over a rise. Walking out of the treeline he suddenly halted, looking ahead. Jak followed his line of sight and saw what looked like clouds of dark black smoke filling the sky.

There was only one thing that the smoke could mean and a sudden dread gripped him. Fen's face had gone deathly pale and for a moment he seemed paralysed by shock. Then something seemed to kick him back into action as he gripped his weapon in front of him and started to run. Jak knew there was no point in his urging a cautious approach — Fen wouldn't have heard. Reluctantly he also brought his weapon to the ready and set off, following.

There wasn't much of the village left: two of the buildings were still burning while the others stood shattered by artillery fire. There was not one home that had more than three walls standing and all the roofs had gone. Jak expected to see bodies strewn around the wreckage, but no. Miraculously it seemed that most of the villagers had been left untouched. A small wave of relief swept through him: all they needed to do now was to find Fen's family and get the hell out.

One of the villagers seemed to recognise Fen and came forward, tears streaking his wrinkled face, his hand clutching a hastily wrapped bundle of all the possessions he could get his hands on before his house was torched.

'Hal,' Fen grabbed the old man by the shoulders to steady him. 'What happened?'

'Some men came...'

'From Balaat?'

'No, no, they said they were from City.'

'City?' Jak saw Fen's face suddenly take on a mask of panic. 'Where is Jeanna? Where are the girls?'

The old man shook his head, hardly able to get his words out in his grief. He pointed to a house a few doors down. Fen began to run, calling out his wife's name. Silent eyes watched from the broken shadows. Jak followed close behind, a sense of foreboding weighing heavy on him. Fen reached the house and stopped dead, almost causing Jak to run into him. He stood staring up at a spot on the inner walls of the shattered dwelling. There, hung from the splintered ends of ceiling joists, were three bodies: one woman and two young girls, their dresses stained with blood from the bullets that had riddled them in their last moments.

Fen fell to his knees, his legs no longer able to carry his weight. He squeezed his eyes shut against the gruesome sight, but Jak knew that the picture would now be burned into his brain — that the horror of this moment would now be his companion for every second of the rest of his life. Watching Fen was like watching a mirror image of himself all those fifteen years ago when he had found his own family lying in their own blood.

Taking his knife, he strode forward and, reaching up, cut down the first body, that of the youngest girl. She was light in his arms, as unsubstantial as a feather on the breeze. Her eyes were shut and her face looked peaceful, as if she were only sleeping, but the drying, sticky blood that felt so cold on his bare arms told a different story, as did the blackened holes in her clothing. For a moment he was holding his own daughter again — the same small limp body gone beyond where he could help or comfort. His throat constricting with grief he gently laid the little figure on the ground and moved on to cut down the other two bodies, laying them all side by side. Fen's wife had something pinned to her skirt; it looked like some kind of note.

Taking it in his hand, he walked back to where Fen was still kneeling and held it out.

'Do you want to read it?' he asked gently, 'or do you want to leave it until later.'

Fen shook his head and held out his hand. 'I may as well know for sure who did this.' His voice was tight, shaky, but Jak saw that the man in front of him was determined not to fall to pieces. Fenim unfolded the note, stared at it for a few seconds, then nodded and handed it to Jak.

Jak read it: *You were warned*. He frowned. 'What the hell does this mean?'

'A long time ago in City, I was recruited as a spy, a sleeper and was given the task of infiltrating into Hellyon. Of course, after a while I realised I could never betray those I fought with and so, after Vallen's death, when I was called upon to perform my duties, I refused. That was what happened at A'dat's palace, why we were compromised. I was warned then that if I turned my back on City, it would be my family that would suffer. I moved them to a safer place but they still found them. It's all my fault.' He covered his face with his hands and began to cry.

Jak placed a hand on his shoulder and then left him to be alone with the bodies of his family for a while.

He walked a few houses away and sat down on what had once been a wall. Any remaining energy drained from his body, seeping into the earth like blood. His mind turned over what Fen had just told him. Never in a lifetime would he have suspected Fen as a City spy: no he had hung that label quite happily on Aris instead. Still, it was no surprise that someone like him — a young, bright doctor — should be recruited by City Intelligence Forces. They had probably thought him quite an asset to their ranks. But what they hadn't bargained for was

Fenim's deep sense of integrity, and of justice. They hadn't counted on his growing disgust at what City had done to Hellyon and its people. And they hadn't counted on the power of friendship. However, in the end he had paid a high price for his betrayal — a price that no man should ever have to pay.

A shadow suddenly blocked the sun and Jak looked up to see Hal, the man that had greeted Fenim earlier.

'May I sit with you?' the man asked.

Jak nodded. 'So what exactly happened here?' he asked.

'They came just before dawn with a lot of noise and shouting. We were frightened, thinking that Balaatan troops had come to kill us all. Instead, they got us all out of bed and rounded us up in the square. One by one they asked us our names and when Jeanna answered they pulled her and her children to one side. They then made us go to the far end of the village while they killed them and destroyed our houses. But why? I just don't understand? What could that woman and those two poor children have done to deserve that?'

'Nothing. They did absolutely nothing,' Jak answered, his teeth gritted against his anger.

'And Fenim? How is he coping?'

'How the hell do you think he's coping? How would you bloody well cope if your family had just been wiped out?' Jak shouted, seeking an easy release for his pain.

The old man lowered his eyes. 'Of course. I am sorry.'

Jak shook his head. 'Never mind. I guess we're all a bit on edge now. Look, if I were you, I'd get your people together and head north, toward the Tribelands. There's plenty of sanctuary there.'

'Do you think they will come back then?'

'No, not City. But Balaatan forces will soon be heading this way. And if not Balaat, then Jerregish. Who knows how those bastards have decided to carve up the pie?'

The old man nodded. 'Thank you. I had better get everyone moving as soon as possible then. What about you?'

'We'll be all right. We've made it this far. I expect Fenim will want to bury his family and then we'll be following you north.'

'So be it. Fair journey to you both then.' The old man shakily got to his feet and shuffled off to round up the villagers.

Jak walked back to Fenim. He was sat, cross-legged, next to the body of his wife, his hand stroking her soiled clothing as he talked in a low voice. Jak hesitated for a moment, not wanting to interrupt, but they would soon run out of time. In the end he didn't have to say a word: Fenim hearing his footsteps, looked up, tears still running from his eyes. He nodded.

'It is time to bury them, I know.'

'Would you like me to dig the graves?' Jak volunteered.

'No. We will do it together.'

As Jerregishan tradition demanded, the bodies were laid to rest at sunset, with their heads towards the east. Fenim said the traditional words of the burial ritual over the fresh mounds of earth and then turned to Jak.

'My friend, I must keep vigil here now until dawn. After that, as my faith decrees, I must take a vow of seven days silence. Once the seven days are over I shall take another holy vow — that to find my family's killers and take my revenge on every last one of them. I am telling you this so that you may make your own choices: you may want to leave tonight, in case Balaat comes this way. You have a future Jak, I do not.'

Jak looked at his friend and frowned. 'I have no more future and no more family than you do. In fact you are as much my family now. No, whatever you decide, I will stay with you. I will help you to avenge what has been done here.'

Fenim took Jak's hand and nodded; the look that passed

HELLYON'S STAND

between them made a bond that was stronger than brotherhood.

'Then will you stay and keep watch with me this night?' asked Fen.

Later, both sat at the graveside and became silent, each one deep in his own thoughts.

Tor sat watching an eagle soar up into the blue sky. His village lay down below in the valley, the smoke from the cooking fires giving the scene a slight hazy look from above. Children played between the huts while the adults sat and socialised or worked together. He hadn't thought he would see it again: when the shell exploded he thought he was dead. When he realised that his arm had gone he wished he was.

Those few hours had been a terrible, terrible nightmare and it seemed to him that for a time he'd slipped between the worlds of life and death, never knowing which was real. And yet, through it all, there was a voice pulling him through, forcing him back to consciousness. He knew it had been his father. Incredibly he had made it back to consciousness somewhere on that ambulance journey and had even found some inner strength. With bandages wrapped firmly around his newly cauterised stump he had declined further treatment at the Marran Hills field hospital and had gone instead to find some food for the journey he now knew he must make. His people would know how to heal him, how to help him accept his new disability. It was while talking to people in the queue at the food tent that Tor learnt about Felson. He had gone to see him, but the man was too far gone for saving—anyone could see that, and he knew he had to move on.

He had made it back to the village on sheer will power alone, or so it felt. Once more he had seemed to live both in this world and the next as the fever took hold of him, talking to ghostly figures who pushed him onwards, wouldn't let him stop. One of them was his father and he knew then that the old man had died. In the mists of semi-consciousness they talked and made things right between them. As his father faded from sight, Tor felt his sister's hands and saw the familiar surroundings of his village around him. He knew things were going to be alright.

Sitting on the edge of the cliff above the village, Tor was suddenly aware of the total peace that surrounded him. Not just the peace of the sky and the earth, but also within his own soul. Gone was his restless urge to wander, to fight, to be different. Now all that mattered was his family, his people, those he loved. He thought about the rest of CU11 and wished he had his full powers so that he could see if they had come through it all too. But his mind was still hazy from the trauma of his injury and Hellyon seemed a lifetime away. All he could do was to sit and wait and hope.

The children below had spotted him and were waving and shouting. He waved back, his eyes drawn to one small figure in particular: Ani. She had fitted in well here and seemed happy enough, but Tor knew that she still cried for her mother at night. Out of all of them, he hoped against hope that Aris had survived—the little girl needed her. If she hadn't, well, there was no question that Tor's family would love her as their own and bring her up in safety. Tor, in particular, felt a certain duty, albeit willing, towards Ani.

With an effort, he pushed himself to his feet and set out on the long trek back down to the village. Maybe it was time he started to tell the children some of the old stories.

18

Aris relaxed in Marissa's house as Ani curled up in the furs on the low mud bench that served as a bed. Tor and Marissa had greeted her with love and relief too when, hungry, thirsty and exhausted, she had turned up on the path just outside the village boundary. Of course, she had hoped against hope that maybe Macker had made it in front of her, but finally she had to accept the woman was dead, or possibly a prisoner of war. And that amounted to the same thing.

Tor appeared with what looked suspiciously like a camp brew. He grinned as he placed it on the bench beside her. 'Thought you might be missing this.'

She nodded. 'There are a lot of things I'm going to miss.'

Tor sat down beside her, his face suddenly serious. 'Yes, me too. But the past is the past and it can't be brought back. In fact, if I had the powers to do it, I'm not sure that I would want to.'

'I wish you had the powers to bring the others back though.'

'Surely it can't be just you and me that got through it?'

'Jak and Fen haven't returned, so we can't say for sure that they are still alive. As for Kris... well, there's still no word.'

'Had you planned to meet here?'

Aris nodded. 'And if he were alive I'm sure he would be

here by now.'

Tor placed his hand on her shoulder. 'Well, at least you have your daughter, and you are welcome to stay here for as long as you wish.'

'Thank you. I might just accept that offer. Ani needs somewhere safe and stable to grow up and I need some peace in my life. For as long as that is possible anyway.'

Tor nodded and gestured to his missing arm. 'Even if I hadn't lost this, I think that I would have come back here anyway. I don't regret what I did, but my place is here, among my people.'

'When do you become ordained as the new leader?'

'Two days time, when the moon Geia reaches fullness.'

'I'll be proud to see that.'

'Thank you.' He dipped his head. 'It'll be hard, and I'll have to learn some of the Sharmsinging powers I neglected when I went to fight for Hellyon, but I know I can do it. With Balaat just over the border, I'll have to.'

Tor became the leader of his tribe during a secret ceremony in a hidden cave that involved only the elders. As he explained it later, he was given a mind-altering brew to drink so that he could communicate with the spirits. During that time he saw and spoke to his father again, who confirmed his suitability as heir. The chief shaman then cut a sacred pattern into his face filling the wound with ground up charcoal and the antiseptic juice of the Millo Berry.

When Tor reappeared for the celebrations after the ceremony, Aris hardly recognised him. Apart from his new tribal scarification, his whole body was painted in red, black and white: circles and wavy lines, lightning flashes and eyes covered his skin. He hardly looked human at all. In fact from the distant look in his eyes, which she later found out was due to the potion he had drank, he hardly looked in this world.

The dancing, drinking and feasting started; huge fires lashed out into the sky as the voices of many drums whipped the dancers' feet into a frenzy. Aris sat back and watched. The whole scene was so alien, even primitive to what she had known before. Looking at Tor now, she tried to remember back to when they were fighting together in Hellyon. Somehow, it was difficult to connect the two: a time line had descended like a curtain and divided Torassin into two different people. Just as she couldn't imagine Tor the warrior allowing his face to be scarred and painted in an ancient ceremony, neither could she imagine this new, dignified leader cleaning his weapon and sharing a brew with a bunch of soldiers in a far land.

She quietly sipped at her drink, trying to adjust herself to what would be her new life. Despite having her daughter back, she still felt as if something was missing, as if she didn't fit in. There again she had never felt at home in City or Hellyon either. She wondered briefly whether she might not feel more at home in the land where she had been born, in Jerregish. But there again, as an unmarried mother, she would have less freedom and respect than here. If only she had Kris, but there was still no word from him: she had to presume that he was dead.

There was a sudden rustling from the bushes behind her and she jumped, her reflexes still strong. A familiar face appeared beside her and her melancholy was suddenly forgotten in her joy of seeing Jak again.

'You're alive!'

'Obviously,' he grunted, then smiled. 'And I'm glad to see you alive too. Tor?'

Aris turned and pointed to the painted figure now holding court. For a moment Jak was speechless. 'I don't believe it. So he eventually became a true Sharm then.'

'And the leader of his people.'

Jak shook his head. 'Somehow I find it hard to think of Tor as royalty.'

'Ah, but this Tor is different from the one you knew. Take it from me—he's grown up. There are even rumours that he's about to marry.'

Jak shrugged. 'Ah well, I suppose there's no helping some people.'

'Is Fenim alive?' Aris asked.

Jak paused for a moment, before running his hand through his hair. 'He's alive physically, but he may as well be dead.'

'What do you mean?'

'He found his family murdered by some old associates of his from City.'

'Murdered? Associates? What the hell do you mean?'

'Fenim's lost his whole family; that's all you need to know at the moment. The rest of the story is rather long winded and I'd rather Fen told you himself.'

'Where is he?'

'A couple of miles back. He is still under his seven-day vow of silence and I don't think this party atmosphere would do much for him at the moment. You'll see him in a few days though. I just came to let you know we're alive.'

Aris nodded. 'I'm sure Tor will be extremely happy to know that too. Tell Fen to take all the time he wants—we'll still be here.'

'So you're settling here?'

'Yes. Ani needs somewhere safe to grow up and I need time to be a mother.'

Jak looked at the floor. 'Well, let's just hope that City and Balaat don't turn their eyes on this piece of land too. Once City has developed its new weaponry there won't be many places it can't reach.'

'I know, but at least for now we are safe here. We'll face the future when it comes.'

Jak looked around him at the revellers. 'Is Macker here somewhere?'

Aris shook her head. 'She didn't make it Jak.'

Jak was silent, taking in this new piece of news. How many more would he have to grieve for? He put his arms around Aris and held her tight for a brief moment before pulling back. 'I need to get back to Fen, make sure he doesn't do anything silly, like take on the whole of City while I'm gone.'

Aris nodded. 'I'll tell Tor that you're both alive.'

'And we'll be back to take the piss out of him in a few days. Or at least, I will.'

Three weeks after Tor's inauguration, the remains of CU11 sat around the hearth in Tor's house, sharing a bottle of kotch. It was like old times. Almost. Sean's absence was a gaping hole in all their lives and Fen was no more than a ghost of his old self. There was a new hardness to his eyes now — a darkness within that wasn't human. Heaven help those who were his quarry.

'So when do you plan to leave?' Tor asked.

'At dawn,' replied Jak. 'We're going to head across the mountains to the Chapterlands, then cross the northern provinces of Jerregish to City.'

'Won't that be risky?'

'We aren't going to just walk in there without a plan. Fen will work his way there as a doctor and I will act as his assistant. With the right clothing and contacts we should soon be able to walk right into City without the slightest hint of suspicion.'

'I'm sure A'dat will help you,' said Aris.

'A'dat is in exile in Chapterland, which is why we're going there — to see him. I'm sure he still has many loyal supporters in Jerregish who will be more than pleased to help us.'

There was silence for a while, as everyone seemed lost in his or her own thoughts. Then Fen spoke up for the first time.

'So what now Tor?'

Tor frowned. 'What do you mean?'

'Hellyon was just the beginning. City wants an empire and with its new technology and new allies in Balaat and Jerregish, it will be sure to push northwards. Your lands and the lands of the other tribes could be next. Are you just going to let that happen?'

'No, but I know that many people in my tribe would rather become vassals of a greater power than actually use violence.'

'Even in defence?'

Tor shook his head. 'To be honest, I don't know. We have not been threatened in living memory: other tribes have been too frightened of our powers and the Constitutional agreement with the Old World people took care of the rest. Maybe I can change their attitude, but it will take a bit of time and patience. I can't rush them.'

Fen took a large swig from the bottle. 'Well, for what it's worth, I'm sure you will succeed. After all, you have seen what those bastards are capable of and I'm sure you wouldn't want it to happen to your people.'

The words hung in the air like a challenge.

'Then maybe that was the whole reason I went to Hellyon to fight,' said Tor quietly. 'Maybe my "difference" was no accident.'

Jak snorted. 'Here we go. Sharm mumbo-jumbo again. You came to fight in Hellyon because that's what your hormones were telling you at the time. It doesn't matter why, Tor — the important thing is that you prepare for the worst, because the worst is usually what happens.'

Aris sighed. 'Tor will have to work this out in his own time and in his own way. Even if the Sharms suddenly decided to fight back and joined with the other tribes and settlers in a defensive coalition, there's still little chance they could stand against the might of a combined City, Balaat and Jerregish. And that goes double if City develops its aircraft. I say we will do better if envoys are sent out beyond the Tribelands to the far territories. We need to find new allies and fast.'

Tor gave her a look of appraisal. 'That sounds extremely wise. It seems I have a lot of thinking to do.'

Aris picked up the bottle and tipped it to her mouth only to find it was empty. 'So,' she said, 'is this our last time together?'

Jak shrugged. 'Who knows? We might meet up again one day.'

'I think we will always be fighting together,' said Fen and punched his chest with his closed fist. 'Here in our hearts, the unit will always stay as the unit, so it doesn't matter if we never meet in this world again.'

Jak raised an eyebrow at him. 'You're beginning to sound like a Sharm now — maybe we've stayed a little too long.'

They all laughed then, breaking the tension.

'We'd better get some sleep,' said Jak. 'Fen and I have a long journey ahead and my old bones need the rest.'

The others nodded and they all stood up and briefly embraced each other. There were no more words between them; there was no need.

Six weeks after Jak and Fen left the village, Aris found herself looking southwards, in the direction of City and

Hellyon. To her it now seemed as if a sleeping monster lay beyond the plains, one that would someday soon wake and swallow the Tribelands. She knew that Tor was taking the threat seriously and had already sent scouts to the north to seek out new contacts. She sighed; despite all her intentions of settling down, there was still part of her that missed the excitement and the adrenaline.

There was a sudden shout and she looked up to see what the fuss was about. Coming down the path was a lone figure, tall and walking with a pronounced limp. There was something familiar in the way he held himself. Aris suddenly found herself holding her breath. Surely, it couldn't be — not after all this time. Then a surge of joy leapt into her throat as she ran to meet him.

'I thought you were dead!' she cried.

Kris shook his head and she could see his eyes glistening with tears of joy. 'No, I just got delayed for a while.'

'Your leg?'

'It was smashed while I was helping A'dat and his people out of Jerregish. Some nice people in the Chapter Homelands helped put it back together again. All I need now to complete the healing is a kiss.'

He drew her to him and she knew that everything would be all right.

At least for a little while.

Made in the USA
Charleston, SC
25 February 2015